SHARON HINCK

W9-BPN-752

Symphony of Secrets

A NOVEL

BETHANY HOUSE
PUBLISHERS

To Verna Hinck,
whose gift of music
in service to her Savior
has blessed so many.

A NOTE FROM THE AUTHOR

Minneapolis and its sister city, St. Paul, are home to a wealth of art and culture. Colleges, theatres, and symphonies abound. Throughout the novel, I've referenced actual locations in the Twin Cities, with a few exceptions. I've taken the liberty of creating a fictional orchestra, dubbed the Minneapolis Symphony, which performs in the also fictional Palace Theatre and Symphonic Hall. These are inspired by some of the great orchestras and performance spaces in Minnesota but are unique creations for purposes of this story.

CHAPTER

1

Agitato: In a restless, agitated style. Italian, past participle of agitare, from Latin agitre, to agitate.

On Monday, I uncovered a drug ring in South Minneapolis. On Tuesday, I spotted a felony theft at a country club in Edina. On Wednesday, I overheard plans for industrial espionage while staking out the back room of a workshop in St. Paul.

On Thursday, my daughter blew all my cases out of the water.

No, my daughter isn't a defense attorney; she's a hopelessly practical girl with no imagination.

We'd agreed on supper together every Thursday night, no matter how busy her fifteen-year-old life became, and I couldn't wait to impress her with my week's discoveries. Clara slipped into the room and collapsed into her chair—a composition of baggy jeans, three layers of tank tops in various colors, and flip-flops. On her long, slim frame, it looked good.

The small wooden table in the kitchen was marred with nicks and stains from all the homework I'd helped Clara with over the years. The curtains on the window over the sink stirred in the spring breeze, kids shouted as they cycled down the alley, and a siren wailed in the distance. I pulled the window closed. Tonight would be chilly. April in Minnesota ran alternately hot and cool, like a Gershwin prelude. "How was school?" I asked Clara as I ladled out some potato soup.

A shrug. "Fine."

"And work? Was the café busy this afternoon?"

Another shrug. "It was okay."

Enough small talk.

"So." I tasted the soup and reached for the salt. "When Susie Nelson came for her flute lesson on Monday, I happened to look out the window. A guy dropped her off—kind of shady looking—and he called her back to the car and handed her a package. She slipped it into her shoulder bag."

Clara rolled her eyes and crumbled a cracker into her bowl. I could tell I had her hooked because she tucked her long, dark hair behind her ears in a subtle Freudian signal that she was listening. I drew out the suspense by reaching for a carrot stick. "When she started her warm-up scales, I glanced in her music bag. You'll never guess what she's up to. No wonder the girl's eyes glaze over every time I explain dynamics to her."

Clara snorted into her glass of milk. "Mom, everyone's eyes glaze over when you go off on one of your music rants."

"I'm serious. Guess what I saw."

"I give up." She yawned.

Like I said, no imagination. "A syringe. Susie is doing drugs, and I bet that guy is her pusher."

Clara pressed her lips together as if stifling a laugh. She reached for the butter and spread some on her roll. "I've gone to school with Susie since first grade."

8

"I know." I waved my spoon at her. "Now do you understand why I want you to transfer to the arts school next fall? There's still time. I know you missed the auditions, but I could put in a good word. They'll take applications until June."

She slammed her knife to the table and skewered me with her gaze. "You promised."

I lifted my hands. "Sorry. It's just—"

She slumped back in her chair. "Mom, did the guy have a ponytail? Blond hair?"

Excitement built behind my ribs, my heart ticking like an overwound metronome. I'd been trying to impress Clara with my detective prowess since I'd read Nancy Drew books to her by her crib. She was finally showing interest in one of my criminal discoveries.

"Yes, that's the guy. He's a dealer, isn't he? Have you seen him around the school?"

"Of course I've seen him. His name is C.J."

Why does my daughter know a drug dealer by name?

Her grin widened. "Mom, C.J. is Susie's brother. He gives her a ride when their mom works late. Sweet guy. You'd like him. Plays classical guitar."

"But . . . but the drugs."

Clara pushed back her chair and shook her head. She threw me a pitying look and sauntered out of the kitchen.

I left the dirty dishes on the table and followed her to the living room. She wasn't going to discount my sleuthing so easily.

Clara sank into a leather wing chair and stared into the vacant, brick fireplace. "Mom, I'm getting worried about you."

Worried about me? She was the one cozying up to an invisible fire in April. I flopped into the wooden rocker and frowned at her. "Because I notice things? I can't help being observant."

She shook her head. "You need a life. And by the way, Susie has diabetes."

"I have a life. And . . ." Her words sank in. "Diabetes?"

"Yep." She picked up one of my *Flute Talk* magazines, flipped through a few pages, and tossed it aside. "How's your audition piece coming along?"

Kind of her to change the subject, now that she'd humiliated me. My cheeks felt warm, as if we really had logs burning in the fireplace. "I'm not happy with the phrasing in the rondo."

She nodded. "You'll get it."

No matter how much we squabbled, Clara remained my number one encourager. A month ago, my friend Lena, who played with the Minneapolis Symphony, had heard rumors there might be an opening soon, so I'd been more obsessed than usual these past weeks.

Clara rested her elbows on her legs and leaned forward, staring more deeply into the nonexistent fire. Her silky hair swung forward to curtain her face, and she sighed.

I pushed away my thoughts about the Concerto in D Major and the troubling rondo. "What's wrong?" Obsessive musician I may be, but when my daughter has a problem, I try to force myself into mommy mode.

Clara wrapped her arms around her middle and sighed again. The posture reminded me of the way her father used to sit when he was worried, and I felt the ache of an old injury.

"Come on." I reached forward to draw back her hair so I could see her face. "You can tell me."

She swiveled away from my hand and slouched back into her chair. "You won't understand."

Her scowl surprised me. She was usually as easygoing as I was moody, enduring my excesses with affectionate humor. A wave of guilt brushed across my skin. I really wasn't cut out to be a mom. I'd been doing pretty well, all things considered, but this past month I'd been neglecting her, preoccupied with the tantalizing hope of the symphony audition. "I'll try to understand. I promise. What's wrong?"

She propped her feet up on the hearth, bare toes flexing. "I had an audition today, and I'm worried. I didn't do great."

I gasped, unable to hide my excitement. Was she finally going to stop drifting and focus her talents? "For what?"

Her chin jutted forward in a gesture that I knew she'd learned from me. "Cheerleading."

Shock and horror made my throat constrict. "What?" I squeaked.

She gave me a level stare. "Told you. You don't understand."

I swallowed hard and picked up the gauntlet. "I'm just . . . surprised." My near-genius daughter with the DNA of two gifted artists wanted to waste time shaking pom-poms?

Clara grinned slyly. "You're not upset? They're deciding next year's squad now, so they can practice all summer."

I gulped again. "I didn't realize you . . . were interested in . . . that."

"Cheerleading. Come on, you can say the word."

"Isn't this kind of sudden?"

Her gaze dropped. "I've been staying at school for practices before work."

"Since when?"

"The past two months. Miguel let me come in later than usual."
Miguel knew about this? And I didn't?

Hurt, anger, and a low chord of shame rumbled in my heart. How had I missed this? She'd been deceiving me. Me, the great observer who could notice any note a fraction off-key and spot every hint in a mystery novel. I'd had no clue about her after-school activities.

Her dark eyes watched me with trepidation, waiting to see how I'd react.

Had I become such a tyrant? Were my outbursts and objections so predictable? I'd show her. I'd be Ultra-Supportive Mom.

I forced a smile. "Sweetie, you're great at whatever you set your mind to. I'm sure you did a terrific job at the audition."

"So you don't mind me doing something that's not artsy?"

"It just surprised me. Of course I want to support you."

She stretched and bounded to her feet with a wide smile. "Glad you approve. Because actually, I didn't do so bad. In fact, I made it." She whooped and jumped into the air, arching her back as if trying to get her heels to touch her head—some strange cheerleader contortion, I figured. Then she boogied across the room and up the stairs, laughing all the way.

I'd been suckered.

I crossed my arms and glared at my Steinway in the corner of the room. Clara played me better than I played Mozart. Her stereo kicked in from overhead, and the sound of thumps accompanied the exuberant passage of Beethoven. She had to be practicing those ridiculous leaps.

A smile tugged my lips, then grew into a wide grin. Seeing Clara this excited was worth the humiliation. I'd named my daughter for Clara Schumann—wife of the great composer Robert Schumann and a gifted musician in her own right. But although my Clara developed adequate keyboard technique, she didn't have the fire to pursue professional music. It figured. She had the opportunities and no fire. I had the fire in abundance. But opportunities? My detective instincts had been getting more exercise than my musical skills for years.

Music was a cruel god who demanded daily sacrifices and gave no promises in return. Even though I'd coaxed Clara to try the arts school, I didn't really want that kind of life for her. Tasting the bliss of performance and then living for years only nibbling crumbs had almost crushed my spirit. I wanted better for my daughter.

Hoping to garner some favor from my own unforgiving deity, I pulled out my flute and settled in for some serious practice, then stared at the magic metal in my hands and shook my head. I set it down gently and headed up to Clara's room instead.

I pounded on her door so she'd hear me over the Beethoven.

"Come in," she called.

After stepping into the room, I waited for her to turn down her stereo. "Time for a visit with Jane."

She grinned. "I have to admit I like her better than the Bronte gals."

Every night, we snuggled and read aloud to each other. Tonight we had a date with the last chapter of *Pride and Prejudice*.

"Hey, I still have to tell you about the thief I spotted, and the spy I overheard yesterday."

Clara laughed—music as sweet as the triplets in a Pachelbel toccata.

The next morning at breakfast, I made one more attempt to impress Clara with my crime-spotting skills.

"I still think I should tell the police about the theft on Tuesday. Or at least the manager at the country club." I stabbed my spoon into the grapefruit, and juice splattered my face. Maybe it would fade a few of my freckles.

Clara handed me a napkin from the ceramic holder she'd made when she was in junior high. "Trust me, Mom. I work the register at Miguel's. It's normal for a waiter to take money out of the till if the restaurant needs it somewhere else. Was it a busy night?"

I winced. "Of course. All the banquet rooms were full." So much for my crime detection skills. The case of the bartender needing change. That would never make it into *Ellery Queen's Mystery Magazine*.

The conversation at Friedrich's workshop on Wednesday? She'd explained that away as well. I thought I'd heard an employee on his cell phone giving away proprietary secrets about seals—Friedrich was the best in the Midwest at shimming new pads when he made flute repairs.

After a few precise questions, Clara suggested the new technician had been discussing the seals at the Como Park Zoo. I had to admit I'd heard him say something about his daughter liking the monkeys, but I'd figured that was a code.

Honestly, who wouldn't have suspected him of espionage? Friedrich guarded his flute-repair secrets with his life.

Clara spoke around a mouthful of whole-grain toast. "I don't get how you can watch the waiters at the club when you're supposed to be playing your flute."

"Oh, please. The pieces they request take about as much concentration as a long nap."

Dimples flashed in the smooth skin of her cheeks, then disappeared. "Yep. You need a life."

A hint of sadness colored her tone. Did she think I was that unhappy? I reached across the table and laid my hand over hers. "I have a life. I have you."

Her nose wrinkled in what I called her "bunny grin." I loved her goofy, squish-faced smile. Then she tossed her hair back over her shoulder. "So why do you keep trying to uncover mysteries?"

"It's a gift," I said breezily.

She tossed a crust in my direction.

I ducked. "Seriously. Musicians are more attuned to detail. We notice subtle things."

"I've never heard Lena trying to solve crimes."

"She's a harpist." I smiled. "She's got her head in the clouds."

"And you don't?"

"Don't you have someplace you're supposed to be? Like school?"

She guzzled her orange juice and grabbed her backpack. "I can tell when I'm not wanted." She stuck out her tongue. "Oh, and I'll be home late."

"Let me guess . . ."

"Cheerleading practice," she crowed. "Have a good day."

"Have a better one."

And she was gone. I poured myself a second cup of coffee and slumped onto my chair, studying my appointment calendar.

Sean Finnegan for voice coaching at ten.

I groaned. I hated tenors—especially this one, whose thick timbre made him sound like he forced the notes through a mouthful of mashed potatoes. But I couldn't afford to turn him away. Daytime students were hard to come by, especially since I only taught adults and a few exceptional teens. I could easily drum up students to fill the after-work hours, but I wanted to reserve most of my evenings for Clara.

At noon, Tessa Williams was coming on her lunch hour for a flute lesson. She wouldn't be half bad if she could improve her breath support. She played with a local jazz group, and I was helping her expand her classical repertoire. She'd probably cut the hour short, as usual, so she could rush back to her secretarial job.

I rested my chin in my hand. A gifted musician like Tessa shouldn't have to work as a secretary, but performing as a musician was rarely enough to pay the bills unless you were in a large orchestra that hired full-time musicians. The competition was intense for those spots. I'd walked away from the opportunity fifteen years ago. I'd had two years at Juilliard and nothing but promise ahead of me.

My coffee suddenly tasted bitter, and I stood to pour the rest down the sink. If I hurried, I could fit in some practice time before Sean arrived. Snatched hours with my flute kept my dream alive. When I played, I could hear the full orchestra filling the concert hall while my descant line soared. Sometimes the imaginary music even drowned out the gremlins in my brain that murmured, "Past her prime. Not enough experience. Too late now."

The hour of playing flew by, and all too soon my progression of Friday students began. I cajoled, coached, and criticized. With each student's clumsy phrasing or ham-handed technique, I reminded myself that I had chosen this life.

No, I hadn't exactly chosen this, but it had been the best alternative I could come up with at the time.

On Saturday afternoon I was more than ready to escape my students and play some music—even if it was for a church basement wedding reception. Lena's van pulled into the parking lot right behind me. I helped her unload and tow her custom hand truck into the church and onto a service elevator.

"Whenever the flute drives me crazy, I thank my lucky stars I don't play a harp." I panted as we pushed the mammoth instrument down the basement hallway.

Lena giggled. "Yeah, and how come you don't see any burly men playing harp? It's not fair."

In contrast to my fireplug physique, she was rail thin, but she carried her long limbs with grace—a grace that vibrated from her when her hands touched the harp strings.

We passed through double doors and into a carpeted church hall. White tablecloths and hundreds of tiny votive candles erased the feeling of being in a humble basement. White covers with satin ribbons camouflaged the folding chairs. Lena directed me to the corner where we'd provide another elegant touch with our harp and flute duets. She happily set up her music.

Lena and I had been roommates at Juilliard, but she'd done everything in the right order. She graduated, built her career, and then married and had children. Now she had a steady job with the Minneapolis Symphony whenever they performed pieces that required a harp. Her husband could watch the kids when she had evening concerts.

Did Lena know she was living my life? The life I was supposed to have?

Unaware of the pangs of envy I was experiencing, she coaxed the cover off her harp, giving a small sigh of pleasure as her instrument was revealed. I wondered if she smiled at her husband, Ken, with the same adoration. Probably. She'd left her position with the Dallas Symphony when he was transferred to Minnesota. Of course it had helped that Clara and I lived in Minneapolis, and it didn't take her long to land a plum job here, as well.

I unslung my music bag from my shoulders and lifted out my flute case.

Lena plucked a string. "Amy?"

"Hmm?" I unpacked my portfolio of sheet music and frowned. "Are you sure we have to play the Canon in D?" If I never had to play that old chestnut again, it would be too soon.

"Amy."

I glanced her way and then continued adjusting my music stand. "What?"

"I'm trying to tell you—"

"Hey, let's do the Galway arrangement of 'Ashokan Farewell,' okay?"

"Amy!"

I plopped my heavy folder onto the stand and stared at her. "What is it?"

She clasped her hands together and stood stiffly, as if about to make a pronouncement. "Cheryl Stinson is moving to Boston."

I wrinkled my forehead. Where had I heard that name? "Cheryl? The flutist?"

Lena's smile nearly glowed. "The very same."

My knees suddenly went limp, and I sank onto my chair.

So the rumors were true! It had been two years since a position had opened up in the symphony's flute section. Back then, I didn't think Clara was ready for me to take on such a demanding job. And government cuts to arts grants made it an unreliable income. I couldn't risk giving up my students to follow my dreams.

But now . . .

I felt dizzy and realized I'd stopped breathing. I pulled in a lungful of oxygen and met Lena's eyes. "When are auditions?"

"They're doing an open call next Saturday."

"One week! I'll never be ready in time."

Lena reached over and tousled the chopped lengths of my hair. "You've been ready for a long time."

I turned away to hide the emotion that swelled until I felt like I would choke. One week. I had one week to find out if my dreams were too far buried to revive.

CHAPTER

> *Determinato: A directive to the performer to play*
> *a particular passage in a determined or resolute*
> *manner.*

The morning of final auditions dawned with streaks of peach in a pale gray sky. I know because I woke up at four and couldn't get back to sleep. I pulled a sweatshirt over my pajamas, slipped into my moccasins, and sat on the back steps waiting for the sun. Being one step closer to my dream made my nerves knot up like bad macramé.

The back alley was dark for the first two hours. I heard occasional rustling sounds, but for once I had no detective urges. Squirrels? A stray, urban raccoon? Burglars? I didn't care. I stared into the shadows, paralyzed.

A place in the Minneapolis Symphony. What was I thinking? I was thirty-six years old. Too young for a midlife crisis and too old to chase after pipe dreams. Why had I agreed to audition?

Sure, my technique was well-honed and of professional caliber. But who would want a flutist with no major orchestral experience since college?

With Lena and Clara both nagging, I had made a call on Monday morning to set up an appointment. Then I had spent the week drilling, polishing, updating my vitae, and feeling sick to my stomach.

On Saturday I'd endured the initial blind auditions. Conservatories and orchestras traditionally blocked the musician from view to prevent any accusation of discrimination or favoritism. The music was all that counted.

The screens had helped me forget the panel hidden on the other side. With the safety of anonymity, I'd nailed the basic repertory. They'd called two days later to invite me to a final audition—and in an unusual twist, this one wouldn't be blind. That news turned my queasy nerves into full-blown panic. Now another Saturday had arrived, and there was no turning back.

I forced myself off the porch, sketched a salute to the sunrise, and marched into the house to prepare.

Clara gave me a pep talk over a breakfast that I didn't eat. Then she skipped out the door for work. At nine, I drove downtown to the Hennepin Center for the Arts. The symphony was renting rehearsal space there. I circled the block several times, determined to avoid paying the crazy fees for the adjacent parking lot.

Okay, so I was stalling.

Snugging my Saturn up to the curb on Fifth Street, I gripped the steering wheel and tried to muster the confidence I needed.

A gaggle of fresh-scrubbed ballet students walked past. Hair in tight buns, mile-long jeans, black leotards visible under their jackets, they strolled with loose-jointed energy.

Just get out of the car. You can do that much.

Angry with myself for the terror gripping my throat, I threw open my door and narrowly missed a kid biking past. Even on a Saturday morning, the downtown streets buzzed with energy.

I launched out of the car and grabbed my heavy shoulder bag. I'd brought my two best flutes, and a thick portfolio of music— even though I had my piece memorized. I planned to be ready for anything.

The stately eight stories of stone loomed over me, and I gave the building my most intimidating glare.

I belonged here. No one could tell me otherwise.

I marched into the lobby and straight into a waiting elevator. Muzak intruded from tinny speakers. You'd think in an arts center they would have more taste.

In the mirrored panel of the elevator, I saw a short woman, overdressed for a Saturday morning in flowing black pants and a white silk blouse, with her brow furrowed in irritation under jutting wedges of coppery hair. I rubbed my forehead to smooth out the wrinkles and tried a demure smile.

Now the reflection looked sickly.

I shrugged. Nothing about me fit the stereotype of a flutist. Musicians had jokes about various instrumentalists. Psychologists had even done research studies on the personalities of each section of the orchestra.

Nothing ethereal or graceful about me. I bucked the trend, in looks and in demeanor.

The elevator doors opened onto a long hallway, and I marched toward a table set up midway to the end. A woman with a clipboard was answering questions for a girl who looked as scrawny as a twelve-year-old. Her small case tagged her as a flute player.

I grinned. I'd grind her into the dust.

The woman behind the table threw a harried glance my way. "Viola auditions in room 312."

A low growl vibrated through my neck. I might not look like a typical flutist, but I was still annoyed at her assumption. "I'm here for my flute audition."

Both women turned their heads to look at me.

Clipboard lady blinked a few times. "Name?"

"Amy Johnson." I sighed to myself. My name wasn't exotic enough for the world-class flutist I wanted to be. How many gifted and tormented artists do you know named Amy Johnson?

"Uh, sure. Down there." She waved a pen toward the end of the hall.

I stomped past her, stoking the fire in my belly. Irritation was a good fuel for anger. Anger burned off my fear.

A sheet of typing paper hung crookedly on the door at the end of the hall. *Flute Auditions* was scrawled in black marker, followed by a thrillingly short list of names and times. No one was scheduled before me, so I pushed open the door and entered.

The room was fairly small. A piano filled one corner, and several chairs waited behind a long table near another door. I cleared my throat. The acoustics weren't bad. I snapped my fingers a few times, testing the echo.

My Pearl flute, definitely. I turned away from the door, opened my case, and assembled the golden instrument.

The far door creaked open. "Miss? The viola auditions are down the hall."

Instead of arguing, I turned and lifted my flute.

"Oh, sorry." The kid facing me was rumpled and carried a stack of scores. He thumped them onto the table.

"I get that a lot," I said, struggling to hide my annoyance.

He laughed—a deep, mature sound—and I looked closer. No, he wasn't a kid. The short stature had fooled me, along with the hair, curly and too long. But he had creases around his eyes and the subtle arrogance of experience.

He dropped into a chair and kicked his feet up onto the table. "Yeah, I've always got musicians asking me to fetch them some water—until I'm introduced."

My pulse leapt into cut time. "You're . . ."

"Peter Cadfael Wilson. They're making me sit in on these. Seem to think they need my opinion."

I caught a hint of an accent. Where had Lena said the new conductor was from? "British?"

He shrugged. "From all over, actually."

I strode forward, cradling my flute in my left arm, and offered him my hand. "Amy Johnson. I'm here for the flute position."

He reached forward to give my hand a quick shake, then leaned back, lifting an amused eyebrow. "Yes, I believe we established that."

My face heated, and I hurried back to my bag and pulled out my portfolio.

The door clanged open and more people entered, sipping coffee, chatting, arranging themselves at the table.

I handed the piano score for my Mozart piece to the pianist, and he yawned.

Yeah, yeah. They'd all heard this piece before. Well, they hadn't heard me play it yet. Today I had to make them forget Rampal and any other flutist they'd heard play this piece. I ran through a few scales. Nervousness corrupted my tone with breathiness.

Shake it off, Amy. Don't let these pretentious kids rattle you.

"Ready?" An angular young woman with long, ash-blond hair tapped her pen on the table. Probably the principal flutist.

"Almost." I handed copies of my résumé to each of the panelists. Semiprofessional chamber orchestras, teaching, and wedding gigs were a far cry from what they'd be looking for.

Peter Wilson kept his feet up, ignoring the onionskin paper I set on the table near him. He crossed his arms and studied me through narrowed eyes. No more amusement on his features. He had become Herr Conductor to the bone.

I returned to the piano to check my tuning. Rehearsal pianos were notorious for going out of tune, but this one sounded fine.

A few whispered directions to my accompanist for tempo, and I was ready. I took a strong stance, poised like a diver on the edge of the board.

The expressions of the panel members were grim, skeptical.

Suddenly, I couldn't breathe. I wanted to run from the room, but my feet were glued to the floor. I did the only thing that could carry me through my terror. I raised my instrument and attacked the opening allegro for all I was worth.

The panel of judges disappeared. The piano faded to a soft supporting background, serving my every whim. My eyes closed as I ignored the music on my stand.

My tempo was daring, and my approach was fierce instead of playful. When I reached the first cadenza, I took the ultimate risk. Instead of playing a familiar and safe arrangement, I took advantage of this rare passage that allowed for improvisation and gave them a fiery interpretation of my own. As the movement concluded, I articulated harsh tonguing in phrases that many flutists would choose to slur.

This was not their grandmother's Mozart.

Somehow, the rage I felt at the course my life had taken, at the lost opportunities, infused my music. When I reached the end of the movement, I looked up, dazed.

The flutist on the panel cleared her throat. "Well, that was . . . interesting. Continue."

I nodded to the pianist and entered the adagio. Purged of my temper for the time being, I floated, soared, and let my music weep for joy. Tone was more important than ever, and I made my notes suspend, growing into a stronger vibrato, then cascading forward to the next fermata.

This movement always reminded me of Clara. Of rocking her to sleep when she was a baby. Of night-lights, the smell of baby powder, and her soft hair against my face.

The closing rondo that had given me so much trouble felt almost like an afterthought. I kept it technically clean and precise, the way Mozart demanded to be played. I stopped rebelling and obeyed the music.

When I finished, I lowered my instrument and forced my eyes to focus on the panel. The flutist was pointing out something on my résumé to her neighbor and whispering.

I hadn't expected a standing ovation, but I had assumed they would at least be attentive. My gaze traveled to the conductor. His feet had transferred to the floor sometime in the past twenty minutes. He was leaning forward, elbows resting on the table, expression shuttered. I couldn't read him at all.

I had always believed that playing my music in the obscurity of my living room while aching for a wider platform was the ultimate pain a musician could feel. But I had been wrong. This supreme indifference in the face of my best performance—this was true torture.

I swallowed back the sudden thickness in my throat and turned to thank my accompanist, already twisting my mouthpiece away from the body of the flute.

"What else is in your repertoire?" The precise diction of the conductor startled me out of my thoughts.

"Um . . . well. Did you . . ."

"Something contemporary?"

I nodded. "J-j-jazz? Celtic? Avant-garde?"

"Wedding music?" the flutist said snidely.

Peter Wilson frowned at her.

I lifted my chin. "How about a little Sciarrino?" Pure avant-garde composer. I would enjoy forcing my tone into the harsh shrieks that the music demanded.

The conductor turned back to me and winced. "How about music instead?"

Okay, so Sciarrino is an acquired taste. "Takemitsu?"

Wilson leaned back. "Really?"

I had his interest. Haunting, atonal—Japanese compositions were a challenge to North American flutists. But I'd had a teacher at Juilliard who introduced me to his music, and I'd never forgotten. I pulled a sheet from my portfolio to refresh my memory. All my pencil notations winked at me, reminding me of the battle I'd fought over intonation and breathiness in each phrase. Now the music was an old friend.

Ignoring the panel, I lifted the flute to my lips. I eased into the melody and invoked a ripple of movement across a still pond, a stately bonsai, and a poignant loneliness.

A chair scraped harshly. "Thank you. That's enough." A woman's voice intruded.

I stopped short and lowered my flute.

Another woman on the end of the table checked her watch. "We'll be in touch."

My gaze shifted to the conductor, but he was scratching some notes and didn't look up. Probably making a grocery list, for all the interest he was showing now.

"Thank you for your time." I choked out the words, grabbed music, case, and bag, and hurried to the hallway, still cradling my flute. The door shut behind me. My fingers fumbled with stiffness as I separated the pieces of my flute, cleaned them, and laid them gently in the case.

I closed the lid before letting my humiliation surge forward, as if I needed to protect my instrument from the rejection.

"It's not your fault," I whispered to the closed case. "You were beautiful."

Head held high, I strode to the elevator. I ignored everyone I passed on my way out of the building and to my car. My chin shook from the effort to hold myself together. Once I was in the driver's seat, I gripped the wheel, lowered my head, and allowed myself one wrenching sob of defeat.

CHAPTER

3

Inconsolato: *A directive to a musician to perform a passage in a mournful style.*

I'll be right over." Lena's calm voice came through my phone. Her children shrieked in the background.

"No, you don't have to—"

"Of course I do. Ken can watch the kids. My call at the theatre isn't until six tonight, so I'm free as a bird."

"But—"

Dial tone.

Great. Why had I called her? Now I had to splash cold water on my face and try to erase any sign of blubbering. In spite of my best efforts, tears had continued to leak from my eyes on my drive home, making my nose stuffy. Maybe she'd believe I was coming down with a cold.

I should have indulged in some solitary chocolate therapy and a long, hot bath. Now that the adrenaline had bled away, I felt exhausted as well as depressed. But I'd promised to call her when I got home from the audition. If I hadn't, she would have shown up on my doorstep anyway.

I slumped on the piano bench and picked out a melancholy etude. I'd been through audition panels years ago—and juried performances. The blank faces, frowns, scribbled notes—I should have been prepared.

The phone rang in the kitchen. I always kept the ringer soft so I wouldn't be disturbed during lessons, but today in the empty house, the sound echoed demandingly. A trill of excitement revived my energy.

What if?

Don't be silly, Amy. They have lots of other musicians to hear today. They couldn't be calling yet.

My pulse ignored my logic. "Hello?" *Why do I sound so young and breathless?*

"Mom? How'd it go?" Dishes clattered in the background and an espresso machine hissed.

"They hated me."

"Mo-thhher. I doubt that."

"I'm telling you, they barely listened. And I'm sure they all had a good laugh at my résumé. I told you I shouldn't have done this."

Clara sighed. "When will they call?"

"Who knows? They probably won't even bother."

"Have you called Aunt Lena?"

Since I had no siblings, Lena had been Clara's honorary aunt since before my daughter's birth. She'd faithfully stayed in touch from Juilliard, and later from Texas. "Yeah, she's coming over to help me lick my wounds." Wait, that wasn't a very appealing image.

"Good. Oh, and hey, she asked if I could baby-sit tonight. She's got a concert and Ken has a photo shoot."

"Sure." Clara adored Zach and Janell. She had unending patience for the two grade-schoolers.

"Will you be okay? Would you rather have me stay home tonight?"

"Don't be silly," I groused, irritated that both my daughter and my best friend saw me as needy.

"Oh, and, Mom? There's a meeting of the cheerleader moms on Tuesday night, okay?"

I pressed my forehead against the smooth surface of the refrigerator. "What?"

"I didn't tell you earlier because you were . . . preoccupied this past week. But you can come, right?" Her voice was infused with enthusiasm.

How could I let her down? She'd been *my* cheerleader since she could talk. "Sure, I can be there."

The buzz of conversation and ping of the cash register sounded through the phone. "Thanks, Mom. Gotta go. Love ya."

I stared at the receiver and listened to a dial tone. A cheerleader mom? I shuddered. Could my life get any worse?

A tap at the back door yanked me out of my pity party.

I pulled the door open, determined to convince Lena that I was fine.

"Hi!" Lena stuffed her keys into the pocket of her jeans. "I parked in your driveway. Couldn't find a spot on the street." She stepped into the kitchen and threw her arms around me, startling me. "Oh, Amy. I'm sure something will work out one day. God made you to be a musician."

God? I stiffened. "Lena, it's no big deal."

She pulled back and nodded, wiping tears from her cheeks. "Right. Let's go for a walk. It's a gorgeous day."

Relieved that she'd stopped emoting all over me, I grabbed my jacket. I preferred putting my emotion into music, not exposing it in real life . . . even to my best friend.

The door locked behind us with a secure click. We crossed my tiny patch of dormant backyard grass and pushed open the gate in the chain-link fence. Graffiti sprawled across the neighbor's garage on the other side of the alley.

"They're at it again. I've got to get a pair of binoculars. Or maybe a zoom lens for my camera. I'm sure I'll catch them in time to call the police next time."

Lena looked around, confused.

I pointed. "The artwork. Couple of punks. They've hit a bunch of Dumpsters and garages in our neighborhood. If the police would just test the paint, I'm sure they could track down the criminals."

Lena giggled. "Yeah, like *CSI*."

"What's so funny?"

She patted my shoulder. "Nothing."

"Stop patronizing me." My words came out sharper than I'd intended.

"All right. I just think the police might be a little busy with murders and car thefts and drug dealers. Maybe spray painting isn't high on their list."

I sniffed. As we passed the Nguyens' pungent garbage can, I wished I hadn't. "Well, they should make it a priority. If they'd lock up the delinquents now, they wouldn't be around to commit the armed robberies and murders later."

We reached the end of the alley and headed toward Minnehaha Creek. The wet smell of leaf mulch heaped on flower beds created an undertone. Fresh spring air provided the strongest note, with subtle higher pitches of stray bus fumes, budding florals, and the fabric softener from my jacket.

We walked three blocks in silence. The South Minneapolis homes had brick chimneys and patterned timbers reflecting the Scandinavian heritage of the founding residents. A wealth of elms and oaks with an occasional pine provided an illusion of a Nordic forest. On one corner, a gingerbread Victorian struggled to fit in.

I'd always loved the artistry and variety of the Twin Cities architecture. The suburbs might surrender to rows of identical townhomes, but in the city you could stumble across a hippie-built geodesic dome tucked between a large brick colonial and a multigabled Queen Anne. Not to mention the dozens of theatres and museums within an easy bus ride. They didn't call it the Mini Apple for nothing.

We dodged across another street, avoiding oncoming cars. The tires made a gritty sound in the sand that coated the street. "Street sweepers haven't been through here yet." I needed to break the silence. I felt the building pressure of the questions that were sure to come.

"Yeah. I hope they get out to our neighborhood soon. My kids keep tracking in grime. What's the city waiting for? We haven't had snow in weeks."

I smiled. "Classic signs of spring. Rain, robins, and street sweepers."

We headed toward a park bench along the creek's bank. Water rushed past. In August, it would be a muddy trickle, but right now the current gurgled and pushed stray branches in a dizzying ride downstream. Lena settled onto the bench.

"This is what makes living here worthwhile," she said with a happy sigh.

"Yeah. May and June."

"And September and October."

"The rest is misery," we said together, and laughed.

My laugh died away quickly.

Lena shifted to face me. "When will they let you know?"

I shrugged. "I didn't think to ask. I thought for a minute that Peter Wilson was interested in my playing, but the first flutist made fun of my résumé."

"Sarah? She's a royal pain. All the woodwinds say so. Don't let it get to you."

I shook my head. "Lena, it's too late for me. I made my choices."

Lena drew a breath to say something, then closed her mouth. After a long pause she shifted to study the creek. "Okay, maybe you won't land this position. But you need to be performing. And not just receptions and galas. Have you checked with the Metro Chamber Orchestra?"

"Stop humoring me. I don't want to keep putting myself through this. Find something else to nag me about."

"Okay. Ken and I want you to come over to dinner next week. And we're inviting a friend of ours."

I groaned. "No. No, no, no."

She toed a cigarette butt near her foot and kicked it into a patch of weeds. "You've hardly dated anyone since—"

"It doesn't work. If he isn't a musician, he doesn't understand my world. And if he is . . ." I exhaled through pursed lips.

Unwanted, the memories slammed into me. Dark eyes intense with emotion as his chin jerked to the bowing of his violin. And later memories—gentle fingers exploring my skin, instead of the strings of his instrument. Had I really ever been that young? My breath expelled heavily.

Lena patted my hand. She knew where my sigh had carried me.

At Juilliard, I had eyes only for music. Until Jason hovered outside my practice-room door.

He told me my Saint-Saens gave him goose bumps. The sweet-talker. Then he walked me to my dorm and we dissected the various music profs. He was as obsessed about music as I was. But his god

33

of choice was the violin. He'd worshiped it faithfully since he was three years old.

I thought I loved him. At least I loved dating someone else who had a passion for music.

Because she was my roommate, Lena saw me float into our dorm room early in the mornings, rumpled and blissfully happy after a night with Jason. She saw my shock when I learned I was pregnant . . . and my devastation when Jason's interest in me evaporated.

She understood what I'd sacrificed when I left Juilliard, and why. How could she encourage me to allow a man to tear apart my life again?

Lena squeezed my fingers. "Have you thought about trying to find him?"

I pulled away, shocked. "Why would I do that?"

"A girl needs a father." She worried her lower lip.

I frowned. "What has Clara said?"

"She doesn't understand why you won't talk about it. She was hoping I'd tell her more, and—"

"You didn't—"

"Of course not. But your answers aren't going to be enough for her forever."

I stood and walked to the edge of the creek, snapping a twig off one of the barren bushes. My hand shook as I twisted the stick in my hands, tamping down a swell of fury. Lena was supposed to be comforting me after my rough audition, not poking into dark closets.

She drifted over to stand beside me. "I'm sorry. I shouldn't have . . ." Sometimes Lena seemed annoyingly fragile. Too gentle. Nothing to push back against.

"He wanted nothing to do with us then. I'm sure that hasn't changed. And I'm thinking I should give up on music, too. Too much heartache."

"Hmm."

"What does that mean?"

She pulled a small envelope from her pocket. "So then, you won't be wanting the comp ticket I picked up for you for tonight's performance?"

I dropped the stick and snatched the envelope from her hand. "What are you playing tonight?" I usually kept tabs on the symphony's upcoming repertory, but I'd been so distracted this week, I couldn't remember what Lena had been working on.

She grinned. "Shakespeare."

"Huh?"

"Mendelssohn's *Midsummer Night's Dream*, Prokofiev's *Romeo and Juliet*." She teased the ticket from my hand. "Unless it will depress you to come."

I grabbed the envelope back. "Maybe this will be my last visit. Then I'll smash my classical records, sell my flutes, and get a normal life."

"CDs."

"What?"

"You have to smash your CDs, not your records."

"Oh." I studied the creek and watched a leaf swirl downstream. "Well, that doesn't have the same ring. I guess I'll keep them."

"That's the spirit. Besides, I've started to think that things happen for a reason. You wouldn't be so talented if there weren't a purpose for it all."

Great. More of Lena's optimism. I'd had my quota for the day. "A purpose?"

"Yeah, you know. Like the reason God put you on earth."

I edged away and looked hard at my best friend. "Are you on a religious kick or something?"

Her pale skin turned pink, and she studied the ground without answering.

"Lena! You are! What on earth have you gotten yourself into now?"

She drifted back to the bench and sat down, rubbing her temples. "It's hard to explain." She shot me a worried glance. "Don't make fun of this, okay?"

I fought the urge to roll my eyes. I'd seen Lena dabble in all kinds of weird things over the years. "Okay . . ." I sat down beside her.

She gave me a relieved smile. "I've been wanting to talk to you, but you've had so much on your mind. See, a friend invited the kids to Sunday school, and they really liked it. Ken and I were worried about what kind of propaganda they were being fed, so we decided to visit and check it out."

I nodded. Made sense. She was wise to be careful. I hurried past most churches with an uneasy suspicion. Maybe people without music to make their lives meaningful needed something to fill the space. But I didn't want to get messed up in a lot of hocus-pocus.

Now her face took on the glow it carried when she played her harp. "Well, we liked it. We started going every week. I can't explain, but . . . there's something so amazing about feeling God's love, and . . ." The gaze she turned on me took on an alarming zealot's gleam. "It makes sense to me now. All of it. Why we're here. Why our lives matter. What happens afterwards." She rushed her words as if afraid I'd interrupt.

She didn't need to worry. I was too surprised to say anything.

"So, anyway, would you like to come to church with us tomorrow? It's just what you need."

Those last words chased away my mild concern for her and the flicker of curiosity I might have felt. "I don't *need* anything. Stop trying to fix me. I'm fine." I jumped to my feet. "Look, it's been a rough morning, and I want some time alone, okay?" I spun away and headed home with strides as long as my short legs could make. I didn't bother looking back.

Lena was always pressuring me to pursue my professional goals, and she often nagged me about my nonexistent dating life. I could handle that kind of meddling—barely. But I couldn't handle her resurrecting the specter of Jason or stuffing religion down my throat.

When I neared my house, I pulled out my keys and the symphony ticket crumpled in my pocket. I smoothed the envelope and stared at it. How could I watch Peter Wilson conduct after my humiliating audition? How could I listen to Lena perform when I was so mad at her?

Prokofiev and Mendelssohn. A free evening of top-notch music. How could I not?

CHAPTER

 Impetuoso: A directive to a musician to perform a certain passage in a vehement or impetuous manner.

I stomped into my kitchen and locked the back door behind me. A hot shower and a nap—that's what I needed. Time enough later to deal with my conflicting emotions and decide about the concert.

While I trudged up the stairs, I heard the doorbell, followed by insistent knocking at the kitchen door.

Call me immature, but I ignored Lena. By the time I had grabbed a change of clothes, I heard her car pull out of my driveway.

A wave of satisfaction flicked through the darker parts of my psyche. Then shame welled up instead. Lena didn't deserve my bad temper. She was just a convenient target because I was feeling so . . .

Defeated? Vulnerable? Afraid?

I raked my hands through my hair. Never. I was tough. I'd proven it over and over. You had to be tough to be a professional musician. You had to be tough to raise a child alone. The audition had been stressful, and that had rattled me—made me overreact to Lena's meddling.

I stepped into the shower and let the water pound me. I'd apologize to her after the concert. She'd understand. She knew I didn't like being pushed.

I scrubbed my skin and wished I could scrub my brain as well— wipe away memories, unsettled nerves, and most of all dangerous hopes. After toweling off, I slipped on a pair of faded jeans and a soft sweater, curled up on my bed, and turned on a CD of Debussy. The music swirled me away to a place of blissful emptiness and gently carried me to sleep.

A scraping sound woke me. I frowned with my eyes still squeezed shut. I could hear the creak of an aluminum ladder. Lena wouldn't be climbing up to my window, would she?

I forced my eyelids open and checked my clock. Two hours had passed. A big yawn made my jaw crackle. Then I heard more sounds from the neighbor's backyard—the neighbor who had moved out two weeks ago.

The new owners weren't moving in until the end of the month. Who was rattling around the vacant house?

My sleep-fog evaporated, and my pulse jumped to high alert. I slipped from the bed, tiptoed across the carpet, and pressed against my wall alongside the window that faced the neighbor's house. I edged the curtain back just enough to peer out.

From my angle, I saw a man in a windbreaker and baggy pants skulking around the backyard. The neighbor's garage door was open, and a ladder stretched up the back of the house.

Talk about an opportunistic thief. He didn't even bring his own ladder. While my eyes widened, the man scaled the ladder toward the top floor of my neighbor's home. He had some sort of glass cutter in his hand.

I fumbled for the phone on the bedside table, dropped it, and grabbed again with shaking hands. I had to try twice before I managed to punch in 911.

"911 operator. What's your emergency?"

"There's a thief." My voice was hoarse from a giddy fear.

"What did you say?"

"A guy is breaking into my neighbor's house," I whispered.

"Ma'am, can you speak up?"

Okay, so the guy probably wouldn't be able to hear me talking inside my house with the windows shut. "I said someone is robbing my neighbor."

"Is there anyone in the house?"

"No. He moved out last weekend. It's empty as far as I know. But the thief is up on a ladder."

"Okay, ma'am. Don't panic."

I am not panicking. I thought I was doing a great job with my first genuine crime report. "Hurry. You'll want to catch him in the act." I rattled off my address and described the neighbor's house. I couldn't for the life of me remember if his house number was higher or lower than mine. All my reasoning power seemed to have left me. "The thief is Hispanic, with a dark blue windbreaker. I think I saw a moustache. He took the ladder out of the garage on the property." I dared another peek. "And he's fiddling around with an upstairs window."

"Okay, stay on the line. We'll have an officer there right away."

"Should I go out and stall him if he climbs down the ladder before the police get here?"

"No!" The dispatcher sounded alarmed. "Wait in your house. The police will check it out and then come and talk to you. Stay where you are."

I tucked the curtain back so I could get a better view. The man climbed down the ladder and began probing the first-floor window on the back side of the house. Talk about brazen! He glanced up and looked around.

I ducked, terrified he had seen my face looking out at him.

Then another thought intruded into my excitement and made me feel a little sick. What if he was a city worker? A house inspector? A meter reader?

I dropped the receiver onto my bed and scampered down the stairs and to my front windows. Lots of cars, vans, and trucks were parked along both sides of the curb, but nothing that looked remotely official.

Nope, the guy was definitely a crook.

I raced back upstairs and apologized to the dispatcher who had been calling for me through the phone line.

"Sorry. I just had to check on something."

"The police are almost there."

"I don't hear any sirens. Where are they?" I felt like I was going to jump out of my skin.

"Is the man still there?"

"Yes. Now he's messing around with the first-floor window at the back of the house. Do something!" Even on the second story, with my doors securely locked, and a solid wall protecting me, my heart thudded as hard as if he were jimmying my window instead of the neighbor's. I grabbed a pillow and squeezed it against my chest—my own version of bulletproofing.

I heard car doors from the street. A uniformed policeman approached slowly along the side of the house, so I had a front-row seat to the whole scene. Wait until Clara heard about this.

The policeman said something, and the man turned, startled, and dropped his tool.

Another younger policeman appeared from behind the garage.

Good, they had him surrounded.

But instead of throwing him up against the house to search him, the police seemed to be having a chat with him. Then the man handed the police a card and a piece of paper.

What on earth were they doing? Exchanging recipes?

Furious, I stomped down the stairs, out my back door, and over to the neighbor's backyard.

"That's the man." I pointed with all the conviction of a witness in a *Law and Order* episode. "He was trying to get in their window. He's not the owner."

The crook muttered something in Spanish and spit into the hostas.

The older policeman turned to me. "Ma'am, are you the one who called 911?"

I drew myself up to my full five-foot-three height, ready to accept their accolades. "Yes. I heard him scrambling around on the ladder. I'm a musician. I have good ears."

The officer rubbed his chin. "Ah, right. Well, it seems there's been a misunderstanding."

I tapped my foot. "Don't let him con you. He's the one who pulled out the ladder."

"Yes, he doesn't deny that. The owner said he could use it."

"What? I don't believe that."

The officer glanced at the younger cop, tugged on his belt, which was heavy with interesting-looking gadgets, and squeezed his lips together as if struggling not to laugh. "Mr. Sanchez is a painter. The new owners hired him."

The younger cop nodded and held up a work order. "He was checking to see what kind of prep work the window trim would need."

Heat flared across my cheeks. "But, but . . . he had a tool . . ."

The younger policeman gave a snort of laughter, reached down, and picked up a chisel. "Yeah, painters often have tools, ma'am."

"Thanks for calling us. It's better to be safe than sorry." The older cop's condescension added to my humiliation.

I slunk back to my house and closed my door firmly, but I could still hear all three men chuckling next door.

Clara was right. My alertness to crime was a sickness. A neurotic distraction that compensated for my unfulfilled artistic passions. And maybe a few other unfulfilled passions as well.

I marched into the living room and glared at the generous row of Sue Grafton books over the fireplace. "That's it. No more. I'm done with solving crimes. I'm sick of making an idiot of myself."

I sank into a chair and studied the large front room. Our two-story stucco house was modest and well-worn—except this pride-and-joy room. Polished wood floors gleamed as late-afternoon sun poured through the arched windows. The triple panes were soundproof so my students could trill a Sousa march on piccolo without bothering neighbors. My Steinway ruled one corner of the room. Music stands, cupboards, and filing drawers clustered along two walls. My flutes held a place of honor in a fleece-lined cabinet. On the near side of the room, Scandinavian bookshelves surrounded the brick fireplace and held my dad's old collection of leather-bound mysteries. He'd passed those down to me along with his artistic temperament and copper-red hair.

My gaze snagged on my flutes: the Gemeinhardt that I sometimes used with students, my beloved Altus with a hand-carved Tanaka head joint, and the gold Pearl flute with the sinfully rich tone. That baby cost more than my two-door Saturn and was worth every penny.

I pulled the silver Altus from the cabinet. The Mozart piece had given me some challenges at auditions, but I'd thought of a new fingering to try. A few scales warmed up my embouchure, then the adagio passage got me into the spirit of the piece. When I reached the rondo, my tempo flew. I coaxed myself to slow down, but the music grabbed me and pulled, like a boat towing a water-skier over the waves.

Until I hit the difficult section at the rapid tempo.

My fingers stumbled. I crashed into the swells. Sputtering and spitting the lake water from my mouth, I surfaced. Slowly, patiently, I rebuilt the measure. Note by note, I repeated the phrase. Then I took a running start and sailed through. Exhilaration flooded me. Better than the first bite of French silk pie. Better than sex. Better than the plunge of a roller coaster.

I returned to the beginning of the piece, the challenging allegro, ready to put the pieces together at the correct tempo. The music seduced me, carried me, invaded me. Over and over.

Close to perfect. So close. One more time through. And then one more.

"Mom? Mo-om!" A hand touched my shoulder.

I jumped, blinked, lowered the flute, and struggled to return to earth. "What?" My voice was too sharp. Clara was used to that. She knew not to interrupt me when I was playing.

"Lena's picking me up soon." Her smile was knowing, as if she'd caught me kissing a date on the front porch.

"Already?" I looked out the windows. Shadows stretched against the sidewalk. I rolled my shoulders, still confused—trapped in the space between the heaven of music and my living room. "When did you get home?"

"An hour ago." She stared at my flute. "Thought you were giving up."

"I plan to. As soon as I hear from the symphony that I didn't make it, I'm going to look for a job as an accountant."

"Yeah. That'll work. Especially with the way you balance our checkbook. Oh, that's Lena's car. See ya!" She dashed out, leaving me still trying to think of a snappy comeback.

I spun on my heel and went upstairs to dress for the symphony. Clara didn't believe me, but this time I meant it. Time to give up on my musical pipe dreams.

Of course, music had a few tricks up her sleeve. She would never allow me to defect without a fight. And music didn't fight fair. Sitting in the dark theatre that night, each note grabbed my heart.

The Prokofiev was lush, rich, captivating. The concertmaster led the violin section in line after line of thrumming power. I sat alone in the dark and wept for the beauty of it. Even the large woman with too-strong perfume on my right, and the old man who kept clearing his throat on my left, couldn't distract me from this time of worship.

How could I have backslidden? How could I have considered renouncing my faith in the arts? I bowed my head in penitence.

Music was my world. It owned me. And I was a grateful servant.

While my deepest soul heeded the call to pursue my musical dreams, the superficial side of my nature studied the conductor.

I was in a cheap seat on the far right of the theatre and could watch his profile. On the podium, his short stature disappeared. He was only a few inches taller than I was, but he led the symphony like a giant. The locks of hair flopping over his eyes made him seem far too young to be a conductor, but he was probably in his forties. Sweat gleamed on his temples as he bounced with energy, coaxing and coercing more and more beauty from the musicians. I saw his jaw clench, his breath pant with the meter of the music. And I understood. He had become the music.

I was so captivated that I almost missed Lena's beautiful harp passage. She did a wonderful job, as always, and I felt another stab of remorse for being such an ornery friend to her. She'd get over her religion kick, just like she'd gotten over yoga, Amway, a vegan diet, no-money-down real estate, the joys of breast-feeding, and saving the whales.

My obsessions had remained more narrow and focused over the years—music, music, and music. And she'd put up with me. The least I could do was forgive her eccentricities and ride out her latest craze.

After the concert, I waited for Lena in the back hallway. I eavesdropped unabashedly on snatches of conversations between the few musicians who clustered around in formal black. There was a general spirit of ebullience. Great musicians loved a chance to shine, and tonight's performance had shimmered. But there were also mutters about their upcoming dislocation.

Symphonic Hall, internationally known for amazing acoustics, needed some painting and general fixing up. The orchestra would be performing at several other local theatres while work commenced.

"Cheer up," one man said to another musician. "It'll be fun playing some different venues."

"Easy for you to say. You don't play timpani."

"You came." Lena's greeting sailed over the chatter. She gave me a firm hug.

"Seamless. Amazing. That second movement took my breath away," I raved. "Although I thought he dragged the tempo."

"That's because you like everything at lightning speed. You need to slow down, Amy. Enjoy the scenery."

A gaunt woman elbowed past. Lena grabbed her arm. "Sarah, have you met my dear friend, Amy Johnson? She was my roommate at Juilliard."

Sarah had the same disdainful lift to her nose that I remembered from my audition. "Oh, really?" She spared me a glance. "Do you play something?"

I let my eyes travel up and down her black gown. "Yes, do you?"

I heard a cough of laughter behind me and turned.

A hand thrust toward me. "Peter Wilson, Ms. Johnson. In case you don't remember."

Heat burned my face. I squared my jaw and shook his hand, refusing to be cowed, even though he'd overheard me slamming his principal flutist. "Oh, I remember." I cast another look toward Sarah. "Although apparently, I didn't make much of an impression."

I made myself sound as if it made no difference to me. As if offers were pouring in and if the audition panel was too stupid to recognize my talent, it was their loss.

The flicker of his smile was almost subliminal before he turned away.

A reporter elbowed closer. "Mr. Wilson, could you answer a few questions? I'm doing a feature for the *StarTribune*."

The conductor was swept away in a tide of congratulations, questions, and invitations.

I turned back to Lena. "I'd better get out of here before anyone finds out you know me, and I ruin your career as well as my own."

Lena only laughed.

I flicked another gaze at the hallway where Peter Wilson had disappeared. "What do you think of this new conductor?"

"He seems to know what's he's doing. Not like that French guy who guested last season."

"Jean Clod?"

She giggled. "Shh. That nickname is just between you and me."

What would I do without Lena's friendship? I felt another throb of shame that I took out my temper on my good-natured friend so often. "I'm sorry about this afternoon." The words had to be squeezed past my reluctant throat. "I overreacted."

"You? Overreact? Now there's a shocker."

I almost glared at her, but then remembered I was trying to be apologetic. "How can I make it up to you? Free baby-sitting? Letting you pick all the music for our next gig? My homemade pepper bread?"

The crowd was thinning out. The florescent lights in the concrete hall were a sharp contrast to the lush magic that the main theatre had provided.

Lena tapped a long finger against her chin. "I've got it."

Oh, no. I didn't like the gleam in her eyes. "Tell me."

"Next week, you and Clara come visit our new church."

I smothered a growl of frustration. "Fine. Once. I suppose it's only fitting after the day I've had. Does your church have a patron saint of lost causes?"

CHAPTER

5

 Verismo: A term meaning "realism", applied to Romantic works, especially operas, of the late 19th century that have to do with unpleasant realities of life.

I remembered the silly head games from high school: trying to conjure a phone call from the cute guy in biology class. I hated to think I'd matured so little since then. But all day Monday, I dashed to the phone each time it rang. I couldn't stop myself.

Even though I knew my audition hadn't been promising, I couldn't completely squelch a stubborn hum of hope. After the blind auditions, I'd gotten word within a few days. Maybe this response would come quickly, too. There was a chance they'd made their decision already.

How much did Sarah's opinion count? She didn't seem to like me, but what about the other panel members? I tortured myself with speculation and replayed my pieces in my head a hundred times.

Monday night I called Lena and begged her to find out when the decision would be announced. She promised to do some checking but wasn't hopeful. The orchestra was disrupted at the moment. They had to replace several musicians who had completed their contracts, organize storage of the symphony's belongings during the remodeling, and arrange new rehearsal schedules around available rental spaces.

"They might not even replace the musicians until next fall. There's so much talk about budget cuts, they may decide to skimp for the summer season." Lena sounded glum. "I know the summer repertory won't be using me much."

She usually appreciated that the harp wasn't needed for all repertory. She enjoyed the lighter schedule because it allowed her more time with her children. But it wasn't a good sign that the symphony was focusing on "lean" works.

"Oh, well." She cheered herself up before I could offer encouragement. "God has a plan. He works everything together for good. That's what they told us in Bible class. Which reminds me, do you want us to pick you up next Sunday? We have room in the van."

"No, no. That's okay." I needed my own car so I could make a quick getaway. "You can give me directions."

"Remember. You promised. The late service starts at ten thirty, but you could come for Bible study at nine."

I made all kinds of faces, knowing she couldn't see me through the phone. "I'll be there at ten thirty," I said, too brightly. "So call me when you find out anything about the flute position."

"Will do. And I'll be praying."

I hung up the phone.

Praying? Whoa. She really had it bad. I hoped this fad wore off as quickly as her knitting phase. She got bored after making one scarf. That experiment had so many dropped stitches it had curves a French horn would envy.

I stared at the receiver, willing it to ring. Then I panicked and picked it up, wondering if I'd missed the call while I had been chatting with Lena. Nothing on voice mail, but maybe they didn't leave a message.

I slammed the phone down again. A few more days of this and I'd be a raving lunatic.

"You could call them." Clara leaned against the kitchen doorframe.

"I don't want to seem overeager."

"Right," she said dryly. Then she walked over to give me a hug. "You're the best musician I know."

"Hmph. Well, you travel in small circles."

"And they'd be fools not to offer you the position."

I let my shoulders sag. "I blew my chances when I was snippy with the first flutist. I'm such an idiot."

"Mom, if they're gonna choose based on personality, you were in trouble before that."

My spine stiffened. "Hey, I'm not about to pretend to be some limpid, agreeable cog in a music machine."

"Exactly." She rummaged under a stack of books on the kitchen table and pulled out several bright-colored papers. "Here are the permission forms you need to fill out for tomorrow night."

"Oh, I don't think—"

"Mom, you promised. You said you'd support me in my cheer-leading. You have to come to the parents' meeting. And you have to fill out the forms."

Forms. I'd quickly learned that parenting was equal parts emotional nurturing and filling out paperwork. Vaccination forms, preschool registration forms, field trip forms, activity permission forms. My life with Clara could be traced by a trail of paperwork. At least the cheerleading meeting would distract me from my obsessive hovering by the phone.

Tuesday night I followed Clara into the school library and realized I had entered Stepford on steroids. A quick scan of the room revealed some moms with polo shirts, discretely highlighted hair, and bright sweaters tied around their necks, and other moms with pin-striped business suits—those who came straight from high-powered jobs. I smoothed the loose black tunic I'd layered with a black cardigan over gray, drawstring pants. My hair clashed with so many things, I usually stuck with dark colors—resulting in what Clara called my retro-beatnik look.

A few dads hovered near the door, running fingers under their collars. Teens with ponytails snapped gum and bounced their heads, iPod earpieces wedged in their ears. I wanted to yank the wires and deliver a lecture on protecting their hearing. Of course if I screeched at them I'd probably do some damage, too.

Clara sailed forward unabashed, greeting her friends and even some of the moms. How did she know so many of them? And where had she developed so much social poise?

"Let's get started," said one of the girls. "I'm Joy Selforth, Lincoln's cheerleading coach. I'm so jazzed you're all here."

The coach? She looked about fifteen in her stretch pants, tank top, and hoodie. She pulled out a chair at the large conference table, and we gathered around and found seats.

"Girls, why don't you introduce your parents, and we'll get down to business."

I forced a smile when Clara introduced me. Acting friendly took more effort than playing a page full of sixteenth notes.

"You're a music teacher?" Dawn Hanson had introduced herself as a stay-at-home mom. Now she reached across the table to shake my hand. "We're looking for a teacher for our seven-year-old, Stephie. Call me, okay?" She said it with an air of doing me a favor.

Clara elbowed my ribs, and I realized my face had slipped into lines of disdain. I quickly looked down and squeezed my short nails into my palms.

It's not her fault she doesn't know the difference between an orchestral flutist and an amateur instructor for tone-deaf ankle biters. At least she's trying to give her kid some culture.

Joy moved on with introductions. Then without pausing for breath she launched into the schedule.

This school took their cheerleading seriously. There was a camp that all the girls were required to attend in July (bake sale to be held in May to help fund the trip), two different uniforms to buy (car wash to be held in June), a tour in November (funds to be raised in a silent auction in September) and a state competition in March (funded by the sale of Christmas trees in December and magazine sales in January).

Joy circulated address and phone lists, schedules, and more medical waivers to supplement the ones I'd already filled out. Soon each parent had a stack the size of an unabridged dictionary.

"We already have co-chairs for our major fund-raisers, and each family is required to participate in at least three events. We also need everyone to sign up to sell concessions at home games." She gave a perky nod. "Which shouldn't be a problem, since you'll be there supporting our teams anyway."

I would? I hadn't thought that far ahead. I'd never been to a football game or basketball game. Never saw the appeal.

Okay, I wanted to be there for Clara. But sit through a whole game? Sell candy?

"I'll pass around the sign-up sheets." Joy sounded as if we'd be delighted about this.

Clara nudged me. "Which events do you want to do?" she asked, *sotto voce*.

A silent auction didn't sound too bad, and I could probably sell some magazine subscriptions to my music students.

But when the clipboard landed in front of us, those events were full.

I wanted to pass the list along, but Joy had her eagle eyes on me. I scrawled my name next to the bake sale, car wash, and tree sale, feeling as if I'd consigned my soul to the seventh ring of Hades.

Clara practically bounced in her chair with excitement as Joy handed out a hot-pink practice schedule. She was revealing a whole side of herself that I'd never seen before, and I wasn't sure I liked it. I glanced at the schedule and passed my copy to Clara.

"You want to do this, you're responsible to keep track of it all."

"No prob."

I tried to get into the spirit of Clara's enthusiasm. I really did. I mingled over weak lemonade and stale cookies for a full ten minutes after the meeting. Then I marched over to Joy and shook her hand.

"We've got to run. I'm expecting an important call."

"Nice to meet you, Mrs. Johnson. Your daughter mentioned you're a musician. I may be calling you to get your advice on music for our dance routines."

Did cheerleaders perform to Mahler or Schubert? Somehow, I couldn't visualize it.

Clara said a few giggling good-byes to her friends and followed me out to the car. "You seem edgy. Did the symphony say they would call you tonight?"

I cranked the ignition. "No. But they might. I want to stay by the phone."

When we reached home, I checked for messages, but there were only a few for Clara. Then I agonized about what that meant. Maybe they waited to speak to someone live and didn't leave a message when they hadn't been able to reach me. Maybe they hadn't called, because they were planning to mail out letters to the rejects. Maybe they tried to call at the same instant that one of Clara's friends was leaving a message, so they got a busy signal.

Oh, the tortuous mind games of waiting for The Call.

On Wednesday, I kept the cordless phone at my side during lessons. Melissa Cleary's piano session was interrupted three times: the dentist reminding me of an appointment next week, an asphalt company who would be in my neighborhood and wondered if I wanted a new driveway, and a time-share company. The third was the cruelest, because the telemarketer responded to my voice with a hearty "Congratulations."

My heart javelined to the sky until I heard the next words. "You've won a set of deluxe steak knives and are qualified for further prizes if you visit our new development near Brainerd."

Is it any wonder I swore at the poor girl before disconnecting? Or that I told Melissa that the way she ignored her phrasing made her music sound like sludge?

No matter. My students didn't mind my abuse. It added to my mystique. They assumed the fiercer the tantrums, the greater the talent.

After I finished my last lesson of the day, I collapsed into my rocking chair, drained. If the music gods were waiting for misery with my current vocation to peak before bestowing my dreams, they didn't have to wait any longer.

Desperate for a mystery to distract my mind, I grabbed my new Sharyn McCrumb novel. Her Appalachian stories were so evocative I could almost hear plaintive folk music drifting across a wooded hollow when I read.

After rereading the same page three times, I tossed the book aside and went to the kitchen to start supper.

Voices in the alley drew me to the window. Laughter and suspicious thumps and scrapes sounded just a few houses down from mine. Someone was dragging garbage bins—probably overturning them—and someone else yelled encouragement. The neighborhood vandals! I'd been waiting for a chance to catch them for weeks.

I reached for the phone to call the police, but then pulled my hand back. No way could I call them again. They thought I was a nut. Instead, I grabbed a meat mallet, pulled on my loafers, and raced out the kitchen door toward the alley.

I rounded the neighbor's garage to face the criminals. "What do you think you're doing?" I yelled in what I hoped was a fierce and intimidating voice.

It worked. I terrified the culprits. Ten-year-old Hien Nguyen and his friend, who had been setting up a skateboard ramp in the driveway, ran screaming into Hien's house.

Okay, so it wasn't the graffiti vandals—only two boys who had shoved aside the trash cans to make room for their play. But one of these days, I'd be right, and then the neighbors would thank me.

In the meantime, I hurried back up the alley to my house, hoping the boys would be too flustered to give an accurate description of the crazed woman waving a metal mallet at them.

I slammed the kitchen door behind me, mortified that I'd jumped into another mistake.

And of course, that was the exact moment the phone rang. This time, it really was the symphony calling.

CHAPTER

Jubiloso: A directive to a performer to play a specific passage in a jubilant or exulted manner.

Ms. Johnson, the Minneapolis Symphony would like to offer you a trial position in our flute section." The woman on the phone sounded disinterested as she rattled off information about an appointment to sign papers and pick up my rehearsal schedule.

After her first sentence, my breath caught, I gasped out some sort of "Thank you," and the universe froze around me. I felt as dizzy as the time I'd challenged a friend to see who could hold a B flat for the most seconds. I'd won, of course. Not from stronger breath control, but from sheer stubbornness.

And apparently, my stubbornness had helped me win again. When I remembered how to breathe, I scribbled down the address for the symphony offices and promised to be there the next day to sign the preliminary forms.

More forms.

So what? My irrelevant thoughts scattered. Numb shock released me. I let emotions roll through me in one intense flood. A smile stretched so wide that my cheek muscles hurt. I hung up the phone and stared at the empty kitchen.

"Yes!" I punched the air, then leapt around the linoleum, wishing I knew more of Clara's crazy cheerleading jumps.

A firm rap at the back door yanked me back to earth. I pulled the door open and saw a woman as short as myself, with jet-black hair and a furious expression. Mrs. Nguyen shrieked at me in Vietnamese.

I tried to look contrite. Instead, I grinned and pulled her into the kitchen.

This made her angrier. "Why you scare my boy? He good boy."

"I know, I know. I'm so sorry. I thought there was a bad guy in the alley. You know? A crook?"

She waved her finger under my nose. "Not a crook."

I gave her a big hug. "I know. But I found out I'm going to be in the symphony."

She pulled out of my embrace and took a few steps backward, eyeing me as if I'd escaped a locked ward. She stabbed her finger toward me again. "Leave him alone." Then she stormed out the door muttering, "Crazy American lady."

I spun around the kitchen and laughed. If this was crazy, I'd retire here any day.

Needing to expend some of my energy, I cranked up an orchestral track of *Pirates of the Caribbean* and grabbed a flute. My rapid upward runs with the booming accompaniment almost matched my exhilaration.

When Clara arrived home after work and practice, I met her on the front steps. "They called. They called! I'm in!"

She did a few wild leaps of her own. "I knew it! I knew it! Let's go out for dinner. We need to celebrate."

"You got it. But first I have to call Lena." I told her the news and enjoyed her shrieks of joy. Then Clara and I headed for Eddie's—our favorite hole-in-the-wall Italian restaurant, with the best pizza in town. After dinner we walked around Lake Harriet, where a bike path and a walking trail paralleled each other in a loop around the large lake, another of the charms of Minneapolis. On the far side of the water the band shell waited for its summer concert series. The skyline of downtown rose up beyond the trees. A few daring sailboarders skimmed across the water, wearing wet suits against the bitter cold water.

"They're nuts." I dodged out of the way of a mom with a racing stroller. Then a warm feeling of kinship flooded me. The boarders, the dog walkers, the in-line skaters. "Isn't it wonderful?" The world was full of fantastic, unique people following their bliss.

Clara took it all in, met my eyes, and smiled.

We watched a few ducks splash up from the water and take flight. "Everyone is celebrating!" I spun around, arms free and face tilted up. Years of struggle and longing slipped from my shoulders.

An elderly couple strolled past hand in hand and smiled tolerantly at my antics.

Clara plopped onto a bench overlooking the lake and stretched her arms across the backrest. She stared up at oak branches overhead. "*Finally* you can get on with your life."

Joy calmed to a sane level in my blood. I sank onto the bench beside her. The intense relief in her voice bothered me, relief as if she'd been holding something sharp and heavy in her arms that she could finally release. She was happy for me, sure, but something else was going on, too. I needed to understand what she was thinking. "It's not like life was so bad before, you know."

She launched to her feet, tossed her hair back, and strode ahead on the walking path without answering.

Don't go there. Leave it alone.

Because I'm a tormented artist unable to sustain too many hours of happiness, I ignored the inner warning. I scampered to catch up with her.

"Clara, playing with the symphony is going to be great, but I'm not sorry that I waited. Teaching gave us a secure life."

"Yeah, sure." She knelt to pet a spaniel that strained against his leash to sniff her toes.

"I mean it." I tailed after Clara as she moved on, wishing I could see her face. "I wouldn't change a thing."

"Of course you would." Her voice was quiet but firm, and her strides lengthened.

"What do you mean?"

Her heavy sigh was strong enough to fill out the sails of the skiffs out on the lake. "You wouldn't have made the same mistake."

"Mistake?"

"Me. I was a mistake. You've told me often enough."

Never. I'd never said that.

"What are you talking about?" My voice sounded shrill in my own ears.

"You know. The whole spiel. Don't sleep around or you'll end up like me. You'll have to give up your dreams."

I grabbed her arm and pulled her to a stop to face me, ignoring the people who walked around us in both directions. "You are the best thing that ever happened to me."

"Hey, I know you love me. But I'm not stupid. I know you dropped out of Juilliard because of me. You switched to a music ed. degree because it was safer than a performance degree."

"Well, sure. I wanted to make a life for the two of us. But . . ."

"But if it weren't for me, you'd have finished Juilliard and spent the past thirteen years playing professionally. Probably touring the world."

I sputtered a denial, but we both knew she was right.

She tugged her arm free and headed for the stairs up to the street where our car waited. "Hey, no biggie. You made the best of it. I can deal with that."

Again, I trailed behind her, puffing as my stubby legs pounded up the steps. "You make it sound like—"

"Mom, we're celebrating. Let's drop it. I'm just relieved. You'll finally get to do the things you've always wanted to."

"I don't want you to think—"

"Hey, Mom?" Clara had reached the top and waited for me to stagger up the rest of the way. "Did you really promise Aunt Lena that we'd go to church with her?"

Oops. "Did I forget to mention that?"

She frowned, with the dark slashes of her eyebrows accusing me. "It's my only day to sleep in."

"I know. I'm sorry. But it's only this once." Besides, after my good news, I felt like singing some praises. Although I wasn't sure to whom. Myself? That felt a bit odd. Lena, for letting me know about the auditions? She wouldn't approve of that. The audition panel? Never.

Oh, well. I'd face that dilemma on Sunday morning.

She gave an exaggerated groan. "Fine. Once. Now we better get home, I've got a killer test in science tomorrow."

She had deflected my worry and skillfully changed the subject. And I'd let her. Maybe it was a cowardly choice, but it was easier that way. If she doubted her importance to me, she didn't want to discuss it, and neither did I. Besides, could I honestly look her in the eyes and tell her I had no regrets?

Thursday morning, I drove to the symphony offices. I expected the Emerald City. Shangri-la. Or at least an artsy loft with a shrine to Leonard Bernstein, Jascha Heifetz, or YoYo Ma. Instead, I reported to a dreary set of rooms in an uninspiring building right off the freeway in the suburb of Bloomington. These complexes had been designed to house corporate offices of boring industries—not those of a symphony. It was so wrong.

A manager—a bookish young man with pale hair and skin—met me in the tiny lobby. He guided me back to rooms that could have held insurance adjusters, or manufacturers of corrugated boxes, or tax preparers. No flair. No life. He pointed out cubicles that belonged to the development department (patrons, endowments, grant-writing), the marketing department (press and other public relations), and general operations (everything else).

Yawn.

We returned to the lobby, where he handed me a clipboard. I sank onto a loose-springed couch and dutifully filled out the paperwork. At least this outer hall held some framed posters advertising past musical events. And the pen they'd given me was decorated with a series of notes. I squinted at it, then hummed the melody line—"Fur Elise."

I had to read through the exclusivity clause in my contract several times. I could still teach, and play in small-ensemble performances outside of the symphony. But I was committing to a three-year term with a non-compete clause, with all sorts of legal and financial penalties for not completing the terms. Fine by me. I would promise them a pound of flesh, and gladly. On the other hand, they had a several-week cushion to make a final decision as to whether I blended well with the orchestra. They could still cut me and go with a different finalist. I braced my shoulders. Not after they'd heard me play day after day. I signed my name with a flourish.

Then I received the Magna Carta, the Holy Grail, my Passport to Paradise—the rehearsal and performance schedule.

"We mail out updates all the time," the manager said, scratching his scalp with the eraser end of a pencil. "Things are a mess because of the painting work over at Symphonic Hall. But this is the most recent. No missing any performance date except for death—yours." He smiled at the joke he'd probably told a hundred times.

I scanned the complicated game plan of sectional rehearsals and full symphony run-throughs with the new conductor. We were renting space at the Minneapolis Institute of Arts, the State Theatre, O'Shaughnessy auditorium at St. Kate's college, and some buildings on the West Bank of the University of Minnesota campus.

The performance schedule didn't return to Symphonic Hall for several weeks. The next series was being performed at the Palace Theatre in downtown Minneapolis. That would be an interesting venue. Broadway touring shows often performed there, but what were the acoustics like for classical orchestra?

"Hey!" My eyes snagged on today's date. "It says there's a full rehearsal this afternoon at the Bloomington Art Center." I glanced at my watch. "I could just make it."

The young man shrugged. "Knock yourself out."

He collected my papers, and I flew out the door. Now that my dream had come true, every second of delay felt like an hour. I dashed home to grab a flute, raced down the freeway back to Bloomington, and quickly found the parking lot for the copper-sided arts center.

When I ventured into the theatre, several musicians were re-arranging chairs and music stands on the stage, a few were tuning, and others were grumbling. Stage lights clicked on and off, and a tall man straddled a row of audience seats, balanced on the chair arms, and shouted up to the lighting booth with an air of being offended that electricity didn't obey his whims.

I made my way up the steps at the side of the stage and toward the flutes. Sarah was yelling at the French horn section to push their chairs back. When she saw me, her frown deepened. "The office didn't tell me you'd be coming today." She rubbed the bridge of her nose. "Well, you can shadow Cheryl. Find a chair and look at her music."

I had hoped for at least a bit of welcome. I didn't even have the comfort of Lena's smile, since today's rehearsal was for part of the Three B's series coming up (some marketing genius had decided an evening of Bach, Beethoven, and Brahms would bring in the crowds), and today's Bach pieces had no harp part. I turned away, eager to introduce myself to Cheryl.

"And, Amy?" Sarah's sharp voice pulled me back. "Don't play anything until I've had you in a sectional. Just listen, study the music, and learn the phrasing."

I swallowed my disappointment. She was right. It would be foolhardy to sight-read a score at a full rehearsal. Still, I was longing for the magic. For full immersion.

Patience. You're almost there.

I edged past the oboes and toward the second flute chair. "Cheryl?"

A model-tall woman with a pixie haircut turned and smiled. "Are you the new viola?"

"No. I'm Amy Johnson, the—"

"Hey! Great meeting you. Lena's told me so much about you. Pull up a chair. Don't let the second violins crowd you."

A robust man carrying a music stand paused in front of us, looking over our heads toward the bassoon section with a grin. "I'm not responsible if you get in the way of my slide," he called to a woman arranging her chair. Then he chuckled, highlighting the round cheeks of a brass musician. "Hi, Cheryl." He shifted his gaze to me. "You're Lena's friend?"

"Yes, I—"

"Name's Leonard Mussorgsky. Coprincipal trombone."

Poor guy. Who would want to share a surname with the drunken Russian who composed tortured nightmares?

"I know, I know, spare me the jokes—and that's my wife, Vicki, the principal cellist."

I waved a hello to the brunette with a square-edged face. She spared me a quick, "Hi, there," and then returned to adjusting a tuning peg. She was an incongruous picture, straddling her cello in shorts and a T-shirt. Orchestra members always looked odd out of their formal clothes. Too human, somehow.

I spotted a folding chair and wedged it in next to Cheryl. The woman on the other side pulled her music stand closer and threw me an annoyed glance.

"Don't mind her," Leonard boomed, resting the music stand over one broad shoulder. "She plays piccolo. You know what they say . . ."

Cheryl rolled her eyes. "Here it comes."

"The higher the pitch of the instrument," he continued undeterred, "the more neurotic the musician. I think they've done scientific studies."

I giggled. "And how can you tell when a trombonist is at your door?"

Cheryl winced. "Don't encourage him."

I grinned and continued. "The doorbell drags."

Leonard groaned, and even the piccolo player chuckled. Vicki tapped her bow against her music stand in appreciation. Shaking his head, Leonard pushed his way between the clarinets and bassoons and settled in his chair in the back row near the trumpets. He grabbed his trombone and blew a raucous glissando that sounded like an elephant laughing.

Something uncaged in the region of my heart. I was with my own tribe again. I'd missed being a part of musical virtuosity all these years. I'd also missed the camaraderie, the bantering. I was home. I belonged here.

Now all I needed to make my place with this group was to play beyond perfectly. My mouth went dry and pressure squeezed my ribs.

"People," a harried woman bellowed from the lip of the stage. The noise dimmed. "Remember to give me recommendations for our patron committee. Costs of everything are going up, and we need more donors. And the librarian said we're missing some parts again. Would you all check your lockers and at home."

"We would if we could get to our lockers," said a French horn player from the back. A general muttering of agreement rose in chorus. "When do we get back into our space?"

"We're right on schedule. But if we don't get the grant we're waiting for, we might never get back into our space."

"Who is she?" I whispered to Cheryl.

"Megan Braunsky. She's supposed to be the development director, but she's more of a Chicken Little," she murmured back.

I listened to the rest of Megan's little speech and marveled at how similar it was to Joy's pep talk at the cheerleader meeting. At least the symphony had a staff to raise money. No car washes or bake sales for us.

When she finished, the cacophony started up again as musicians tuned, tweaked, and tested a few passages.

A door burst open behind the back row of audience seats, and a form marched down the dark aisle toward the stage.

"Look sharp," Cheryl whispered. "You playing?" She nodded at the flute case on my lap.

"No, I'm supposed to listen today."

She nodded and arranged the pages of her music, angling the stand so I could see.

Peter Wilson jogged up the steps and ignored the chaos, fidgets, and preparation going on around him. He opened a bulging satchel and pulled out a score to set on the podium. He nodded to the violinist closest to him—the concertmaster. A lanky man with sun-kissed hair stood and pointed his bow at the oboe.

As he tuned each section, I had the luxury of studying the symphony members. Some wore blasé expressions that were poor disguises for the pride they felt in being here and the competitive drive to remain. Others had the near-psychotic fervor of those more comfortable with their instruments than with humans. After everyone else was ready, a string bass player ambled onto the stage. Without a word of apology for arriving late, he adjusted the glasses on his lugubrious face and planted his instrument against the stage floor.

When Peter stepped into place, all movement and sound stopped. Postures lengthened, eyes zeroed in on the baton, dozens of silent musicians played the opening measures in their minds with such concentration I could almost hear them.

The conductor surveyed his kingdom. "Ah. I see one of our incoming musicians is with us today. Welcome, Ms. Johnson."

I sketched a salute toward the other musicians as they shifted their focus for a second to assess me.

Peter Wilson frowned. "Your instrument isn't ready?"

"No . . ." I glanced at Sarah for rescue.

She ignored me.

I cleared my throat. "I was planning to follow . . ."

He waved that away with a commanding gesture. "Ridiculous. You can't learn without playing. Trust me. I'll let you know if you should stop." His attention swerved from me to the percussion section. "Not so heavy in the Prokofiev next time, right?" He gave a few more notes on last weekend's performance.

I scrambled to assemble my flute and quietly tuned with Cheryl.

The conductor raised his baton, and I drew in a breath and lifted my flute. Then I realized Cheryl's was held alert, but in her lap. I squinted at the music stand. We had sixty-four measures before we came in. I surreptitiously lowered my instrument.

Peter Wilson's slow scan of the symphony paused at the flute section. He indulged a flicker of a smile.

My face felt sunburned. I could be wearing a scarlet letter A for *amateur*.

Then he gave his downbeat and coaxed the violins into play, and my self-consciousness dissolved. Lush music washed over me with so much power that I thought I might shatter from sheer pleasure.

Bach was a perfect piece for my initiation. Mathematical, pure, calming.

The sixty-four measures swept past. It was time for me to put up or shut up. Would they fire me if I botched this? I glared at the music, daring it to thwart me. Then I lifted my flute.

CHAPTER

7

 Virtuoso: A person who excels in musical technique or execution. A person who has a cultivated appreciation of artistic excellence.

Imagine being a member of a neighborhood tennis club and suddenly squaring off against Serena Williams at Wimbledon. Or daring to display sketches from an art class in the Museum of Modern Art. Or leaving a community theatre to play opposite Robert DeNiro on a Broadway stage.

Juilliard was a lifetime ago, and I hadn't played this Bach minuet in years. Cheryl was flawless, each run clear and brilliant. I barely kept up. Good thing I'd been hired as second flute. I could blend into the background a bit more easily until I was up to speed. And speed was the operative word. The violins bowed a relentless pace while our flute melody scampered over the top, skipping lightly along difficult intervals, trying to make them sound effortless.

When we finished, I leaned forward and struggled to catch my breath.

"Yes," the conductor spoke. "But not so heavy."

I forced my head up and was relieved to see he was speaking to the cellists on his right and not to our flute section.

"More *a-ta-ta-ta*. You see? Not so much *bum-bah-bum*. From eighty." The baton lifted, and we all flew back into motion. He cut us off after a few measures.

"Better. Keep that feel throughout. Violins, too. Light. Sharp. Tiptoe. No heavy boots."

I smiled at the analogy. How many times had I tried to convey that to my flute students who sometimes strangled a note, trying to wring out the tone by sheer force?

"We go again."

The next few hours flew by in an adrenaline rush. Pushed beyond my limit, I pulled the skill up from my toenails. Even the few brief breaks were a time of focused concentration as Cheryl gave me a crash course on her intonation choices, and I jotted notes on tempos. I'd transfer those from my notepad into my own music when I received it.

When Peter Wilson glanced at his watch and declared the rehearsal finished, I was coated in a sheen of sweat that had little to do with the stuffy theatre. My muscles felt rubbery, and I wasn't sure I'd be able to stand.

"Great job," Cheryl said, running a cloth through one of her flute pieces. "I'd have been terrified jumping in that way."

Sarah, on the other side of Cheryl, slammed her music folder closed. "It wasn't terrible, but come early to the sectional tomorrow. You need work." She stood and stalked off into the wings.

Insecurity grabbed me for a second, but anger rescued me. *Yeah, well* you *need work—at acting human.*

"Don't let her get to you," Cheryl said.

"*Ja.* She wanted her friend for the chair." The concertmaster pushed aside a music stand and made his way toward us. "Good to know you." His hard consonants sounded German, but his vowels had a Scandinavian tone that pressed against his palate. Or maybe Austrian? Dutch? He reached out a hand.

Since my flute rested in three pieces on my lap, I offered my hand without standing. His grip on my fingers lingered longer than necessary, and he leaned forward. "You will be a nice addition." His gaze coasted over me with appreciation. Charm or smarm? It was hard to tell.

"Amy, this is Stefan Kronenberg." Cheryl's warm voice put him in the first category. "He joined the symphony about a year ago."

He chuckled. "Much to the sorrow of David Tanner."

"David's the first associate concertmaster," Cheryl explained. "He thought he was moving into the big chair."

Stefan's shrug was self-deprecating but the gleam in his eye showed his comfort in the supreme role. Supreme, but for the conductor.

I glanced around, but Peter Wilson had vanished. After forcing me into a cold playing of the repertory, he could have at least said a few words to me.

"So, can I buy you a coffee to welcome you to this circus?" Stefan slipped into his jacket and turned up the collar in a gesture that seemed automatic, probably developed over the years to hide the violin hickey under his left jawline.

I glanced at my watch. "Sorry. I need to get home."

He shrugged. "Some other time. Cheryl?"

"Sure. Is there any place around here?" She slipped her flute case into a shoulder bag.

They drifted off stage right, brainstorming places for a good cappuccino on this end of town. Cheryl stopped and turned back toward me. "I'll see you tomorrow at our sectional."

I took my time cleaning my flute. Sitting alone on stage I breathed in the echoes of rehearsal that still hung in the air. When I closed my eyes, the music resonated through my memory. I smiled widely and let the joy warm my veins. I had done it. Sure, it was only a rehearsal. But I had played with the Minneapolis Symphony.

A growling voice offstage interrupted my savored moment. " . . . and that's the third time this week." It was Leonard's deep voice, but it sounded like his sense of humor had deserted him.

A higher pitch answered him. "You're jealous. Admit it. You think Stefan is making a play for me . . ."

A backstage door slammed, cutting off the argument. So much for marital bliss. I had wondered how married-couple musicians managed. Sounded like Leonard and Vicki didn't. Maybe Vicki had only married Leonard for his money (if he had any) and now she was interested in Stefan. Or maybe Leonard was in trouble with the mob and was trying to distract Vicki by pretending to be jealous. Or maybe both were really international spies using the symphony to . . .

None of my business. I was through with observations and mysteries. I didn't need the diversion anymore. It was time for me to focus on my music. Nothing else mattered. I didn't want drama or symphony politics. I'd give Leonard and Vicki a wide berth. I'd also do all I could to smooth Sarah's ruffled feathers. It made sense that she was irritated her friend hadn't won the position, so I'd have to work extra hard to win her over. Stefan seemed far too distracting, so I'd avoid him. With all that resolved, I packed up and headed home.

Several hours later, I filled Clara in on the day. "And then Cheryl said she was happy to know she was leaving the second chair to a gifted flutist. Did I tell you she's going to the Boston Pops? She's over-the-moon excited about it. I would be, too. And she told me that the string bass player is always late, but he's so good, no one says anything about it. And tomorrow Sarah is going to get her claws into me at the sectional." I paused to take a sip of the decaf latte that Clara had brought home from work.

"So it's official. We hate her?"

"Nope. Can't."

"Why not?" Clara pulled out the rubber band to release her ponytail. She massaged her scalp, releasing a gentle aroma of coffee grounds.

"She's amazing. She totally earned her principal flute chair. I can't hate anyone that can nail her trills like that."

"Whatever." Clara prowled to the fridge and yanked open the door. "You know, some moms have supper waiting when their kids get home," she muttered.

"Yeah, but can they make your soul melt when they play Debussy?" I wiggled my talented fingers in the air with a grin. "Leonard and his wife seemed nice. He's one of those class clowns that helps everyone let off steam. And I'm not sure what I think of Stefan. The conductor is great. They've had some that Lena didn't like. Wouldn't it have been horrible if I'd joined right when they hired a bad conductor? And did I tell you that—"

"Mom!" Clara's voice was muffled because it was deep inside the fridge. She pulled her head out and smiled at me. "What do you always tell your voice students?"

I scrunched my forehead. "What?"

"Breathe! You haven't taken a breath since I walked in the door. How old is this yogurt?" She waved a carton in my direction.

"Who knows? Do we have any frozen lasagna? Check the freezer."

She closed one door and opened the other. More rummaging. "There's something wrapped in foil, but there's no label. I can't tell what it is."

"Okay. Freezer surprise it is." I bounced up, took the packet from Clara, loosened the foil, and popped it into the oven. "You should have heard me. I don't think I've ever taken the minuet at that tempo before. I didn't know I could play like that. But I'll need to practice like crazy to get ready in two weeks. I'm supposed to perform when they debut the new repertory."

I set the oven temperature and turned to face my daughter. For me, excitement is a froth that dissolves quickly, leaving murky insecurity. "Unless they drop me after this trial period. What if I can't do it?"

She flopped into a chair and peeled a banana. "Mom. They wouldn't invite someone who couldn't play. Don't start freaking out. You can do that on opening night. Not before. Now, what should we read tonight?"

I pushed aside my churning doubts with effort. "Elementary, my dear Clara."

She groaned. "Not another Holmes."

"Come on, we haven't read one in weeks. We left off at *The Adventure of the Solitary Cyclist*. You'll love that one."

"Here's the deal. You watch one of my episodes of *Gilmore Girls*, and then we read Sir Arthur."

"Deal. I'll even make the popcorn."

"Wow, you *are* in a good mood."

And in spite of artistic anxiety, I remained in a good mood until the following morning.

"No, no, no!" Sarah's badgering seared my eardrums. She'd been at it since I arrived. "Your phrasing is all off. I told you we're breathing right before the upbeat at measure thirty."

"Sorry." I penciled in a bigger apostrophe to indicate the breath, and a long phrasing line to remind myself not to breathe until the mark. My annoyance at Sarah was tempered by frustration with myself. I'd worked alone so long, a lot of my orchestral skills had slipped. Sarah was brutal, but I was glad for this chance to go through all the music with her before the woodwind sectional.

"I told him you wouldn't fit in," she murmured.

"What?" I dropped the pencil onto the lip of my music stand. "Told who?"

"Peter Wilson. He pushed for you to get hired." She gave me a sour look. "But you knew that, didn't you?"

I shook my head, furious. *You're still only in on a trial basis. Don't lose it. Don't give her the satisfaction.* "Of course not."

"Right." Sarcasm dripped from the word. "Well, don't count on a relationship to keep you in if you can't cut it. Relationships between musicians never work."

Pain throbbed behind my eyes. *You probably never had a relationship in your life.* I forced myself to stay calm. "The only thing I'm interested in is playing my flute." My voice held barely a tremor. I reached forward to jot another note on my music, and my pencil lead snapped.

"Oh? Well, don't think you can fool me." When I ignored Sarah's taunt, she sat back and studied me. "We lost a decent second violin that way."

Puh-leeze. Who cared about the second violins? The last thing I wanted to hear was symphony gossip. Couldn't we just make music? Art would be much less complicated if people weren't involved. I pointed to the last bar of music. "How dramatic is the ritardando here? Could you show me?"

"Stefan lobbied for his relationship-du-jour to get the open violin spot. And to be fair, she was great. But when he dumped her, she couldn't handle working under him anymore." Sarah smirked. "She blew up at him during rehearsal one day. Quite the scene."

My fingers clenched around my flute. "Look. My guess is that Mr. Wilson wants the best symphony possible. He wouldn't recommend a musician unless she was the right choice. The only relationship I'm interested in is with my fifteen-year-old daughter. Now could you play the ending so I can hear where you begin the slower tempo?"

She narrowed her eyes, then flicked her long hair back behind her shoulders. "Fine. But if I don't think you're ready, I'll have my coprincipal play the second-flute part when we debut the Three B's."

No one would have blamed me if I'd bashed her over the head with my flute. But I'd never do that. The flute was too valuable. Instead, I shut out everything but the music and worked with the laser intensity that had always served me well.

Music demanded more than technical perfection. True music also required heart—open, bleeding, vulnerable heart. I'd heard a thousand instrumentalists who hit every note but left me empty— automatons with no understanding of how to let their deepest yearning and most secret pain leach into the music and give it the resonance that made an audience weep.

Heart—my greatest challenge, and my greatest strength. I refused to hide behind the notes. Even in front of Sarah, I lost myself in the music and held nothing back.

After several repetitions, Sarah glanced at her watch. "Okay, time for the sectional."

I gathered up my case and music. Time to get out of the stuffy practice room and head for the auditorium, where we'd rehearse with the oboes, clarinets, and bassoons. Though it was a relatively small subgroup of the orchestra, at least I wouldn't be alone with Sarah any longer.

"Amy."

I hated the way she barked my name. "Yes?" Maybe my hard work had garnered some grudging respect.

"Don't you dare miss that repeat we cut. And get your phrasing right. There are at least ten people who hope you flop so they can take your place."

Gotta love those encouraging folk.

I stood to my full five-foot-three-inch height and glared down at Sarah where she sat. "They can hope all they want. I'm here to stay." I spun on my heel and stormed out the door and toward the auditorium. My declaration would have carried more punch if I hadn't turned the wrong way in the hall.

I slunk onto the stage a few minutes later after wandering unfamiliar corridors. I couldn't wait until we moved back into Symphonic Hall.

"Ah, there you are." An arm dropped over my shoulders. Stefan Kronenberg steered me away from the flute section and back toward the wings. "After your rehearsal, we can have that coffee and be acquainted, *ja?*"

"Mr. Kronenberg," I slipped out from under his arm. He smiled down at me, blond European elegance in a pale blue turtleneck that made his eyes the shade of high-altitude sky. "Why are you at the woodwind rehearsal?"

"Ms. Johnson." He bowed his head in mock formality. "I believe the concertmaster should keep an eye on all musicians." He leaned closer with a teasing smile. "Besides, I thought someone should protect you from Sarah."

A laugh escaped me, destroying my efforts to remain stiff. I felt warmed by his concern. "I can handle her."

"I am sure you can." His expression grew more serious. "Be careful. Not with Sarah only. Something is—"

"Amy!" Sarah called. "Are you rehearsing or not? Get over here."

"The general speaks," Stefan said. "We must talk later."

I hurried to my place beside Cheryl. Stefan headed down the steps at the side of the stage and took a seat in the dark, empty rows.

"Be careful." What did that mean?

No, Amy. Don't be an idiot. Focus on the music. This is your big chance.

I had no intention of going out for coffee with Stefan. I didn't need to "be acquainted" with anything except my musical score. I planned to run the other direction from anything that stirred my mystery-solving impulses. Besides, what deep, dark secrets could a symphony possibly hold?

CHAPTER

> *Religioso: A directive to perform a certain passage
> of a composition in a devout, solemn, or religious
> manner.*

n the excitement and exhaustion of my new job, I almost forgot
about my promise to Lena.

She didn't. She called Saturday night to be sure I had directions to her church. "And I'll watch for you near the main doors."

Great. "So what do we wear?" I had vague notions of patent-leather shoes and bonnets, but I couldn't see convincing Clara to wear such things.

Lena laughed. "Nothing fancy. Think business casual. Don't worry. Nobody cares how you look."

In spite of her reassurances, when I parked my Saturn in the big lot Sunday morning I scoped out the other people swarming toward the church. A few women looked dressed for a garden party, and some men wore suits. But Clara and I would blend in pretty well with the rest.

"Let's get this over with," Clara grumbled.

We made our way toward the entry. Raucous music carried from deep inside the building. I stepped up on the sidewalk, then stopped and grabbed Clara's arm.

"We're sitting in the back, okay?"

"Check. And near the door." Clara twiddled a long strand of hair near her cheek and held herself as tight as an overstrung violin.

"Roger Wilco. Ready?" I smoothed down my hair.

An indrawn hiss came from Clara. "I guess."

We strolled through the open doors into a large space that felt like a theatre lobby. Lena stood on tiptoe, scanning over the heads of the crowd. She lit up when she saw us and began swimming upstream in our direction.

"You made it." She winged her arms around Clara and me like a mama swan and steered us closer to the noise coming from the far side of this first room. "Ken and the kids are saving us seats right up front."

Clara and I exchanged alarmed glances, but before I could stop Lena, she guided us through the inner doors and into sensory overload.

People sang, clapped, and waved their arms. A few even jumped in place, looking like they'd misplaced their pogo sticks.

Lena must have been pulling my leg. This wasn't a church; she'd coaxed us into some sort of rock concert.

We maneuvered down the aisle to empty seats by Ken. The sea of beaming faces worried me.

"If they pass out Kool-Aid, I'm outta here." Clara spoke against my ear as we took seats.

I nodded and turned my attention to the platform in the front. Drums, guitars, and an electronic keyboard pounded out a three-chord progression. Again and again.

Simplistic melody. Insipid lyrics.

Lena stood and swayed side to side, eyes closed, lifting her palms in front of her. Was she kidding?

No, she was really getting into this.

I forced my face into what I hoped was a pleasant expression.

The song leader segued into another piece. Another three chords. A line that repeated over and over like a commercial jingle.

This was church? I shuddered.

Finally, the overamplified noise concluded and a young man in a suit bounded up to the platform.

"Lord, we just want to thank you," he spoke into a microphone, looking at a spot on the ceiling. "Just come and inspire us today. We're hungry for your Word. Just open our hearts."

Just, just, just. Was this special prayer jargon? Before I could figure it out, the music leader grabbed the man's last words and sang them—leading into yet another repetitive song.

We stood, we sat, we stood again. Finally, another guy in a suit made his way to the front and adjusted a lapel microphone. Another prayer.

"Lord, open our hearts today to hear from your Word . . ."

These folks were really obsessed with opening hearts. I smothered a snicker as I wondered if any of them were cardiac surgeons.

" . . . Amen. Let's turn to the book of Ephesians."

Instantly, everyone pulled books from purses, pockets, or under their chairs and hundreds of pages ruffled. Lena handed me a Bible to share with Clara. Curious, I leafed through a few pages. I'd heard the Bible included some good literature, but I'd never had a chance to examine one.

"Today I'd like to talk to you about the mystery of God."

Mystery? My head jerked up. Maybe this wouldn't be a wasted hour after all.

The pastor pointed to a page in his book. "Many people think that faith is about getting God's attention, hunting Him down, earning His approval somehow. But Paul says here that God's purpose is to reveal the mystery of His plan . . . His love. 'And He made known to us the mystery of His will according to His good pleasure, which He purposed in Christ.' Yes, God is so awesome that He is beyond our complete understanding. But He still wants us to know Him. And the exciting part of the story is that He doesn't wait for us to reach out to Him. He is pursuing us."

Goose bumps rose on my arms. My neck prickled as if someone had blown across it. It had been years since I'd given much thought to what I believed. I figured there might be some sort of benevolent force beyond the realm of everyday human existence. Something unknown and unknowable. I followed the pastor's ideas about God being mysterious.

But the notion that God was interested in me, personally . . . pursuing me . . . wanting to let me in on His mysteries . . .

I shivered and shoved the book into Clara's lap. No thanks.

Sure, I liked mysteries. But I liked them in part because of the symmetry. The bad guy was always caught and punished. Balance restored. God, on the other hand, didn't make sense. Evil people got away with things. Where was the symmetry in that?

After the church service finally wrapped up, people hugged and chatted over the noise of yet another song. Lena introduced us to a few families, beaming all the while. Did this church give people points for bringing friends? She sure seemed excited to have us there. We made our way out of the lobby and to the parking lot.

Lena trailed us to my car and looked at me with overeager eyes. "What did you think?"

Telling her the truth would be like swatting a puppy.

Clara stepped forward. "It was kind of interesting. Thanks for inviting us."

I glanced at my watch. "We've gotta run. This . . . it's not my thing, you know?"

Lena's light dimmed. "Well, I'm glad you came. You're welcome any time."

Clara gave Lena a hug. "Maybe I'll come again sometime."

We got into the car, and I burned rubber pulling out. "You shouldn't get her hopes up like that."

Clara grabbed her sunglasses from the dashboard and settled them on her nose. "Come on. It wasn't *that* bad. Maybe we should go again."

Alarm thrummed in time with my growing headache. "Listen, chickadee. I've known Lena a lot longer than you have. She'll get over it. So, are you practicing first, or am I?"

Clara had no passionate music ambitions, but I'd insisted she study piano. She was fairly proficient, now that I'd found her a teacher other than myself.

She yawned. "I better do my time first. Once you get going, you'll forget to give me a turn."

After a slapdash lunch, she settled at the piano, and I relaxed at the kitchen table, read the Sunday paper, and listened to her work on a Haydn sonata. The room was sunny, a few sparrows fluttered outside the kitchen window, and I had an afternoon of practice to look forward to. Yet every now and again the creepy thought from the church service intruded into my peace.

"He is pursuing us."

Later, when Clara left to do homework with Ashley or Chelsea or Brittany—one of those cheerleader friends—I picked up my flute, determined to shake off the haunting.

Focused attention on the repertoire shut out all other thoughts. Repetition of difficult phrases soothed me like meditation. I always told my students, "Practice makes permanent." Playing a phrase wrongly embedded it in kinetic memory. It was vital to take each piece in small bites and play the difficult passages over and over correctly before stringing the entire work together.

The wedge of light from the front windows sundialed across the wood floor as hours passed. When I finished, I drooped in my chair, sated and cleansed. I basked in the vibrant silence.

Then, as if I'd left a window open, I felt a ripple in the air. A presence.

Sometimes having a creative imagination was a curse. I deliberately cleaned my flute and put it away. The fridge compressor kicked in with a soft whir. Subtle creaks sounded from a variety of directions. Normal house-settling? Or something more?

Anger gave some muscle to my nerves. I wasn't going to be spooked in my own house. I padded quietly from room to room . . . catching my breath for a second before peering around each doorway.

Just as I suspected, no one was there.

"He is pursuing us."

That's what I got for visiting Lena's church. Now I had a major case of heebie-jeebies. I planted myself in the center of my music room. "Go away."

CHAPTER

Attacca subito: A musical directive for the performer to begin the next movement (or section) of a composition immediately and without pause . . . subito meaning suddenly or quickly.

I'm going to throw up. I'm absolutely going to heave my guts out." I picked up my car keys, then dropped them back on the kitchen table and turned toward the hallway.

Clara blocked my exit from the kitchen. "Mom. Get a grip. You're going to be fine."

"I can't do this. I didn't have enough time."

"Right. Just your entire life. You're ready." Clara adjusted the collar on my formal black dress. "Now go get this concert under your belt, and don't freak out. Remember, we have the bake sale tomorrow."

For two weeks, I'd shut out everything except music. A few nights ago, I came up for air long enough to help Clara bake several misshapen loaves of banana bread for the upcoming fund-raiser.

But otherwise, I'd done the horse-with-blinders thing. I learned the names of a few more orchestra members, but made no attempt to sort out the politics or power structure. I shut out Sarah's carping and Stefan's flirting. I refused to acknowledge Peter Wilson's indifference toward my skill. As long as I could ignore the people, the time had been heaven. Music, music, and more music.

But in my tunnel vision, I'd blocked out what I was working toward. Music had gifted me these past two weeks, but now it was payback time.

My stomach knotted.

"Mom, if you don't leave now, Miguel and I will get to the theatre before you do."

"You've got your tickets?"

"Yes." Clara fanned them out. "Miguel, his wife, and me. They're really excited." She grabbed my shoulders and steered me toward the back door. "We'll see you and Lena backstage afterwards. Now go!"

It had been Clara's idea to invite her boss, Miguel, and his wife, Anita. Thoughtful gestures weren't part of my DNA. I wasn't bubbly, warm, or sociable like the other moms at the high school. I wasn't compassionate like Clara. I wasn't ethereal and gentle like Lena. I wasn't patient—though my students didn't mind because my tough approach made them better musicians.

My only redeeming quality was my music. No wonder I was terrified. What if tonight was a disaster? If I didn't play the flute well, I had nothing.

In spite of my nervous stalling, I arrived at the theatre far too early. A stage manager answered my tap on the back door and let me in. The Palace was a restored, neoclassical theatre complete with a Phantom-of-the-Opera chandelier. The lush curtains, murals, and gilt-covered carvings were a bit garish for my taste.

After a quick peek at the empty rows, I returned to the backstage area. The drawn curtains muffled sound. Stepping out on stage,

I felt protected from the demanding expectations of the outside world. Our chairs and stands were in place. The edges of the timpani gleamed in readiness. A gap in the oboe section stood ready for our wheelchair-bound coprincipal.

I took my chair and arranged my music with clammy hands. Then I closed my eyes and tried to remember the thrill I'd felt when I'd gotten my acceptance call. When had joy turned into terror?

"Odd place for a nap." Peter's crisp syllables jolted my eyes open. "But, then, I try never to criticize a musician's process."

"I wasn't . . . I just . . ." My dry teeth got in the way of my tongue.

He ignored my sputtering and stepped up to the podium. He tugged on the cuffs of his tuxedo shirt while he stared at the pages of the score I knew he had memorized. I could barely keep my single melody straight. What kind of mind could hold all the threads of each section, each instrument? I had glimpsed his brilliance at rehearsal, even though he had looked ridiculously average in jeans and rolled-up shirtsleeves. But now I felt a tinge of awe. He was in his element.

I rose to leave him to his preparations.

"Do you have someone coming tonight?" He spoke without looking up from the music.

"My daughter, a few friends."

"Brilliant." But his attention remained on his score, and he whistled a line of Brahms through his teeth.

I smiled as I slipped away. I wasn't the only artist fighting nerves. Although he'd filled in during the last concert series, tonight was his debut as senior conductor. Tonight was technically a preview show, but there would be local critics attending. I'd bet anything he was feeling the pressure.

More musicians arrived, and soon the backstage was a comforting chaos. As an old theatre, the building had a warren of dressing rooms, makeup rooms, and prop storage in the basement. Several large dressing rooms had been updated with lockers where we could store personal items during the show. Lena found me, her blond hair looking white against her black dress. "Isn't this fun?" She flexed her fingers a few times, then looked at me more closely. "No offense, but you're looking awful pale."

"I'm fine," I snapped.

She grinned. "Must be the black dress making you look so white. Couldn't be nerves."

"Don't. Even. Go. There."

Stefan wove around other musicians toward us, cradling his violin. "How is the new flutist?" Tall and commanding in his tuxedo, his warm smile instantly loosened some of the nerve-knots in my stomach.

"I'm wondering why I thought I could do this," I confessed.

He met my eyes with confidence. "You have this gift. You must play."

I blinked, and he moved on to encourage the new viola. I also heard him give some reminders to one of the other first violins.

"What's the difference between a violin and a viola?" A deep voice grumbled behind me.

I spun and saw Leonard's generous grin. "Wait, I know this one . . ."

"There's no difference," he plowed ahead. "The violin just looks smaller because the violinist's head is so big."

Lena and I laughed, but Leonard's gaze tracked Stefan with something darker than humor.

Stop noticing. Blinders, Amy. Don't pay attention to the undercurrents.

"Amy!" Sarah snapped at me from a doorway to a rehearsal room. "I want to go over some problems with you. Our tones didn't blend well in the Brahms yesterday."

Probably because I put a little *oomph* behind my playing. No, that wasn't fair. She had a mellow and lyrical tone, and it was my job as second flute to meld. I trailed behind her to a bare, concrete makeup room. Her bony shoulder blades pressed against the ebony silk of her dress.

"Do you ever eat?" *Whoops. Did I say that out loud?*

Sarah smirked and ran her hands down the straight lines where her hips ought to be. "I know. I've always been thin. I used to model in high school. My parents were furious when I stopped."

"Because of your music?"

She nodded. "Modeling took too much time away from flute practice."

"And what do they think now? Now that you're a principal flutist?"

The hollows of her cheeks deepened. "They tell me I'd make more money modeling."

I snorted, and we shared a moment of exasperation over the folks who didn't get it. Then she flipped open her music folder. "Let's try it from measure one twenty-eight." And we reviewed the section until we sounded like one instrument.

Time dragged, then compressed, then stalled out again as I found myself under the lights, flute in hand. Curtains parted. Stefan strode out and led a final check of tuning. Polite applause greeted Peter as he walked on stage.

Savor this. You made it.

The baton lifted. Bows readied on the strings. Chests expanded with an intake of breath. The audience watched from the darkness—a predator beyond the circle of light, waiting to be soothed by our magic.

We launched into the Brahms. Some part of my brain slipped into automatic, well-trained by hundreds of repetitions. Another part of me seemed to float outside myself, watching the magnificent moment unfold. The cellists' hands vibrated like hummingbirds on their strings, a bead of sweat rolled down Peter's temple, dust motes hovered above the footlights, and an exhilarated red-haired flutist played her first professional concert.

A rush of emotions broke through the surreal scene. I channeled the joy into my music. I couldn't smile. That would ruin my embouchure. I couldn't leap from my chair and dance around the stage. So while my heart was turning cartwheels, I sat firm and tall.

And I played.

I played cleanly, with precision, carefully blending with the first-flute line, anticipating each attack.

We were glorious.

The applause was an unnecessary afterthought. We basked in the reward, and relaxed during the brief intermission. Now that I'd survived, the constricting fear had dissolved, and I was ready to completely enjoy the final two acts—the Beethoven and Bach.

A stagehand mopped the spit from the floor near the brass instruments. Sarah swigged water, and an oboist sucked his reeds to keep them ready. String players adjusted their bows. In no time, the house lights dimmed, the murmurs quieted, programs rustled, curtains parted, and we poised, ready for the second part of the Three B's.

Peter smiled as he faced us, probably enjoying the same flush of victory that I felt. This debut could not have come off better.

He gave the downbeat, and the strings attacked. Since I didn't come in for several measures, I was watching the violins when it happened.

Right after their first page turn, Stefan and his stand partner David Tanner moved their bows in opposition to the other violins. David glanced to his left, and his fingers stumbled as he saw his arm move counter to the rest of the section. The shocking sound of David's wrong notes carried throughout the orchestra.

Musicians in every section glanced over to the violins to see what was going on. Peter's eyes widened. Everyone kept playing, but the damage was done. Confidence shaken, confusion affected the violin section. The rhythm felt uneven. Stefan closed his eyes and began to play from memory. His bowing slipped back into unison with the violin section.

The monster beyond the footlights mumbled in dismay as the first movement limped to a close.

In the brief pause before the next movement, one of the first violins behind Stefan and David passed his music forward. Stefan nodded to the conductor, and Peter continued the piece. I had to concentrate on my own playing, and had no chance to guess at what had occurred. Even though Stefan and David were now in sync with the other violins, the whole orchestra was distracted, and it showed in our playing.

When we finally reached the second intermission, Peter's face was thunderous, and Stefan was livid. I slipped into the wings to find Lena and ask her if she knew what had happened. A French horn player pushed past me, and I squeezed into the folds of a back curtain, which made me an inadvertent and invisible observer for the confrontation.

"What were you thinking?" Peter cornered Stefan, a pit bull growling up at a Great Dane.

"Some person changed my bowing." Stefan rattled his music in front of Peter and then flung the papers to the floor. "See? See there?" A serious charge. The concertmaster set the bowing choices for the violin section, coordinated the downstrokes and upstrokes, and led in precise unison. To erase the penciled marks and change them would be like someone moving my breath marks and phrase lines. But this problem was even more obvious to the audience.

Peter mopped his forehead with a handkerchief. "Who would do that? And why?"

"How can I know? Tonight critics come. I have an enemy." Stefan's accent became more pronounced in his agitation.

"Or I do." Peter rubbed the back of his head, mussing his hair further. He raised his chin and glared at Stefan. "Check the rest of your music. We'll hold the curtain."

Stefan gave a curt nod and began collecting his scattered music, still clutching his instrument in one hand.

I glanced across the wings. I hadn't been the only person spying on this encounter. Leonard stood in the shadows near the giant ropes that rose up into the fly space. A smile of satisfaction played around the edges of his lips.

CHAPTER

10

Glissando: Sliding between two notes.

"Mom, I thought you were done with the conspiracy-theory stuff." Clara slouched near the kitchen table with her feet up on a chair.

"Conspiracy theory is for grassy knolls and alien abductions." I stirred sugar into my coffee, hoping it might sweeten my mood.

"And this is . . . ?"

"Sleuthing. Someone sabotaged the concert last night. I want to figure out who did it."

"Aren't you being a little melodramatic?"

"They ruined the concert."

"It wasn't that bad. I didn't even notice the big crisis."

I thumbed the crease in the variety section of the newspaper and turned it to face her. "The critics did."

She skimmed the review, which contained words like "clumsy, insecure, uneven."

"Ouch," she said. "Did you think it was that bad?"

I nodded. "We never regained our edge after the problem with the bowing. Everyone was out of sorts."

Clara pursed her lips and blew out a slow breath. "Okay. Explain it to me again."

"The concertmaster—that's Stefan—makes the bowing decision in the rehearsal process. Everyone marks their scores with little V marks for the up-bow, and a little square missing the bottom side for the down-bow. To up-bow, they start at the tip and push through. To down-bow, they start at the frog—that's where they hold the bow—and glide downward. They have to fit all the notes in a certain phrase during that pull . . . kind of like a flute player finishing a phrase before taking a breath."

"Wow. Did you study violin in college, too?"

I shook my head. "I had a . . . friend who played."

"Ahh. Your freckles are turning pink. That means it was a guy." She gave me a cheeky grin.

"Let's get back to the point," I said, eager to distract her before she gleaned truths I wasn't ready to share. "Someone erased the bow marks and reversed them. Not right at the beginning, where he might have noticed before playing. After the page turn."

"So the saboteur understood music. Who would have anything to gain in messing up the concert?"

I sipped my lukewarm coffee and made a face. "I don't know. David Tanner wanted the concertmaster position and didn't get it. He could be jealous. Leonard is always joking around, but his dislike of Stefan is pretty serious. But it couldn't be someone in the symphony. The problem made us all look bad."

Clara thumped her feet to the floor and sprang up. "Well, you can solve the case of the Maniacal Musical Misanthrope later. We have to get to the bake sale."

I shuddered. "I don't bake fancy stuff, and I don't schmooze. How is this a good thing?"

Clara laughed. "You managed banana bread. And I'll help with the schmoozing. Let's go."

I hesitated. "They added a rehearsal before tonight's concert. I'll have to leave early."

She planted her fists on her waist. "Then you'd better plan on some serious selling. We're not leaving until we make our quota."

The gym echoed with animated conversations, the scrapes of folding chairs, and the whoops of younger siblings chasing each other around the booths. I stalled in the entryway. Garish crepe paper dangled from ceiling and tables, and plastic flowers stood guard over displays of cookies, pies, and cakes.

I wanted to put in my time and get out of here as soon as I could. If I had my druthers, I wouldn't be here at all. But I also wanted to make Clara happy and ease the growing guilt tumor that had been pressing against my diaphragm.

Worse than the pain of labor and delivery, mommy guilt was a constant companion. It went into remission when I was able to stay busy enough to avoid the malignant thoughts—how many things we scrimped on because I funneled our meager budget into musical instruments, how Clara grew up without a father because I wasn't appealing enough to hold a man, how I didn't have the personality of the storybook mom and had probably scarred her for life with all my neuroses. Most of the time, I was preoccupied enough to push those worries away.

Today, as I watched cheerful moms bustling around the gym, the guilt burned in my gut.

Clara checked in at the registration table, where Joy bounced around answering questions. "Mom, over here. We need to decorate our booth."

I hefted our grocery box of banana breads and followed Clara to a lunchroom table with a wobbly leg. She set about adorning our space with a paper tablecloth, a ubiquitous bouquet of plastic tulips, and a careful arrangement of our loaves. I propped up our folded cards that listed the five-dollar price. A ridiculous amount, in my opinion. I'd wanted to price them at two dollars, hoping to get rid of them so I could leave early.

Joy Selforth prowled the gym checking on all the cheerleaders and parents. When she reached our table she gave a toothy smile. "I've sure enjoyed having Clara on the squad. She is so focused during practices. It's awesome."

Maternal pride expanded under my ribs. "Well, her musical training taught her that."

"Oh, that's right. You play something, don't you?"

"Yes, and I've been scheduled for an extra rehearsal today, so I may have to—"

She patted my arm. "That's all right. I'm sure they'll understand if you have to be late." With another beaming smile, she scampered on her way.

Clara smothered a burst of laughter.

I whirled to frown at her. "Not funny."

" 'You play something, don't you?' " Clara mimicked. "You should have seen your face."

"Ha, ha. Look, I'm serious about the rehearsal. I have to leave by three."

"Then you'd better start hawking those banana breads."

I rolled my eyes. The public was just arriving, and I needed to lure them to our table quickly. I pasted on the most inviting smile I could conjure and barked a friendly "hello" to each family that walked past. One baby in a stroller startled and began crying, but it was hardly my fault he was so jumpy.

"Mom, stop making that face."

"What face?"

"You look all fierce."

"This is not my fierce face. This is my friendly-but-determined face."

"Trust me, Mom. Friendly it's not. Watch me." She moved to the side of the table and struck up conversations with everyone who came within a ten-foot radius. She chirped greetings to children and answered questions for adults. Charming and poised, she seemed like an alien in my daughter's body.

Clara had been a bookish little girl, which suited me fine. We had led an insulated life with fine music and good literature. Clara never ran around screaming like some of the little tyrants here today. Because it was always just the two of us, I treated her like a small adult, and she acted like one—albeit a shy one. Today I couldn't see a glimpse of my timid little girl with long braids and large glasses. Her hair swung free, her eyes sparkled behind contacts, and no hint of awkward shyness remained. I was startled to realize I envied her.

I let her attract customers, while I quietly took money and made change. Within an hour, our sale items were depleted, and I glanced at my watch. I might even get to the orchestra rehearsal early.

"Why, you're doing great, aren't you?" Joy was back, rah-rahing our efforts and carrying a large carton. "The Parents' Auxiliary League baked plenty of extras, so I thought it was time to restock your table. Have fun."

She dropped the box of baked goods on our table and galloped away before I could protest.

Clara winked at me. "Back to work."

After another string of sales in the noisy and crowded gym, we hit a lull. I bought us each one of the bear claws we hadn't sold yet. We sank into crooked metal chairs, and I took a huge bite of pastry. "You know what doesn't make sense?" I licked my fingers. "Musicians take good care of their music. Stefan would have had his folder with him most of the time."

Clara swigged from her water bottle. "So when did someone make the changes?"

"That's what I'm trying to figure out. Someone must have slipped onto the stage after Stefan set up his music on the stand."

Clara rotated an ankle. "Did you see anyone hanging around the stage?" She lifted her other foot to flex and point it several times. Apparently I wasn't the only one getting sore feet.

"Well, I was out there for a while trying to gather my nerve."

She grinned. "Did anyone see you? They might decide to suspect you."

"There was a stagehand in the hallway. The only person I remember talking to on stage was Peter Wilson." A headache pulsed behind my eyes, and I massaged my forehead. "He stayed out there after I left."

Clara's chewing slowed. "Could he have done it?"

"Never. He cares too much about the music." But in spite of my firm tone, a sickly fear crawled through my stomach.

"Hey!" Lena approached our table with her son, Zach, running laps around her legs. "I heard this is the place to get the best banana bread."

Ken followed close behind with Janell piggybacking, using a choke hold on his neck. "Lena said you guys were doing a bake sale, and I had to see it for myself."

I crossed my arms. "Har, har. We're doing fine. We sold all our banana bread."

Ken leaned toward Lena. "That's a relief. We won't have to buy any after all. You didn't make that cherry pie, did you?"

"Get real," I said.

"All righty. We'll take two."

Zach slingshotted away from Lena and toward a table with cookies, and Ken charged after him with Janell still on his back.

Lena smiled as the three disappeared deeper into the gym and then turned back to give me a once-over. "Seriously, how's it going? We thought we'd come out as a show of support."

I glanced at my watch. "Not as bad as I thought. But I'm supposed to be at the theatre in forty-five minutes."

Clara gazed out at the other parents and daughters manning the tables around the gym. "It's fine, Mom. I can stay for the last hour by myself." But there was a forlorn look behind her words.

Was being a mother supposed to hurt this much? I seemed to disappoint her more with each passing year.

"I've got a great idea." Lena took her purse from her shoulder and stowed it behind the table. "I don't have to get to the theatre until six. I'll send Ken home with the kids and stay with Clara for the last hour."

Clara threw her arms around Lena. "That's awesome. You sure you don't mind?" She looked over her shoulder in my direction. "Isn't that great, Mom?"

My face felt tight as I smiled. "Terrific." I'd baked the stupid bread and sat here most of the day. But Lena offered to hang around for one hour, and she got to play the saint.

Clara tugged Lena toward a chair. "The cookies are three dollars per dozen, and we have extra bags under the table . . ."

They'd both forgotten I was there. "Okay, then. I better get going."

No response.

"See you later," I said loudly.

Clara glanced up vaguely. "Yeah. Have a good concert."

Suddenly I couldn't wait to caress my flute, to breathe life into it. It was the only thing that could push away the loneliness that throbbed more insistently than my headache.

The mood in the theatre was grim. As a new, trial member, I wasn't invited into any of the conversations. But as I wove my way through clusters of musicians, I overheard plenty of speculation.

"... worst possible time, with that big grant up in the air."

"Leave it to the strings to ruin the preview night."

"Why didn't he give an interview? Taking all the blame as the conductor might sound noble, but ..."

"If I find out it's someone in our orchestra, I'll ..."

"... but who would target him?"

I took my place beside Sarah and set up my music.

"Check it over." She jerked a nod at my sheet music. "And keep it with you."

"Will do." Sarah was so prickly and annoying, I wished I could find a way to blame her for yesterday's disaster. But no true musician would pull a prank like that, even if she had a grudge against Stefan. Maybe if I spent more time with Stefan, I could figure out who his enemies might be.

"Cut the chatter." Peter snapped from the wings. "We have work to do."

Musicians hurried to take their places. Leonard eased past me and winked. "What's the difference between God and a conductor? God knows He's not a conductor."

I hid my giggle behind my music. I'd be crushed if I found out the burly trombonist had anything to do with the sabotage of Stefan's music. He made the tension around here bearable. Once again the string bass player shuffled in last, and the musicians around him sighed with resignation. It was so similar to the orchestra at

Juilliard. There was always a musician who clowned around and always one who dragged in late.

Today Peter Wilson lived up to the God-complex of a conductor. As he drilled sections of the Beethoven, he demanded the impossible and was furious when we didn't give it. He berated each section of the orchestra. We gave our best efforts but never coaxed even a small smile from him, much less a word of approval. All he was doing was frustrating us—right before our concert. How was that supposed to help us play well?

He finally glanced at his watch and cut us off midphrase, leaving us a miserable stage-full of artists. When I hurried backstage to get some water, I wasn't the only one carrying my music with me.

Lena had arrived near the end of the rehearsal, and I met her in the wings. "That was brutal," I whispered.

Her eyes were wide. "Yeah. I hope everyone can shake off this mood."

"How was the end of the bake sale?"

"Fun." Her happy grin turned uncertain. "Um, but I need to tell you . . ."

"What?"

"Well, that coach came around at the end to have everyone sign up for a sewing day next Saturday."

"Hey, I don't mind. Honest. If you want to help Clara sew costumes, it's fine with me."

She shook her head. "No, that's not what I mean. I had to pick a time, so I put you down for ten in the morning."

"What?" My voice rose to a shriek.

Lena took a step back. "I'm sorry. I thought that would be the best time for you—"

"The best time would have been none at all. What were you thinking?"

She bit her lip. Lena was a tuning fork, vibrating in the frequency of whatever influence surrounded her. When I lost my temper at her, she practically trembled. "I didn't want Clara to feel bad. All the other moms were signing up. Look, I'm sure you can call her . . ."

"Ms. Johnson?" The voice behind me struck my last nerve.

"What?" I turned and channeled all my frustration into a killer glare. And found myself eye to eye with the conductor.

This time there was no amusement in his eyes. "I need to discuss something with you after the concert. Find me."

"Ah, all right, I . . ."

He had already disappeared.

I swallowed hard. Maybe my trial period was about to run out.

CHAPTER

11

Tacet: An indication in the music that a performer is to be silent for some time.

Tension crippled the lyrical sections of our pieces, but Stefan played with fierce intensity as he led the violin section. Halfway through the concert Peter's jaw began to relax, and his conducting became less stormy. The audience was appreciative. Probably more than we deserved. But at least we had no further mishaps.

During the applause, I waited for the rush of happiness—the dream-come-true elation. Instead, a cloud hung over my first non-preview, opening-night concert. If Sarah, Peter, or the powers-that-be decided my tone didn't blend, or my skills weren't adequate, or they just wanted to go with another candidate, my dream would be stillborn.

After the concert I lost myself in the hubbub backstage. If Peter planned to cut me, I didn't want him doing it with others around to hear.

Stefan sailed through the milling bodies and aimed my direction. "Amy! Now you must come out with us to celebrate, yes?" His face shone with triumph. He looked like a tourist ski poster for a Scandinavian country—all energy, bright eyes, and impossibly good looks.

If this was my first and last concert, I should commemorate the evening. "Okay. Where should I meet you?"

"We are walking to Solera. They have a tapas bar. I will wait for you in the lobby."

Leonard and Vicki reached me next. "Now that was more like it." Vicki tucked her hand around her husband's arm. "I love the Beethoven. Folks should hear it the way it's meant to be played."

"I have a new one." Leonard cleared his throat. "Why does the viola player stand outside the house?"

A man carrying his viola past us snorted and walked away. Leonard called after him, "He can't find the key and doesn't know when to come in."

Vicki covered her face with her hands and moaned.

I shook my head. "You need to work on your material."

Lena glided toward us, dark skirt swirling around her ankles.

Leonard's eyes squinted over his rosy cheeks. "Lena, I've got one for you. How long does a harp stay in tune? About twenty minutes or until someone opens a door."

Lena giggled. "How many trombones does it take to change a light bulb? Just one, but he'll do it too loudly."

"No, no. Don't start him on the light-bulb jokes," Vicki said. "He'll go on for hours."

Leonard guffawed. "I'll save some for the restaurant. You coming?" he asked Lena.

"I need to get home to the kids." Her cheerful tone held no hint of regret.

Her glib contentment annoyed me. She was equally happy in both arenas: consummate professional, and nurturing wife and mother.

"How about you?" Vicki asked me.

"Yeah, I'll meet you in the front lobby."

The couple moved on, and Lena pulled me aside. "I'm sorry about signing you up for the sewing thing. I didn't know what to do. That Joy lady can be pretty persuasive."

"It's not your fault. I'll figure out something. Can I borrow your cell phone? I forgot to recharge mine, and I want to let Clara know I'll be home late."

"I'm glad you're going to have some fun."

I winced, ignoring the avid curiosity in Lena's eyes. "Yeah. I figure I need the distraction. Peter said he wanted to talk to me." I shrugged. "Either I'll be celebrating tonight or holding a wake."

Lena dug in her purse and handed me her phone. "You don't think they decided on someone else, do you? They usually give a musician a few weeks before making the final decision, after they see if the blend will work."

Sarah stalked past and disappeared into the dressing room. "Maybe someone's put in a bad word on my behalf." I punched in my phone number.

"If she did, I'll wrap that flute around her scrawny neck," Lena muttered.

Her virulence startled me. "Hey, leave that honor to me. Besides, the way I played tonight, I probably deserve to get canned."

"Stop fishing for compliments. You know you're good. Sarah's been around so long that she resents any decisions that don't go her way. She better not ruin it for you."

Clara answered the phone. "Brad? Mom's gone. Come on over. She'll never know."

My lips twitched. My little smart aleck. "Okay, and I'll bring Orlando and Johnny, too, if they're done shooting that new pirate movie." Lena stared at me as if I were nuts, but I ignored her. "Sweetie, I'm going out with a few of the musicians. Will you be okay if I'm an hour or so late?"

"But what will the neighborhood do without you here? What if a house gets TP-ed or someone parks too close to the fire hydrant? Who'll keep the police informed?"

"Make that three hours late."

Clara laughed. "If you bring some guy home, hang a sock on your doorknob as a signal, okay?"

"Keep that up, and you aren't leaving for college until you're thirty."

She was still giggling when she hung up.

I snapped the phone shut and handed it back to Lena.

She shook her head. "You guys are nuts."

"Yeah? Well, talk to me when Zach and Janell are teenagers, okay?"

Lena smiled. "If they turn out as great as Clara, I'll be thrilled." She waved good-bye and headed up the hall toward the theatre lobby.

A sour taste burned in my throat. I should feel pride at Lena's assessment of my daughter. But she was encroaching on my territory. Lena fit in perfectly with all the other cheerleader moms at the bake sale. She functioned well with normal people. She took to motherhood effortlessly when her kids were born, and it irritated me. I'd wrestled with each stage of parenting the past fifteen years . . . and still did.

I struggled to shake off my dour mood and went down the metal stairs in search of Peter. A locker rattled in the large warm-up room, then slammed shut. I paused outside the door. I didn't want to find Peter if he was in a bad temper.

"Why does he keep requesting you for these quartet parts?" It was Leonard's voice. "There are plenty of other cellists."

A woman sighed. "He appreciates my technique. Trust me, that's all." Vicki's voice.

"I do trust you. It's Stefan I don't trust."

I tiptoed backward. More domestic squabbles. One advantage of being a single mom—I didn't have to deal with a husband.

"Are you looking for me?"

I jumped at the sound of Peter's voice. I'd backed myself into the threshold of a small dressing room.

His.

He'd cast off his penguin jacket and unbuttoned his cuffs, which flopped around his wrists, making him more boyish than ever. A gleam of sweat on his face made the hair at his temples curl in dark ringlets.

Play it calm. Professional. He's not going to fire you. "Oh, there you are. You said you wanted to see me?"

"Right. Come in, come in."

I stepped into the small room, hands clasped like a schoolgirl called to the blackboard. By contrast, he looked completely relaxed, sprawled in a chair that he angled to face me. He wouldn't be this casual if he were about to kick me out, would he?

He raised an eyebrow. "For someone who can play Mozart with so much fire, you're a nervous little thing, aren't you?"

I released my breath in a huff. "I'm not little and I'm not nervous and . . ." My mind snagged on the important part of that sentence. "You liked my Mozart?"

"Are you busy on Wednesday?"

My stomach did a roller-coaster dip. Stefan's friendly flirtation was one thing. But I knew better than to encourage any interest from the man who could shape my career. "Look, I'm flattered, but—"

"I'm doing a lecture demonstration at Concordia University—Structure of the Sonata Form. I want to use a flutist. Are you free? Ten o'clock."

A lecture demo? Embarrassment gave way quickly to another happy climb. He'd chosen me? "Well, I'm honored. If you think . . . Why—"

"Good. Sarah was busy, and Cheryl is already out of town."

Oh. Last resort choice. The coaster leveled off.

He was still talking. "We'll use the Bach Sonata in E Minor. That was on your repertoire list, yes?"

"Sure. And I don't think I have sectional Wednesday morning." I rummaged through my bag looking for my pocket calendar. "I might have a student . . . but of course I can reschedule . . ."

"You're dithering."

"No. I mean, yes. I mean I can be there. Who's accompanying?"

He yawned, rolling his head to one side with a crack of vertebrae. "I'll take care of it. You know how to find their music auditorium?"

My head bobbed. "I'll be there." I sounded as breathy as when the Youth Symphony offered me a solo in high school. What was wrong with me? I was an experienced musician. I hitched up the strap of my bag, scrambling for something smart to say.

"So, um, the concert went better tonight," I said. Not smart, but at least cool and casual. Now would be the perfect time for him to tell me that my trial period was over and they were offering me a full contract.

"Barely."

"Can you think of anyone who would want to hurt the symphony?"

He stopped scowling, and his face took on the bemused tolerance I'd seen Clara wear so often. "Playing detective? Poor technique is hardly a crime. Though I've worked with a few musicians I'd like to see hanged."

"But Stefan's music—"

"Probably pulled out an old part by mistake, and his ego won't let him admit it." Peter turned his chair away. It scraped against the concrete floor. "Good night." He flicked his hand in a careless wave.

Subtle as a train wreck. I was dismissed, along with my questions—spoken and unspoken. Fine. I'd make myself indispensable to the orchestra so I could lock in this job, and as far as the mystery, I'd get more clues from Stefan.

Several musicians were gathered in the theatre lobby. "There she is." Stefan's warm smile soothed my jangled nerves.

"What took you so long?" Vicki asked.

"Sorry, sorry. I'm ready now."

A dozen musicians descending on a restaurant to unwind wasn't quite as raucous as a rock concert after-party, but we came close. Relief made us giddy, and a few rounds of drinks pushed giddy into the goofy zone. Even Leonard's jokes made us laugh.

Stefan had wedged himself next to me at one of the tables. As the chatter grew louder, he turned toward me. "So how do you find our orchestra?"

"I love it. I just hope I can keep up." Performing professionally was a whole different world. I was good, but that might not be enough.

He waved away my insecurity, stirring the air over our votive candle and making it flicker. "Your selection was not mistaken." His voice lowered. "Like others."

I leaned closer. "What do you mean?"

"This conductor. Not enough experience. He will not take the symphony into more . . . renown."

"He seems pretty sharp. And he's choosing some great repertoire."

Stefan raised his glass. Ice cubes tinkled over the noise around us. "We will see."

No mutual admiration society between the concertmaster and conductor. Not uncommon in this world of Hindenburg-sized egos.

I smiled. "You played with a lot of power tonight."

He gave a courtly nod. "My thanks." The blue in his eyes turned grey as he sat back and a shadow caught his face. "I am capable of much more." He stared down into his glass and shook his head.

Now would be a good time for some delicate probing. "So do you have any enemies? Any idea of who could have ruined your music yesterday?"

His laugh was rich and full. "Any violinist who is not in my chair. But tell me about you. Did I hear you were at Juilliard?"

We shifted into an easy conversation that took us quickly through all the getting-to-know-each-other formalities and on to music.

"Next weekend, we will debut my violin solo." His fervor was contagious. "Vivaldi."

"I can't wait."

His face clouded. "I hope no more problems will . . ." The words trailed off, and he stared into the candle that guttered and went out.

Sympathy wove a soft bond between us. "I'm sure it'll go fine. Besides, maybe it was a mix-up. Could you have put out some old music by mistake yesterday?"

He met my eyes, his face very still. "Would you set up wrong music?"

I sighed. "Never."

He nodded. "Let us hope that we will find this enemy before more damage is made."

I raised my glass. "I'll toast to that."

CHAPTER

12

 Con brio: A directive to perform the indicated passage with vivacity or spirit.

"I want to hear every detail," Clara said at breakfast the next morning.

"Well, he's really nice when you get to know him. He's traveled a lot, of course. Had some great stories."

Her mouth sagged open. "I meant the concert. But now that you've mentioned it . . . tell me about afterwards."

I picked up my coffee mug and tried to hide behind it. "Never mind."

"No, no, no. The witness has opened the door to this line of questioning. Who's nice when you get to know him? And how well did you get to know him?"

"Stefan. We talked. That's all. He's been really supportive. And I want to help him figure out who wrecked his music."

"Stefan? The concertmaster? Whoa . . . aiming high, huh? And speaking of high, isn't he a little tall for you?"

I clamped my teeth together. "It's not like that. I'm just trying to make friends. And everyone's too tall for me."

"Not the conductor. He looked just right." She waggled her eyebrows.

"That's so wrong. For about a million reasons."

"Whatever. Can you drive me to Ragstock this afternoon? I need a dress."

"Why?"

Clara's skin pinked up, and her gaze darted around the room. "Ryan asked me to the end-of-the-year dance."

I leaned forward, ready to move from defense to offense. "Ryan?"

"He's a football player. Of course, this time of year he's on the baseball team. . . . We got to talking after my practice one day, and—"

"I knew it. I knew cheerleading would lead to other things. Now she wants to date a football player."

Her giggle didn't reassure me. "Mom, he's in my honors lit class. He's a great guy."

"Right. Well, he won't keep up with honors classes if he insists on bashing his head into people as a hobby."

"Yes or no on the lift to the store?"

"Yes, but I want to meet this jock before the dance."

"Will do." She shoved away from the table and dropped her cereal bowl into the sink. "I gotta get dressed."

I glanced at the clock on the stove, confused. "It's only nine."

Again her gaze skittered away. "Lena's picking me up. I said I'd go to church with her again."

I choked on a mouthful of coffee.

She gave an innocent, wide-eyed smile. "Wanna come?"

I ran a major scale up and down in my head—my version of counting to ten. "No. And why would you want to?" When she started to answer, I held up my hand. "Look, if you're curious, we can get a book on world religions and study it together, all right?"

She stood up and planted her palms against the table, staring me down. "I feel like going. No biggie. Enjoy your coffee, read the funnies, solve a few mysteries. I'll be back soon." She sailed out of the room.

I wanted to grab for her. Hold her down. Hold her back. Hold her.

She was right, it was no biggie. Except that it was. Because every experience that separated us brought the inevitable closer. I'd felt twinges when she got her first haircut, started kindergarten, went to her first slumber party. I'd seen the warning light blinking. She was growing up.

But did anyone stop to think about what that meant? All the love, all the investment. All so the child could say good-bye. I hated being reminded that Clara had her own life. Each passing year her life contained a little less of me.

She avoided the kitchen, and ten minutes later I heard her dash out. The front door banged shut—a hollow sound in the front room.

I clenched and unclenched my hands. Then I marched into the living room and grabbed my flute.

On Wednesday morning, I hit all the rush hour traffic and was afraid I'd be late for the lecture demonstration. The main freeway between Minneapolis and St. Paul ribboned its way past hospitals, across the Mississippi, and toward the cluster of colleges scattered on the east side of the river. I had to park a few blocks away from the music building, so I jogged through a mid-May drizzle, arriving damp and out of breath.

Peter wore a suit and tie and looked as stiff as he did in his concert tux. I had chosen a midlength black dress—a bit less formal than concert attire. The empty auditorium scooped upward in a jumble of orange- and rust-colored seats.

I pulled out my music and adjusted the music stand at center stage near a grand piano. "So, who's accompanying?"

Peter cracked his knuckles, pulled out the piano bench, and sat down. "I think I can manage to keep up. Let's try a few transitions, yes?"

Wasn't he just full of surprises? Why hadn't he mentioned that he'd be accompanying when I'd asked him about it earlier?

"During the lecture, I'll be stopping at the end of some of the sections to discuss them. Be ready."

I nodded and asked for a tuning note. We checked a few of my entrances. Was he still evaluating me? Was this all a test? I tilted the music stand, then grabbed as pages fell forward off the stand. I'd drop my flute next if I didn't calm down.

Students began streaming into the auditorium. One of the music professors introduced Peter, who then launched into his talk. As he spoke in his rich baritone voice, his appreciation for composers kept the students scribbling notes. His colorful anecdotes coaxed chuckles from them. We played the first section, and then he signaled me to stop. From the piano bench, he chatted with the students, explained the form, and told them what to listen for in the next movement. Then we were off again.

A strange feeling fluttered inside me along with the trills in the presto section. This was fun.

Fun was not part of what I taught my students. Fun was not what made me a good musician. Intensity, discipline, urgency, and sacrifice drove my relationship with music. Yes, I loved it. But it was a desperate, compelling sort of love, with little room for whimsy. Yet somehow, today, I had fun. I almost laughed as we finished the last reckless section and the students applauded. A few people lingered to ask questions. Some even approached me, wanting advice.

"Not as bad as I feared," Peter said after the last student disappeared. "I'm not much good at teaching, but you know . . . public face for the symphony and all that. Everything is public relations these days."

"You were great."

Small creases deepened around his eyes. "Thanks for your help."

I stood, expectant.

Come on. Tell me if I'm still in the orchestra. You've heard me enough.

He gathered his music and wedged it into his satchel. When he turned to leave, he saw me still planted on the stage in his path. "Something wrong?"

Irritation prodded me. "Look, it might not be appropriate to ask, but I need to know. Are you kicking me out or what?"

He cast a confused look toward the auditorium doors.

"Out of the orchestra," I snapped. "Give it to me straight. In or out." I cleared my throat, wishing for an ounce of diplomacy, but that schooner had sailed. Still, I softened my tone. "Please."

Understanding crossed his face slowly. "They didn't send you the letter yet? Of course you're hired." His teeth flashed against the dark stubble of his jaw. "That's why you've been so jumpy?"

His grin sent me over the edge. "Well, you could have said something." I struggled to keep the screech from my voice. Not the attitude a musician should convey when addressing a conductor, but I was full of after-a-crisis adrenaline. "Do you have any idea how stressed out I've been?"

He seemed genuinely puzzled by my ranting. "How was I supposed to know you hadn't been told, or that you're so insecure?"

"Hello? I'm a musician!"

He rubbed his chin. "Point taken. My apologies."

Ready to mend fences, I took a deep breath. "Well, I'm honored to accept the position." As I said it, pure joy crackled through me like static. I was in. It was real. It was happening.

His smile was tired. "Well, if this new grant doesn't come through, it'll be a short run, so enjoy it while you can."

I stepped aside and watched him leave. Were things at the symphony really that bad? Maybe someone at the office was embezzling funds. Maybe the other orchestras in town were out to get us and had bribed the arts council. The theories jumping through my head sounded like a far-fetched episode of an old crime show. "Columbo Goes to the Symphony." Still, stranger things had happened. Could the orchestra really close? No. No way. My lifelong dream had come true, and nothing was going to cut it short.

As I walked to my car, the drizzle eased up. Water dripped in a syncopated rhythm from the gutters. I enjoyed the muted shade of a cloudy spring day more than the glaring vibrancy of summer.

Then a jacked-up junker rolled past with hideous rap music blaring through open windows.

My mood soured. The Twin Cities had passed no-smoking ordinances. Why couldn't we protect people's health by banning bad music?

"Enjoy it while you can."

Peter's words rang through my mind as I watched Clara that afternoon. We'd been prickly with each other for the past few days. She'd never said anything after the church service with Lena, and I refused to ask.

Ryan had given her a ride home from school and stuck his head in the door to meet me. I drilled him about his vocational goals, his hobbies, and his driving ability. Then I warned him of the dire consequences if he kept Clara out past eleven. The longer I talked, the rounder his eyes became. When I paused for breath, he said a hurried good-bye and ducked out, disappearing in a squeal of tires.

Clara draped herself over the arms of the wing chair and groaned. "Mom, he's just a friend. You don't have to go all Homeland Security on him."

"Too many questions?"

"Just a tad."

"Sorry." And I meant it. "I only do it because I care about you. There are guys out there who—"

Her eyes darkened.

I backpedaled. "I mean, I like getting to know your friends."

She rolled her eyes, then stretched her head back until her long hair brushed the floor.

"Clara-bird, I've got news." I waited until she hauled her head back up from her half-backbend and looked at me. "My trial period is over. I'm in the symphony for keeps."

She lifted her hand for a high five. "Way to go." Her smile was genuine, and she seemed suitably happy for me, but right after our hands slapped, she pulled back into herself—eyes distant, body angled away—as if she were wearing invisible headphones that shut me out.

I hated it. And I hated that I didn't know what to do about it.

"I made a hot dish." I twisted the soft belt of my cardigan. "You hungry?"

Clara swung her legs down and sat at attention. "You cooked? On a Wednesday?"

I shrugged. "Thursday doesn't have to be the only night for a family dinner."

She bounded to her feet and followed me into the kitchen. A steamy casserole of rice and chicken eased away some of her stiffness—and she really loosened up after I suggested Ben & Jerry's Cherry Garcia for dessert. When she snitched a few of the chocolate chunks from my scoop, I didn't swat her hand. Sometimes the simplest thing turns me into a good mom again.

"Are you practicing tonight?" she asked around a mouthful of ice cream.

"Naw. I played a lot today already. What are you up to?"

"I need to finish the autobiography project." She cast a sideways glance at me. "I could use some help. If you have the time."

"Sure." I stood up and stretched. My back was sore, probably from all the tension gripping my muscles in the past weeks. I scraped the plates and loaded the dishwasher.

Clara disappeared upstairs and returned in a few minutes with an armful of supplies.

"Okay, I've got my baby book and my notes. But I have some questions."

Questions. My shoulders tightened and a cramp traveled down my spine. She spread her colored pencils out across the kitchen table, and unrolled a lopsided diagram of a family tree. I sat down and pulled the baby book toward me, tracing the Beatrix Potter drawings on the cover. I remembered my strange mix of feelings when I'd first held this book. Wonder and dread. Hope and disbelief. The confusion lasted through the entire pregnancy but dissolved the day she was born and her eyes met mine for the first time. In that moment I knew I'd made the right choice.

"Mom, can I ask you something?"

My throat was gripped in a fist. "Sure."

"What was your dad like?"

I blew out a sigh of relief. "My dad? He was really smart . . . a bit absentminded. When he had his nose in a book, you could do a production of *A Chorus Line* in front of him, and he wouldn't know you were there. He loved you to bits. Used to hold you on his lap and read poetry to you. Not Mother Goose. The real stuff."

The lines of her face softened. She looked up from her notebook and gazed into space. "I remember that his sweaters always smelled like pipe smoke."

"Yep, he loved his pipe. I'm surprised you remember that. You were only four when he died."

"I remember his voice. It was rumbly and would go on and on when he read to me. But I don't remember him talking other times."

A deep hidden wistfulness waved to me from my long-ago past. "He hid behind his books. He was brilliant, but shy. Making conversation made him nervous."

She asked more questions, and I dove deep into the waters of nostalgia, revisiting places I usually avoided—my mother's death my junior year of high school, my father's further withdrawal, the salvation that music provided, the thrill of getting into Juilliard. Beyond the kitchen curtains, sunset mellowed until the kitchen became a safe and gentle womb. Both our voices softened as we talked.

When it grew too dark for her to see her papers, Clara stood to turn on the light. With one click, the room jumped back into harsh reality, and I rubbed my eyes.

Clara paused by the wall with her back toward me. "Thanks for all your help. I'm almost done." When she turned to face me, her eyes were sympathetic but resolute. "Now, tell me more about *my* dad."

CHAPTER

13

Crescendo: A steady increase in force or intensity.

Even during my pregnancy with Clara, I'd wrestled with the question. What would I tell my daughter about her father? I avoided the dilemma for years. When Clara came home from kindergarten one day and asked why she didn't have a daddy, it was easy to say, "We'll talk about that when you're older." Later, when the questions became more persistent, I was tempted to create a story for her. He was killed in a tragic car accident before we could get married. He went off to war to protect our country and died on the battlefield. But I suspected a lie would come back to bite me. So, I kept it simple. "I dated a guy in college. He wasn't ready to be a father. And we've managed fine without him. No, I don't know where he is now. Yes, he was handsome and talented and fascinating and I loved him. No, he didn't really love me. That's all you need to know." Those conversations never ended well, but since I shut down every time Clara brought it up, she finally stopped asking.

Now the chair creaked as Clara sat down across from me. She ripped a blank sheet of paper from her notebook—a harsh, determined sound. She'd been asserting herself in a lot of ways recently. Cheerleading, dating, church. I had the feeling that I wouldn't find it so easy to dissuade her from her renewed curiosity about her father.

My stomach lurched. Was this really what she needed from me? Would it seal our relationship? Or would she have further proof of my failings and shift her love toward a mythic father?

Clara picked up her pen. "Was he a musician? You must have met him at Juilliard. An actor? Oh, please tell me he wasn't a dancer." Her half-laugh didn't fool me. Her body was strung as tight as Lena's harp.

"That's not important." I wanted to get up and busy myself. Put on the teakettle, dust away toast crumbs on the counter. But I couldn't move.

"Maybe it's important to me. Please. Tell me about my father." She said the last word with tenderness—as though she had already taken his side.

Hot pain drove into my chest. My nails pressed into my palms. "He was never a father," I hissed. "Just a biological donor." Even I was surprised at the fury that unlocked inside of me as I thought of Jason. "He's never been in the picture. You have no idea—"

"No, I don't." Clara leaned forward. "So why don't you tell me?"

I clenched my jaw and looked away.

"Did you love him?" she prompted.

"I thought I did. I was an idiot. We've been over this before. The subject's closed." I finally convinced my legs to move, shoved my chair back, and headed to the sink where the glass baking dish was soaking. I scrubbed it with all the anger roiling inside my heart.

"You're serious? You think you can make this go away by saying 'subject's closed'?" Her pitch and volume rose. "Why are you so stubborn? I have a right to know."

"There's nothing to know."

She lifted her notebook paper, then calmly and precisely tore it straight down the middle and let the pieces fall. "This whole 'secret past' thing is not working for me." Her eyes raked me with scorn. "Who are you really protecting? Him or you?" She ran out of the room.

You. I'm protecting you.

A door slammed overhead.

I lowered into my chair, holding the table for support. I felt scalded, the skin around my world blistered by her words. I could call Lena, but she'd take Clara's side. I considered storming out for a walk, but it was getting dark. Getting mugged would be the perfect cap on the day.

Instead, I did the only thing I could. I went into the living room and picked up my flute.

Clara's stony glare made for a cold start to Thursday morning. For once, I was relieved when she rushed out to catch her bus.

In contrast, the symphony dress rehearsal went well. Spirits were high, and I could finally relax. Hard work felt especially good now that I officially belonged. Making music with the other talented orchestra members gave me power. I'd get through this phase with Clara. I'd be able to help her with school events and still juggle rehearsals, performances, and my students. Lena would stop being religious and go back to normal. And I'd solve the mystery of Stefan's music. Strength surged through me as I played.

During the rehearsal for Stefan's solo concerto, I watched him play and admired his artistry. His blond bangs shifted with each jerk of his head. I felt brief pangs, as memories flashed of Jason handling his bow with a similar flourish. But I was able to slam that door and enjoy the Vivaldi. Tomorrow's audience was in for a treat.

Peter left the theatre at the same time as I did and thanked me again for helping with the lecture demonstration. As I walked toward my Saturn, I noticed Leonard peering through the window of a Lexus a few rows away.

"Lock your keys in?" I called.

He started and pulled away from the car. "No, no. Just admiring." He hurried away to a nearby PT Cruiser and climbed inside to wait for Vicki.

I got in my car and took my time adjusting my mirror and the radio. Vicki pushed her way through the stage door, lugging her cello. She got into the car with her husband, and they pulled out of the lot. I lingered a little longer, enjoying the feeling of being on a stakeout.

Sure enough, a few minutes later, a man sauntered to the Lexus, clicked his keylock, and climbed inside. Stefan. So what had Leonard been doing at Stefan's car?

I filed the question away and drove home, humming Vivaldi. Here I was, returning from a rehearsal with the Minneapolis Symphony. Living my dream. Happy warmth stayed with me all day—until Clara got home from practice.

"How was school?" I asked from the living room floor. Music books and sheets surrounded me. Somewhere in these piles was a fingering exercise I needed. The contents of my music bag rested in frightening mounds waiting to be sorted. Cigarette paper for cleaning pads, duster brush, pieces of soft flannel for swabbing my flute after practice, a Dictaphone so I could play a difficult passage into it and play it back to check my intonation, spare mini-tapes, notebooks, pencils, a couple different brands of key oil, cork grease, and a silver-polishing cloth.

Clara scanned the mess and walked across the room toward the stairs without answering my question about her day at school. Her foot landed squarely on one of the pages and left a dusty shoe print.

"You hungry?" I rescued the page and tucked it into my folder.

She continued up to her room without a word.

Beware the easygoing child when she decides to hold a grudge. Clara continued the deep freeze all evening. Another bedtime passed without our traditional reading time. How were we going to handle the upcoming sewing morning if she wasn't speaking to me?

After I brushed my teeth, I stood outside her closed door. I let my fingertips touch the wood but didn't reach for the doorknob. She'd get over this. I was doing the right thing.

I padded to bed, refusing the sadness that pressed in around me. Instead, I drifted to sleep with images of Stefan's bow gliding through space while beautiful notes captured the air.

Friday was long and lonely. Clara didn't even wish me luck on the concert when she left in the morning. I left for the theatre before she got home from practice, eager to head for the place where life made sense. Musicians tuned and played random bits of repertory. Stagehands navigated the wings with hushed urgency. I took comfort from the rhythms of preparation and made my way through the now-familiar backstage area to find a quiet corner to warm up.

David Tanner raced up to me red-faced and sweating. "Amy, have you see Stefan?"

"No. Why?"

He pushed past me. Curious, I followed him down the stairs at a distance. He knocked on several doors and stopped each person he saw. Finally, he spotted the stage manager. Chris was a small, wiry perpetual-motion machine. When David grabbed him, Chris squirmed. He probably resented having to stand still long enough to listen. After some animated conversation and arm waving, Chris consulted his clipboard. His eyes darted over the page. Then he gasped in a breath and froze.

I strolled closer, trying to act casual. It would be easier if I had a newspaper to hide behind. Instead, I stooped to adjust a buckle on my shoe.

Chris pulled a cell phone from his pocket and jabbed in a number rapidly. "Where are you?"

He couldn't be calling Stefan. The audience was already arriving, droning like bees out in the theatre.

"What?! Why didn't you call? Do you realize what time it is?"

Now I didn't need to sneak closer to hear. Several other musicians heard him yell and turned to watch.

After pacing back and forth, with the phone pressed to his ear, Chris stopped short and took several breaths. "Yes, yes. Call after you talk to the doctor."

He snapped the phone shut and glared at David as if the situation were his fault. "He's at the emergency room. Some sort of allergic reaction. His left hand swelled up."

David looked shocked, and flexed his own hand. Anything that would stiffen the fingers would be horrifying to a violinist. "When is he getting here?"

Chris shook his head. "He's not. You'll have to play the concerto."

"What? Wait. I haven't rehearsed it. No . . ." But David was talking to an empty hall. Chris had already charged off.

I tagged along after Chris. The agitated stage manager stormed into Peter's dressing room and left the door open. From my stakeout in the hall, I heard Peter groan when Chris told him the news.

"So"—Chris spoke quickly—"should I announce that David Tanner will be playing the solo?"

"No! He can't do it. We have press coming tonight."

I ached for Peter. Another disaster on his watch. He had to be furious.

"Announce that we'll have a change in order. Move the concerto to the end of the program. Give me your phone." Peter used a voice that no one would dare disobey.

I hovered outside the door to listen. Peter's one-sided conversation with Stefan consisted of a terse attempt at sympathy, followed by an order to get to the theatre, which must have been refused—judging by the colorful British curses coming from the dressing room.

"What do we do?" Chris sounded apoplectic.

"Find Rich and send him to me. Hurry."

Chris raced past without seeing me. He also ignored the other musicians gathering like agitated hens in a chicken run. Word spread fast backstage, and everyone was upset, milling, hovering near Peter's door without getting too close.

Peter must have heard all the worried murmurs. He stepped out in full regalia and gave a curt nod. "You may have heard. Our concertmaster has been taken ill. David will take his role tonight, except for the concerto, which has been moved to the end of the program."

The gathered musicians nodded like bobble-heads.

"Go on with you." A tendon jumped along Peter's jaw. "Get ready. Focus."

So, what was he planning to do for the concerto? Moving it to the end of the program only postponed the inevitable. I offered Peter a sympathetic look, but if he saw, he didn't react.

When the conductor stepped out onto stage, his face didn't betray a single flicker of emotion. He calmly led us into our first piece. But though he willed us to think of nothing but the music, the symphony members were rattled, and it showed. Even Sarah wavered on one of our entrances. We were adequate. Most of the audience enjoyed the music and wouldn't hear the subtle differences. But we all knew better. Peter's expression darkened the longer we played.

At intermission, Peter disappeared with Rich, the pianist, and didn't come back until it was time to return to our places. We prepared for the second half, not knowing the plan for the end of the concert. Without the concerto, it would be a short program. Maybe he'd heard from Stefan and the concertmaster would arrive in time.

I struggled to push the problem from my mind and simply play. Right before the concerto, Peter left the stage. The cellos exchanged glances. The oboist readjusted her music stand. Stagehands pushed the harpsichord into place. Rich walked out to a smattering of applause and took his seat on the bench.

I stared into the wings for a glimpse of Stefan. Instead, Peter marched out carrying a violin. A voice announced that there had been a change in the program and the concerto solo would be played by the conductor, Peter Cadfael Wilson. Curious buzzing carried from the audience, along with the flutter of pages as people rechecked their program.

Without waiting for them to quiet, Rich played the introduction.

Peter's playing was deft and confident. Not brilliant. How could he be on such short notice? But the piece was clearly no stranger to him. When he attacked his strings with unnecessary ferocity, it only added to the excitement of the piece. Angry Vivaldi. A new concept. But he made it work fairly well. At least the concert wasn't a disaster.

Another near miss. What were the odds that Stefan's allergic reaction was an accident? Solving mysteries had once been simply entertaining. Now it had become essential. Someone had to save the symphony.

I couldn't wait to get home and tell Clara about this latest drama. She'd help me sort out theories. Then I remembered my daughter was no longer speaking to me. The thrill of tonight's music dampened. The audience drifted out, and musicians gathered up their things.

I'd just have to find Stefan and drill him about what happened. Once I made sure the symphony—and my career—was secure, I could work on my relationship with Clara.

CHAPTER

 Dissonance: 1. Inharmonious or harsh sound;
discord; cacophony. 2. An unresolved, discordant
musical chord or interval.

The hunt to track down Stefan took no time at all. He was backstage, looking pale and exhausted. I elbowed my way past the gaggle of string players around him. "Are you all right?"

He held up his red, swollen hand. "The doctors gave to me an injection and cream. Then I came here to play."

A show-must-go-on musician. "You couldn't play like that. You look like you have mumps in your fingers."

He frowned. "When I came, people were leaving. Did they cancel the concerto?"

"We managed," a dry voice answered from behind me. Peter strode up to Stefan. "Are you surprised we survived without you?"

Vicki inserted herself between the men. "I'm sure Stefan feels terrible about this. Don't make it worse."

Leonard barreled forward to edge her away. "Thank heavens you've performed the Vivaldi before," he said to Peter. "You were terrific."

"Adequate." Peter turned dark eyes toward Stefan. "Your hand?"

Stefan waggled his stiff fingers. "The swelling already is less." When Peter's piercing stare continued, Stefan hunched his shoulders. "I should have called sooner, but I hoped I could play."

More musicians crowded closer. Peter glanced at the rubberneckers, then drilled Stefan with a glare. "Come with me." He marched toward his dressing room without waiting to see if Stefan was following.

I wasn't averse to using my friendship with Stefan to get the inside scoop. I trotted alongside him. "Do they know what caused it?" My breath came faster as I struggled to keep up with Stefan's long strides.

"They asked if—"

"In here," Peter's terse command interrupted.

I trailed behind, hidden by Stefan's tall frame. Maybe Peter wouldn't notice me.

As soon as he stepped into the room, Peter whirled to face Stefan. "What did you do?"

He'd be good at an interrogation scene in one of my mystery novels. Same intensity and righteous anger. I stepped forward and put a hand on Stefan's arm. "Be fair. It's not his fault."

Peter's scorn shifted my way. I should have kept my mouth shut.

Stefan sank onto a chair with a weary sigh. "They said it is like . . . the ivy. Poison."

"Poison ivy? What were you doing in the woods the day of a concert?"

"I was not. I came here to rehearse on the stage."

"Alone?" I pulled up a chair and sat across from him.

Peter shot me another glare. "When did the swelling start?"

"As I left here. So I went quickly to the doctor." Stefan cradled his damaged hand in his other arm. "Could there be this ivy in the theatre?"

Poor Stefan. His hand was clearly in pain, he'd missed his big solo, and now Peter was browbeating him. "I don't think so," I said sympathetically. "Can you remember what else you touched?"

"My violin, my case, my bow, the locker handle . . . the usual." He flexed his hand again. "I don't know. You think someone did this to me?"

"Some strange things are going on," I answered.

"Too right." Peter raked his hand through his hair and took a deep breath. "Go home. Call me in the morning."

Stefan nodded and stood up, his skin a concrete gray under the fluorescent lights. "I am very sorry."

Peter waved him away. Stefan paused to rest a hand on my shoulder. "Thank you for your concern." Then he hurried out.

"So you're his new fancy?" Peter's tone was bland.

"What?" I jumped to my feet. "Of course not."

He shrugged. "You seem very . . . involved."

"Don't be ridiculous." Then I tried to match his coolness. "Besides, it's none of your business."

"As long as it doesn't affect your playing. You're under contract now. You can't get a broken heart and jump ship."

I snorted. "Get real. I'm just concerned about the symphony. I think this is related to his part being changed. Someone is out to get him." A bit of my enthusiasm for this genuine mystery may have revealed itself.

Peter's eyebrows lifted and his lips curved. "Or he's allergic to the soap in the men's room." Peter took off his tux jacket, shook it out, and dropped it over a chair.

"Who would want to ruin his career?" I grabbed the jacket and positioned it on a hanger, smoothing the wrinkles the way I did when I picked up after Clara. "David Tanner has a motive."

Peter watched me hang his jacket. Then he blinked and shook his head. "Moving up a chair? He didn't even want to fill in tonight."

"Leonard is jealous of him. He might want to teach him a lesson."

"What? Why would a trombonist be jealous of a violinist?"

I sighed. "Don't you pay attention? Vicki."

It took a few seconds for the lights to come on. "Oh." He loosened his collar and sat on the edge of the makeup counter. "No. Why would he risk harming the whole orchestra?"

"Jealousy can make people do strange things."

"This is ridiculous. Stefan's the concertmaster. Plenty of people dislike him. You could just as well suspect me." One side of Peter's mouth quirked upward.

I coughed out a laugh but suddenly became aware of how quiet the backstage area had grown. The musicians and stagehands had cleared out. I was alone with someone who might have—

He stood up, and I stumbled back a step. "Go home," he ordered. "A few pranks won't destroy the orchestra, but a bunch of nervous musicians will. I don't want you upsetting people with your theories, understand? Play Miss Marple somewhere else."

Miss Marple? I am way too young for that comparison.

I planted my heels. "Aren't you going to call the police?"

"And tell them what? A violinist got his music mixed up and has a rash?"

I wanted to blast him for his sarcasm, but he had a point. Fatigue weighted my bones. I was supposed to be enjoying my dream life, but everything seemed to be going wrong. Clara was at home ready to give me more of the silent treatment, the orchestra was floundering, and Peter thought I was a nervous Nellie. Not that his opinion of me mattered—only his opinion of my flute skills.

"Good night," I said stiffly.

He didn't seem to notice when I walked away.

The next morning, I pulled ready-to-bake cinnamon rolls from the freezer. Gooey frosting and hot pastry might help thaw my daughter.

Clara trudged into the kitchen, looked in the oven, and shot me a suspicious glance.

"I've been looking forward to this sewing day." I chirped like a piccolo. "It'll be fun to meet more of your friends."

"Uh huh. You were *thrilled* when Lena signed you up for this."

Okay, she was a walking lie detector. Time to change the subject. I asked her about school, but she answered in monosyllables. I told her about the latest drama at the symphony, and she kept her eyes dull with disinterest.

Once we were both digging into the rolls, I tried again. "So, what are we supposed to bring this morning?"

She licked her fingers. "Sewing kits. You know. Fiskars, measuring tape, straight pins, marking chalk."

Tension squeezed the back of my neck. "I don't have any of that."

"What?" She feigned shock. Then she gave me a half-smile. "Relax. Mrs. Biederbock said she'd have extra stuff. She has a quilting business, so her basement is full of extras."

Now that she was speaking to me, I worked to keep the conversation going. "And her daughter is . . . Chelsea?"

"Ashley."

Ashley, Brittany, Chelsea. Her new friends sounded like the cast of a CW television series. I sipped my grapefruit juice. Sour.

"Mom, no judging them, okay?" Clara pushed aside her plate and leaned onto her elbows. "They're bubbly. They're popular. So are their moms. That doesn't mean they're idiots."

I wadded my napkin and flung it onto the table. "I never said they were." But wasn't that exactly what I'd been thinking? Shiny, happy people made me nervous. Give me an angst-ridden artist any day.

"Clara!" Janie Biederbock squealed when she opened the door to greet us. "And you must be her mom."

Drat, she was a hugger. "Yes," I mumbled while being squeezed against Janie's shoulder. "Nice to meet you."

Janie drew us into the living room where a few other moms and daughters were chatting. The upholstery on the overstuffed couches and chairs sported pink roses. Lace trim adorned every curtain. Watercolor prints of cottages filled the walls. "It looks like Laura Ashley exploded in here," Clara whispered. I stifled a snicker and felt a wave of hope. If we could laugh together, all was not lost.

Liszt twinkled out through hidden speakers. I glanced around looking for them.

Janie walked up behind me. "I tuned my stereo to NPR in your honor. Classical music to sew by." She giggled.

I felt oddly touched. I didn't generally approve of playing great musicians as background music. When the music was true art, it deserved full attention, not to be treated as a superfluous soundtrack. But at least I wouldn't have to hear hideous pop music all morning.

"Ladies, I think we're all here now. At least the first shift." Janie giggled again. She tossed her honey-brown hair, and the flip on the ends curled up even more. "Let's go downstairs. I have the patterns laid out on my cutting table."

Dawn Hanson maneuvered behind me as we filed down to the huge finished basement. "You haven't called me yet about giving flute lessons to my little Stephie. But Chelsea told me you got a job with the Minneapolis Symphony."

I had hoped she'd forget about our conversation at the cheer-leading parents' meeting. "Yeah. Sorry we haven't had a chance to talk."

"That's all right," Dawn said warmly. She seemed to be impossible to offend. "Besides, now she's thinking about taking up figure skating instead."

"Ah." I nodded, as if that made perfect sense.

Janie clapped her hands. "All right, everyone, we need folks to cut, baste, press, sew."

Moms and their daughters volunteered for various jobs. Clara moved across the room, where she sorted through a box of ribbon with two other girls. I chewed my lower lip and walked closer to Janie so I could whisper. "I don't really know anything about sewing."

"No problem. You can serge the straight seams. It's easy."

She sat me down in front of a machine with more dials and buttons than a 747 cockpit. But she was right. After a quick explanation, I found it wasn't too difficult to match up edges of fabric and seal them together with a quick run through the serger.

While I worked, I listened to Clara and her friends.

" . . . and then Brittany said she didn't like Tom, but she really wanted to go out with Jamar. And then when Tom heard, he said—"

"Aren't they cute?" Dawn handed me another pinned-together skirt. "I love watching them. It brings back memories of our high school days, doesn't it?"

What kind of high school days was she remembering? After Mom's death, Dad retreated further into the dusty stacks of his university library. My anger twisted me into a clumsy, lonely teen. Music understood me when no one else did.

I should have felt happy that Clara was so comfortable with people. Classmates, their moms, Miguel and Anita, Lena's children. Instead I felt envy.

My daughter's voice floated across the room, rapid with excitement. "The dress is amazing."

"You should get your mom to do your hair in a French twist," Brittany said.

A French braid? Clara's attention swung toward me, her enthusiasm draining. My fingers were nimble on my flute, but Clara knew I was no good at froufrou hairstyles. I cleared my throat. "Maybe you should go with a simple style. I have to leave for the theatre by five."

"No." Janie rolled her measuring tape briskly, clearly a take-charge woman. "Brittany's right. Clara would look great with her hair up."

I opened my mouth to explain again.

"I know," Janie said brightly. "Clara can come back over here to get ready for the dance with Ashley. I love doing hair."

Clara lit up. "That'd be awesome. Mom, can you drop me here on your way to your concert? I'll call Ryan and let him know."

"Sure." I tried not to sound sour. I was good enough to chauffeur, but not good enough to enjoy pre-date preparations with my daughter. At least I was holding my own with the sewing circle. I held up the skirt I'd been stitching. "I finished this one."

Janie came over and shook it out. Then she held it closer to her eyes with a squint of confusion.

"Is something wrong?" Defensiveness poked through my politeness like needles through fabric.

Clara swiveled her head to see what Janie and I were talking about. Janie patted my shoulder. "Well . . . you stitched the waist shut."

I groaned and covered my face with my hands. Janie reassured me that she could fix it, and switched me to pinning pattern pieces. When I looked over at Clara, she had turned away.

After several hours of struggling to fit in with normal soccer-mom types, I was exhausted and eager to head home. The windshield wipers beat a sleepy 4/4 time as we drove through spring drizzle. "It's okay with me if Ryan picks you up at Janie's, but I still want him getting you home at a decent hour."

Clara nodded. "Will do."

"And no driving anywhere else. Just from the school to our house. Got it?" I had some qualms about letting her go on a real "car date." Ryan had had his license for several months, but this sort of official date was another rite of passage I wasn't ready for.

"I know, Mom. Don't worry. He's a careful driver." The prickles had left her tone. I had earned some points with her for enduring domestic torture all day.

"Besides," she continued, "I can't stay up too late. I'm going to church with Lena again tomorrow morning."

I chewed the inside of my lip and imagined playing a G minor scale—two octaves up and down. If I let my temper blow up now, I'd destroy our fragile truce. "I don't get it. What's the attraction?" I was proud of how level I kept my tone. I nosed into an open spot along the curb in front of our house and shifted into park.

Clara unbuckled, then picked at a worn spot in the armrest. "It's hard to explain. Did you know that God is supposed to be like our father? That's kind of cool for someone like me." She jumped from the car and jogged up to our door, feet slapping on the wet sidewalk.

"Someone like me."

Fatherless because of her mom's mistakes. It was bad enough that she had to turn to Lena and Janie for the things she didn't get from me. Now she was turning to God. How was I supposed to compete with that?

I stared through the droplets on the glass. *Okay, God. What about me? My dad wasn't always a picnic, you know. Why weren't you a father to me? At least Clara has me to look out for her. Who do I have?*

The sound of rain on the car's hood was hollow and empty.

"Right," I sneered. "That's what I thought."

CHAPTER

15

Rattenuto: A directive to perform a certain passage of a composition in a restrained manner, or held back in rhythm or time.

L ook. Not so bad, *ja?*" Stefan waved his hand in front of my face. The skin looked red but less puffy.

Poor guy had been through a lot in the last few days. On general principle I didn't believe in coddling, but he deserved some sympathy. I glanced at the violin cradled in his arm, the lacquered wood rich and warm even under harsh backstage lights. "Are you going to play tonight?"

His chest swelled. "Of course. I'm even doing the Vivaldi."

He deserved a chance to regain some status. "That's great." I smiled widely.

"And I am grateful for your kindness last night." Instead of leaving to warm up, he scuffed a foot like a shy boy. "So may I take you for dinner? A thank you?"

European charm was potent, but I shifted into automatic man-repellent mode. On the rare occasions over the years when I had attracted male attention I had been adept at cooling the interest quickly.

"Oh, I don't think so." I should have launched into my "single mom, dedicated musician, don't have time to date" spiel. But I didn't have the heart. Besides, I was exhausted. A week of tension with Clara, my marathon day of sewing with cheerleader moms, followed by my tirade at a God I didn't believe in, had left me drained. Why did Stefan have to pick a moment when my defenses were down?

"Please?" Stefan's gentle smile further weakened my resolve. Clara was at a dance tonight enjoying a little heart fluttering time with a guy. Maybe I deserved some, too.

"Let me think about it, okay?"

He winked. "After you hear my concerto, you won't be able to refuse."

I laughed, glad to be back on safe territory. "We'll see. I've heard some great violinists in my day."

He chuckled and turned away.

A draft from an outer corridor chilled my ankles. I shivered. What was I thinking? Even if I'd break my rule about not dating a musician, I certainly couldn't get involved with a string player. Way too many ghosts. I forced my feet to move and stomped to the large dressing room where other women were stowing their bags or changing into performance dress. I'd give Stefan a firm "No" after the concert. For now I took comfort in the silver keys of my flute.

My fatigue washed away as I walked onstage. Once again the work took complete focus, and any outside anxieties vanished. I enjoyed every minute. Peter conducted with the confidence and supple movements of an athlete. Sarah offered me grudging respect with a nod as we finished the first piece. Leonard only told three jokes during intermission. Best of all, nothing weird happened. No sandbags fell from the ceiling, no music disappeared, no trapdoors swallowed one of the percussionists—although the way they rushed the tempo in the Beethoven, I almost wished for that.

Stefan played the Vivaldi flawlessly. I'd admired Peter's pinch-hitting, but Stefan was in a different league. The music curled up behind my heart, and the beauty made me ache.

"You were right," I told Stefan backstage when the concert ended. "You were amazing."

"So. Dinner Tuesday night?"

None of my reasons for avoiding men seemed compelling at the moment. "You're on."

Sarah walked past and overheard our exchange. She shot me a dark look, sniffed, and moved on.

Great. Back to square one with her. She'd been quick to warn me about Stefan's failed relationship with the second violinist. Now she'd assume I would be the next indiscretion. Come to think of it, her intense scorn of the second violin seemed out of proportion. Maybe Sarah had a thing for Stefan the concertmaster. Maybe she was a woman scorned. If so, I should add her to my list of suspects. I needed to get this mystery solved.

"Stefan, did you find anything to explain your allergic reaction?"

"Eh?"

"Could you show me your locker?"

He laughed. "Ah. You are being the American detective, yes? Sam Spade?"

He seemed to find the idea highly amusing. I ground my teeth. He could tease all he wanted as long as he let me search his shelves for clues.

Stefan opened his locker and pulled out his case. "Be my guest." He waved toward the cabinet. Wishing for the penlight that everyone on *CSI* carried, I pulled items out and studied them. Rosin. Spare strings. A sweater for chilly rehearsals. A dog-eared book of scales and drills. A few pencils. Nothing unexpected.

Stefan leaned against a locker and watched my meticulous search. "When you are done investigating, please pass me the cloth for my strings."

I grabbed the square of fabric. I'd seen him use it frequently. His routine was to wipe off his strings, put his violin to bed in the plush lining of its case, and then rub the rag over his fingers to remove stray rosin.

Detective goose bumps rose on my arms. "Wait! You use this on your hand."

He gave me a tolerant smile. "Yes. Is this sinister?"

Ignoring his mockery, I stepped to the center of the room where the light was stronger and held the cloth up. Tattered, red-plaid flannel, the fabric looked like it had been torn from an old shirt. I caught a whiff of an unusual scent.

I held it under Stefan's nose. "Do you smell that?"

The smile disappeared. "No." He watched me as if doubting my sanity.

"It's like cloves and cinnamon. I've smelled this before. Where was it?"

"I do not understand."

"Last summer!" My pulse pounded rapidly through my temples. "Clara and I got henna tattoos at the art festival."

Leonard walked in and pulled a few things from his locker. He glanced at us, raised his eyebrows, and then lumbered away. Once he was out of sight, I turned back to Stefan.

"Clara and I both got a bad rash." I rubbed my forearm at the memory. "The doctor said it wasn't from the henna. It was the clove oil that had been mixed with it." I took a deep breath, relishing the dramatic pause. "Lots of people get a bad reaction to it.

It irritates the skin. I think someone put some sort of oil on your rag—someone who's seen your routine. The way you wipe off your hands when you're done playing."

All amusement washed from Stefan's face. He squeezed the bridge of his nose. "This is not good."

"No. We should make a list of people who want to harm you. And who have backstage access."

He pulled out a handkerchief, used it to take the rag from my hand, and stuffed both in his pocket. Then he threw his coat over his shoulders like an impresario. "I am too tired to think. We can talk on Tuesday."

"Of course."

"And do not speak of this, yes?"

"Don't you think we should tell the police?"

His smile was weak and resigned. "They were not helping when my car was broken into."

Another attack? "When was this?"

"A few weeks ago. Good night, Amy." Firm, but affectionate. "We will talk later."

Driving home, I congratulated myself on uncovering an important clue, and I mulled what I knew. Someone had sabotaged Stefan twice. Three times if I counted the car break-in. Sarah had warned me away from Stefan, so I suspected she was a little moon-eyed over him. Leonard was jealous of Stefan's relationship with Vicki. David could be angry that he hadn't landed the job of concertmaster. I had too many suspects. Even Peter seemed to have a strong dislike toward Stefan, although I couldn't figure out why, unless it was just the natural animosity of two bull elk butting antlers.

Any one of them had access to the stage before the concert. But would Leonard or Sarah know much about violin notation? I should focus on David and Peter. But David hadn't wanted to play the concerto. If David hurt Stefan, wouldn't he also want to take over the solo?

That left Peter as my prime suspect.

And I didn't want him to be. He was talented, tolerant of my blunders, and had fought for me to get the flute chair.

I left the lights of downtown behind and merged onto the freeway. No good detective let personal feelings interfere with an investigation. My next step should be to find out all I could about Peter and his history with Stefan. Then Stefan and I could discuss the case when we had dinner on Tuesday.

Satisfied with my plan, I coasted down the exit ramp to my neighborhood, humming the Bach minuet all the way home.

After a quick shower, I cozied into my rocking chair with a mug of cocoa and an M. C. Beaton novel. I'd recently discovered the Agatha Raisin series and felt kinship with the cranky, blunt solver of mysteries.

Two minutes before Clara's eleven o'clock curfew, I heard the slam of car doors, the uneven tap of Clara's heels, and murmurs at the door.

I tossed aside my novel, hurried to the entryway, snapped on the porch light, and yanked the door open.

Two startled faces blinked at me. Ryan's bow tie dangled open, and his cummerbund was crooked. With his bristle-top hair and freckles, he reminded me of a mischievous six-year-old. Clara looked closer to twenty-six—too sophisticated in her spaghetti strap dress. Janie had done a beautiful job with the French twist. I felt a funny squeeze in my chest.

"Hi! Come on in. I was hoping to get to chat with you both. How was the dance?"

I expected Ryan to blush and run. Instead, he put a gentle arm around Clara's waist and guided her inside. "It was fun." He offered an open, friendly grin. "How was your concert tonight?"

I struggled to hold on to my resistance toward him. I didn't want to like any young man who spent time with my daughter, especially a dumb jock. But he was making it difficult.

"The concert went great. And I found a clue."

Clara kicked off her shoes and curled up in her chair. Ryan wisely left the rocker for me and settled on the ledge of the fireplace. "Clara said you're trying to solve a mystery. What did you find?"

"Now you asked for it." Clara's tone held affection as well as resignation.

"No, really. I'd love to hear about it."

Eager, interested—this guy was quickly thawing me. I filled them in on the clove oil clue, and we batted around theories. Maybe it was the late hour, or Clara's softness, or Ryan creating a buffer, but I relaxed and enjoyed the conversation.

"And Tuesday I'm going out to dinner with Stefan, so I'll try to get more information."

"A real date?"

Clara didn't have to sound so shocked.

"Sort of. He just wants to thank me for supporting him."

"I still think he's too tall. But, hey. Different strokes." She yawned and stretched.

"Whoa." Ryan glanced at his watch. "I've gotta go."

"Yeah. I need to get to bed. Aunt Lena's picking me up early so I can go to the Youth Bible Bash before church."

Bible Bash? I chewed the inside of my cheeks to keep myself from commenting.

Ryan reached for Clara's hand in an easy, familiar gesture. "Walk me out?"

She untangled her legs and surged to her feet.

I stood up to follow them to the door, but Clara shot me a warning glare, so I sat down and watched them step outside. Clara was barefoot, and it was a chilly night. She couldn't stay out too long.

Sure enough, after enough time for a kiss, but not long enough for any serious necking, Clara came back in, spun across the floor, and collapsed into her chair. "That was fun."

The dance? The chat? The kissing? I knew better than to ask.

"He's growing on me," I said instead.

Clara smiled. "Told you." She pulled herself up, dropped a quick kiss on my forehead, and floated up the stairs toward the bedrooms, a picture of crushed carnations, rumpled silk, and teenage dreams. Halfway up, she turned. "Tuck me in?"

My heart warmed, and all the prickles of the past few weeks melted away. "Sure. Let me lock up. I'll be right there."

She caressed the banister. "I knew you'd like Ryan, once you got to know him. You've gotta trust me. I know what I'm doing." She blew me another kiss and continued up the stairs.

I know what I'm doing.

I had believed that once about myself. And look what a mess I'd made. Reluctant to spoil tonight's mood, I swallowed my fears. At least Ryan was providing a good distraction. Clara had stopped asking me about her father.

CHAPTER

16

Fugue: A polyphonic composition based upon one, two, or more themes, which are enunciated by several voices or parts in turn.

Quiet Sunday mornings. Sipping coffee without the need to rush, doodling around with the crossword puzzle in the paper, enjoying silence—at least until Hien Nguyen and his friends tore up and down the alley on their skateboards—and watching Clara shuffle sleepily into the kitchen around noon in an old knee-length sweatshirt and bunny slippers. Sunday was usually my favorite day. We might take a picnic to the creek and toss crusts to the ducks. Or hit the Linden Hills Co-op to stock up on organic produce for the week. We'd pop into Great Harvest Bakery for a free sample of cranberry-pecan bread and to buy a loaf of whole grain, too. Other weeks we might stop in at the Paperback Exchange so I could pick up a few new mysteries. Unique neighborhood stores added character to our gentle urban setting and provided countless options for a low-key Sunday.

Today, I sat alone at the kitchen table, knowing Clara wouldn't be coming down the stairs rubbing sleep from her eyes. She'd left hours ago for church. The house was empty.

And the silence laughed at me.

In a few short years, Clara would be off to college. This would be my life. I glanced at the clock over the stove. 12:30 blinked into 12:31.

I picked up my coffee, swirled the last inch of murk, and dumped it in the sink. Clara might leave, but I'd always have my music. That's all I needed. I pushed open the kitchen curtains, trying to shove away my lethargy. When Clara got home from church, she wasn't going to find me moping.

I washed out the coffeepot and wiped down the counters. Then I opened a can of broth and started mincing every stray vegetable I could find in the fridge. Homemade soup would be great on a cool spring day. My knife made satisfying taps against the wooden cutting board. I paused to turn the radio to NPR. Robust marches lifted my mood, and I chopped in time.

When Clara breezed into the kitchen a few minutes later, I was able to smile. "How was church?"

She dropped a pile of books onto the table and gave me a wary look. "It was okay." She watched me decapitate a stalk of celery and tilted her head. "How ya doing?"

"Fine."

She narrowed her eyes and studied me for another moment. Then she shrugged. "Good. Hey, guess what? The youth pastor had a great idea for my science paper. We were in these small groups, and I mentioned that I still hadn't come up with my topic. He lent me all these books on Intelligent Design."

I scraped the vegetables into my stockpot and came over to look. "You talked about science projects at church?" That place sounded weirder all the time.

149

"At Bible Bash. Anyway, nobody else in my class has this topic. Besides, I know it will totally freak out Mr. Davis." She pulled a pencil from her shoulder bag and began jotting notes on a sheet of paper.

I glanced over the titles. "What is Intelligent Design?"

"It's a theory, like evolution. Except instead of believing things just happened, there are scientists who believe that someone started it all."

Oh, boy. I could see where this was heading. "What difference does it make?" I tried to sound reasonable, but it came out flippant. "We're here now. Who cares how we got here?"

She rubbed her forehead with the eraser end of her pencil. "Well, I guess it matters because if someone did make all this"—she flung an arm open, apparently indicating our kitchen—"then there's a reason for it."

"Willow Construction made all this." I mimicked her arm gesture. "And they should have included more outlets and a bigger pantry. And of course there's a reason for it. We need to eat."

Clara glared at me. "Forget it." She gathered up the books and fled the kitchen.

What was with her? Those religious types were getting to her. She couldn't even take a joke anymore.

The soup didn't have enough time to simmer, and it tasted flat as we ate a silent lunch. I reached for the salt. "I'm sorry. I didn't mean to be snide."

She gave a one-shoulder shrug. "You can't help it."

I wasn't sure how to take that. "I've gotta run. Wish me luck on today's matinee."

"You'll be fine," she said automatically, her eyes remaining on her bowl.

With that less than glowing encouragement, I grabbed my garment bag and flute and headed to the theatre. The concert went well, but it didn't completely soothe the ache in my heart.

Afterward, I changed back into my charcoal-gray slacks and sweatshirt. We had one more concert of this repertory, so I left my garment bag in a locker. Sarah barely spoke to me. Leonard and Vicki hurried off. Everyone cleared out quickly—places to go, people to see. Emptiness nagged me with growing strength.

In no hurry to leave, I snatched a moment to sit alone in the quiet, plush theatre. The gilt-edged cherubs and mammoth chandelier were a bit much, but I liked the vast, ornate space. I liked what it said. Our music was important. It deserved an important place. This was the only part of my world that made sense.

I hugged my flute case to my chest, tilted my head back and closed my eyes. I was losing Clara. First cheerleading, then Ryan, and now God. It wasn't just that she had new interests. What bothered me most was that her view of me was changing. I saw her looking at me differently. She measured me in different ways. In her mind, I came up short. A moan escaped my throat.

I felt someone settle into the seat beside me. "Are you ill? You look rather . . . subdued."

Peter. I straightened and opened my eyes. He had changed into jeans and looked like a rumpled kid again. The creases between his eyebrows deepened. With all the problems the symphony had experienced lately, he was probably worried about a musician keeling over.

"I'm fine." But I didn't sound convincing and couldn't summon the energy to jump to my feet and exit. When he waited, my chest rose and fell heavily. "It's my daughter. We always used to get along, but lately . . . we're fighting about everything."

"Mmm."

When he still didn't leave, I kept talking. "See, patience isn't my predominant quality."

"I hadn't noticed," he said dryly.

"So I say things that upset her, and then . . . and being a single mom, I get tired of having to figure things out by myself."

He gave a soft whistle. "Single mum and professional musician. Can't be easy."

"It's not. I seem to disappoint her all the time. And now she's on this God kick." I tilted my head back. "I can't make sense of half of what she says. She's talking about how things didn't just happen. That there's a reason."

"You don't agree?" His voice was carefully passive.

I closed my eyes. "I have enough trouble figuring out the world I can see. The other stuff gives me a headache."

After a long silence I opened one eye and glanced at him. "Why? Are you into religion?"

He laughed. "Hardly. But it sounds like she's asking some good questions."

I smiled. "She's always been good with questions. Trouble is, I'm not so good with the answers."

We sat in silence for a few more minutes, looking at the stage. Maybe he was remembering the music, as I was, letting the hovering echo sing to us one more time. Then he shifted, leaned forward, and rested his chin on his fists. "I keep thinking there has to be something behind all this. The planet, people."

"So you believe in God?" I couldn't completely hide the scoff in my voice.

Another low chuckle. "I don't know. But think about it. The notes don't put themselves on the score. And someone has to direct."

"Ah. So you're comparing yourself to God? The grand conductor?"

He grinned. "Are you accusing me of a big ego?"

"Occupational hazard. Brain surgeons, jet pilots, conductors—it's in your job description, isn't it? The God complex?"

He folded his arms, muscles flexing beneath his rolled-up sleeves. "You mean skill, confidence, and leadership," he said with mock sternness.

"Whatever. Come on. Next you'll tell me you believe in Santa Claus and the Tooth Fairy."

"And Neverland," he insisted.

I smiled, bemused. It felt comfortable to sit here, to banter, to relax in the after-concert glow.

"There you are." Stefan's voice jarred the peaceful moment. He stood in the aisle, again wearing his coat over his shoulders. "Do you like Thai food? Or would you prefer Italian? I want to make reservations for Tuesday." He flashed his teeth, then shifted his gaze to Peter. "Good concert. Maybe the problems have stopped."

Peter shoved to his feet. "Too right. We can't afford more bad press." His voice had gone all cold and stony. "Good night." He walked away without a backward glance.

"I'm sorry. Did I interrupt something?" The smug current of humor in Stefan's tone overpowered any attempt at sincere apology.

I frowned and watched Peter disappear down a side aisle. "Why doesn't he like you?"

Stefan rubbed at a callus on his fingertip. "Professional jealousy?"

"He's a respected conductor. That doesn't make sense."

"Because I know secrets from his past?"

I stood up. "Do you?"

He laughed. "We can talk on Tuesday." And he disappeared in a swirl of his long coat.

I sank back into my chair and kicked the seat in front of me. I was tired of never getting straight answers. Stefan wasn't taking the sabotage seriously enough. If the symphony kept having problems and bad reviews, we'd lose the grants we needed. Maybe it didn't matter to Stefan or Peter. They could work anywhere. But this was my one chance.

"I'm locking up, Miss," Ed called to me from the far aisle. He frowned, rattling the large key ring at his belt. A wizened man with shocks of gray hair, he looked like he'd been working at the theatre since it was built—and it seemed he wasn't thrilled to have his space invaded.

"Yeah, yeah. I'm heading out."

He nodded and trudged to the back of the theatre. A low rumble sounded overhead. A storm was moving in. I shivered. Once bereft of people the theatre air had cooled quickly. I'd left my jacket backstage in my locker and didn't want to freeze on my way to my car. Some parts of the country might allow for sunbathing in May, but Minnesota could deliver anything—including icy rain.

Guided by the red glow of exit signs, I carefully climbed the stairs at the edge of the stage, then fought my way through a seam in the curtains to enter the wings. The tall fly space, crisscrossed with metal catwalks, loomed overhead. I picked my way forward, but a coil of wire reached out to snag my ankles. Sidestepping, I knocked against a jumble of music stands. Silhouettes of lighting trees and old flats propped crookedly against the back wall created a scene from a Poe short story.

Every instinct told me to hurry, but I didn't want to crash into anything. With careful maneuvering, I made it to the stairway, down the metal steps, and entered the corridor toward the dressing rooms. The lights here were off as well, and the dim emergency lights transformed the concrete into a surreal tunnel of lurking shadows. Instinctively moving on tiptoe, I trotted past several doors.

Suddenly, I heard a rattle from behind one of the closed doors. I froze, my skin turning cold, then suddenly hot. Someone else was backstage.

"Ed?" My voice came out as a constricted whisper.

No one answered.

The clang of a locker door echoed with exaggerated volume in the silence of the empty backstage area. Sweat beaded along my hairline, and I pressed against the wall. Someone was in the room where Stefan and the other string players stored their supplies. I squeezed my eyes shut, trying to draw courage from the pebbly wall behind me. This was my chance to surprise the saboteur. Indecision paralyzed me.

Another slam was followed by crisp footsteps heading toward the door. Toward me. Gasping in several shallow breaths, I looked up and down the hall for an open doorway that I could duck into.

Too late. The handle of the dressing room door squealed. If this were an episode of *Alias*, I would have grabbed an overhead pipe and swung up out of the bad guy's line of sight.

But this was real, and I had nowhere to hide. I was so close to the door that I thought I could hear the breathing of the person inside. I eased back, sidling along the wall in a crouch.

Then the door opened with a *whoosh*.

CHAPTER

17

Battaglia: Battle. A piece suggesting a battle.

I dropped into a lower crouch, hoping I'd disappear. A dark figure swept out into the hall and crashed into me.

My breath escaped in a *woof* at the impact against my ribs. But the prowler was more surprised. My huddled body acted like a hurdle that he couldn't clear. He sprawled headlong, flew over me, and hit the ground with a thud. Unfortunately, his body blocked my escape route back to the stairs.

So I spun and ran deeper into the darkness. Stupid. There was no exit this direction. But I didn't have many choices. Further down the hall, I darted into a storage room. A musty smell of vaudevillian greasepaint and sweat-stained costumes lingered in the air. In the faint light from the hallway, I felt my way past a garment rack and some crates, then ducked down to hide.

"He ran back here." A man's angry voice thudded against the walls.

With a click, overhead lights flared. I lifted a hand to shield my eyes, and my elbow bumped a prop sword that clattered to the floor.

"Who's there?" Ed's gruff call accompanied the sound of jangling keys.

Relief surged through me. Ed hadn't been the prowler who bolted from the dressing room. He wasn't the man after me.

"Just me." I popped up.

Ed and Peter both stood in the doorway and glared at me. Peter was rubbing his elbow. Ed rattled his keys again. "I told you I was lockin' up, Miss."

"I know. I was getting my jacket."

"Back here?" Peter's cold suspicion stung me.

I drew myself up to my full five foot, three inches. "Someone was breaking into Stefan's locker."

His brows lifted. "You know that because . . . ?"

"I heard the locker door rattle. It must have been the saboteur."

Peter took a step forward and winced. He stopped rubbing his elbow and bent to massage his knee. Logic tied the pieces together. A sick feeling burned in my stomach.

"It was you." I choked the words out past my horror and disillusionment. A conductor ruining his concertmaster. That was beneath evil. "What were you doing in there?"

"Oh, no you don't. The problems started when you joined the orchestra. I want an explanation."

"What?" I stomped out from behind the crate. "I've been trying to help Stefan—and the symphony."

"Says you." Peter took a step forward, and I skittered back, knocking over a faux Renaissance candle stand.

Ed charged forward to pick it up, keys clashing. "And I thought the City Opera was bad," he grumbled. He plunked the stand down and pointed to the door. "I'm locking up. Now."

"After you." Peter stepped aside, allowing me just enough room to slip past him.

"Sorry," I said to Ed. "Just a misunderstanding." I marched toward the door.

Peter's hand shot out and grabbed my arm. "This isn't over." His anger burned through my skin and straight into my bones.

"Mom, I don't have any jeans to wear tomorrow." Clara had listened to my garbled description of the drama at the theatre without much sympathy.

I paced the kitchen. "Haven't you heard a word I've said? Who cares about jeans?"

She pulled plates from the dishwasher and shoved them into the cupboard with unnecessary force. "Sure I heard you. You've already made an enemy of the principal flutist and now the conductor. You're off to a great start. But I need jeans for school, all right?"

"Well, you know how to do a load of laundry."

Clara threw a fistful of silverware into a drawer and rounded on me. "It's way beyond that. Have you been in the basement this week?"

"I've been busy. Rehearsals, concerts."

"Yeah, well I'm busy, too. Why should I have to do all the cooking and cleaning and laundry?"

"That's not fair. I usually—"

"Oh, really?" She crossed her arms and leaned back against the counter. "What are we having for supper?"

"Um . . ."

"And did you happen to notice the layer of crud on everything in the bathroom?"

"Hey . . ."

"The only room you bother cleaning is your precious music room. Maybe I should just get my own place."

"Don't be stupid." As soon as the words were out, I wanted to grab them back.

Clara's eyes widened, the skin around them turning pale. "Nice to know what you really think." Her words were dangerously quiet. She walked stiffly past me.

I reached for her, stammering apologies.

She jerked away and out the back door, letting the screen slam behind her.

I kicked at the table leg, then yanked out a chair and sank onto it. This was all because of cheerleading. She was hanging out with kids whose moms spent the whole day cleaning and baking cookies. Clara knew I wasn't like that. She'd never minded before. Why did she have to pick the worst possible time to get so demanding? She had no idea the pressure I was under.

I reached for the phone and called Lena. "Clara and I had a fight."

Lena's sigh carried through the connection. "Again? Now what?"

"I had a horrible afternoon, and when I got home she attacked me for not doing more housework."

"Clara attacked you?" Lena sounded sad but not very indignant on my behalf.

"Sort of. She's mad that I'm not like all the other moms. But I have to work. What does she expect? And my work demands a lot."

"Amy, she knows that. It's just that sometimes . . . well, it's hard on her, too, you know."

I rubbed my forehead. "What has she said to you?"

Lena paused. "You guys just need to talk, okay? Next time try listening to her."

"I do listen."

"Amy."

"Okay, so I'm not the best listener. But I never signed on to be Supermom. This wasn't my idea."

Another long silence. "I know you feel overwhelmed sometimes. I do, too, and I've got a husband helping me. I don't know how you've managed all this time as a single parent."

Mollified, I relaxed against the chair back. "I wish she understood that. And, hey, I haven't even told you the other problem."

I filled Lena in on my backstage investigations and the dubious outcome.

Strange noises came from the phone. Muffled sputters. Finally I realized my best friend was laughing.

"It's not funny."

"Oh, Amy. How do you do it? Do you enjoy having people mad at you?"

"Hey, it wasn't my fault."

"Mm-hmm." She choked back another giggle.

"You think it's funny that Peter is out to destroy the symphony?"

Lena groaned. "Amy, use your head. Why would a conductor pull pranks like that?"

"So what was he doing in the big dressing room?" I huffed. "He has his own private one."

"Who knows? But it's none of your business. Seriously, you better stop poking into things. Symphony jobs aren't easy to come by."

"I know. That's why I'm trying to help. I keep hearing rumors that we're going under . . . and the bad reviews aren't helping."

Lena sobered quickly. "Yeah. We had Megan and her husband over for dinner last week. She's sending out résumés for new development jobs. We lost our major national grant, and if she can't drum up some local corporate support, we're in trouble."

Defeat poured over me, and I sagged under the weight. It had taken years for a flute position to open up. There were a few other professional orchestras in town, but the experienced outgoing musicians from the Minneapolis Symphony would snatch up any openings. I didn't want to move, and Clara wouldn't want to up-root with only a few years of high school left. This could be my last chance to establish myself as a professional orchestral flutist. "We've gotta do something."

"No. You have to fix things with Clara. Saving the symphony is not your job."

She was right. I was letting my stress pull me away from my daughter. "You're right. Thanks, Lena."

"Anytime."

I hung up and pulled open the closet where I kept cleaning sup-plies. Was it a bad sign that the mop had cobwebs on it? Maybe Clara was right. I had let a few things slide. I'd get the place spruced up and prove that I could be a responsible mom.

After two hours of dusting, scrubbing, and vacuuming, I re-membered the laundry. When I flicked on the lights down in the basement, I moaned. Piles of clothes created foothills worthy of the Himalayas. Instead of sorting, I turned on the machine to hot water and started picking out everything white. That seemed like an easy place to start. I pulled out everything denim and got it ready for the next load, then headed upstairs.

My hands were red from scrubbing bathroom tile, my back ached from torquing it into unfamiliar positions, and my hair smelled like furniture polish because I'd accidentally sprayed myself. I hated housework. It was so futile. If I washed the dishes, they got dirty again the next day. Dust bunnies reproduced faster than I could vacuum them. And every minute of frustrating cleaning was one less minute of practice time.

Still, I wouldn't stop at half measures. I surveyed the fridge and cupboards. We were out of everything. I'd have to make a trip to the grocery store. After a heavy sigh, I made a list and slammed out of the house. If I hurried, I could stock our kitchen and prep ingredients for stir-fry tomorrow night. I'd pick up some Fudgsicles, too. Clara's favorite.

Was I trying to buy her love? Sure. Whatever worked.

When I got home from the store, I made several soggy trips in the rain lugging bags in from the car. Clara was conspicuously absent. Before unpacking the grocery bags, I checked my voicemail.

"Amy, this is Janie Biederbock. Ashley's wondering if Clara could spend the night. They're having such a good time working on their history project together, they said they didn't want to stop now. Don't worry, we've got spare jammies for her, and I'll drive them to school tomorrow morning. Talk to you later." Her chipper voice drove pins into my skull.

I tore open the box of Fudgsicles. *More for me.*

On Monday afternoon, I arrived at the Palace for our student matinee. Busloads of elementary school kids were wending their way to the theatre. We were scheduled to play *Peter and the Wolf*, and the ever popular *1812 Overture*.

Megan, the development director, was on hand to welcome the kids and give a short talk about the sections of the orchestra. After she explained how musicians warmed up, she introduced Stefan and stepped aside. He smiled, playing up to the rows filled with kids. The oboe set the pitch and each section tuned. Finally, Stefan lifted his bow to give a tuning note for the violins. As he pulled his bow, the clear note suddenly howled downward like a sick cat. Stefan stared at his violin in shock. Then he quickly adjusted the peg for his high string. He tried again, and again the string slipped, sending the pitch sliding. Children began to giggle. After a few more fumbling attempts to hold the string, Stefan stalked offstage. David watched him leave and then looked over at Megan. She made a rotating gesture with her hand—clear sign language for "Keep it moving."

David stood up and tuned the violins. Then he sat down in Stefan's chair, chest high, assuming the role of concertmaster without even hiding his smile. In the wings, Stefan held his violin, stabbing a finger at one of the tuning keys and talking angrily but inaudibly to Peter. Peter grabbed the violin and studied the problematic string. Then he looked out at the musicians waiting on stage. When his gaze intersected mine, his eyes darkened.

Since the orchestra had tuned and the conductor hadn't entered, Megan stepped back up to the microphone and chattered about the role of the conductor. Finally, Peter entered and the kids whistled and stomped—probably more excited that Megan would stop talking than that they were going to hear music.

We managed the short concert sans Stefan. As soon as we finished, I hurried downstairs to find him. He was slumped on a chair in the large makeup room, holding his violin in his lap and running a finger silently up and down a string.

"Now what?" I demanded.

"The string wouldn't hold. Someone put extra oil on the key."

This was getting scary. "But you keep your violin with you."

He nodded. "I don't know when it was done. Some time after I warmed up, but before we came on stage."

"Or someone sitting next to you on stage." I pictured David turning his head to cough, covering his mouth with a handkerchief that hid a tiny vial of oil. Could he have done it?

Leonard came into the room. I expected a joke or even some gloating. Instead, Leonard straddled a chair near Stefan. "Good thing we're getting back into our space this week. Maybe it'll be easier to protect our instruments."

Stefan looked at Leonard with grateful surprise. "Maybe."

Other musicians poured into the room. The brave ones asked Stefan directly about what had happened. Others got the scoop from the whispers swirling in the hallway. Suddenly Peter strode into the room. Stefan put his hand over mine. "See you tomorrow night."

I squeezed his hand. "Don't worry. We'll solve this." I stood up and threw a defiant look at Peter.

"More of your handiwork?" he asked me, nodding toward Stefan's violin.

Idiot. I pressed my lips together hard to keep from saying anything. Peter's suspicions of me were nothing short of stupid.

Stefan seemed to share my opinion, because he barked a laugh. That cheered me up until I glanced at Peter. His eyes raked me with pure disdain.

He might have appreciated my flute playing when I auditioned, but clearly his opinion of me had tanked.

A few minutes later, I trudged to the parking ramp lugging my garment bag, flutes, and portfolio of music. Even if things started looking up for the symphony funding, Peter could have me fired. The way things were going, my career could be over before we moved back into Symphonic Hall.

CHAPTER

18

Interlude: Any intermediate performance or entertainment, as between the acts of a play. . . . An instrumental passage or a piece of music rendered between the parts of a song, church service, drama, etc.

So, how was the matinee concert?" Clara licked the last of the chocolate from her Fudgsicle stick. She'd arrived home after school, looked around at my homemaking efforts, and declared an unspoken truce. A freezer full of treats didn't hurt the cause, either.

"Someone messed with Stefan's tuning peg, so his string wouldn't hold its pitch." I poured rice into a kettle and hoped Clara would note that I was making a full dinner from scratch. Well, close enough: instant rice, a bag of frozen stir-fry veggies, and a can of sauce.

"You're right. This is starting to sound like more than accidents and coincidences."

165

"What did you say? I missed those first two words."

She grinned. "You heard me." She picked a water chestnut out of the bag of veggies and nibbled it.

"That's not the worst part." I adjusted the burner under the rice. "The symphony didn't get renewed on its largest grant."

"Because of the problems?"

"I don't know. But all these fumbles sure don't help. We're coming off like a bunch of amateurs. I've got to figure out who's doing this."

"Mo-om. Are you determined to self-destruct?"

I put the lid on the rice. "What are you talking about?"

"You can't keep poking around."

I opened my mouth to argue, then closed it with a smile. "I don't have to. Stefan is taking me out tomorrow night. All I have to do is help him brainstorm who would have a reason for doing this."

"Ooooh. That's right. A real date. I should go buy some fireworks."

"Huh?"

"It's a big event." Clara reached into the bag and pulled out a frozen pea pod.

I swatted her hand. "Cut that out. If you want home-cooked meals, at least let me cook them. So how do I get more clues from Stefan?"

She sprawled back in her chair. "You're hopeless, you know that? You should be worrying about which dress makes you look sexy, but all you can think about is clues."

"Come on. When was the last time I worried about a dress looking sexy?"

"My point exactly." She stood up. "Let's go."

"But the rice—"

"Let it simmer. You need my help." Clara dragged me upstairs and threw open my closet. I sat on the bed watching as she pushed the hangers to one side and rifled through dresses, skirts, and blouses. She pulled out a dress, shook it out, and frowned. "Too old."

"I got that one less than a year ago. It's practically new."

"I didn't mean the dress is old. The look is old. It makes you look pruney instead of hot." She returned the dress to the closet and pulled out a flared skirt in a soft batik. "This has possibilities. If I can find a decent top. Something clingy."

"I've got turtlenecks in my dresser," I said wryly.

She snorted and kept pawing through the clothes. "This is hopeless. You'll have to borrow a top from me. And what are you doing with your hair?"

"Hair? I'm having dinner, not going to the Oscars."

"All right. I'll take care of that tomorrow. The color's great, we just need to spike out some of the layers to make it trendy."

Trendy? I grabbed a pillow and buried my face in it, muffling a scream. Coming up for air, I saw Clara poking through the seashell-covered box where I kept my jewelry. She'd made the box in third grade. Some of the shells had broken off and the design was crooked. I loved it.

"I'll have to lend you a necklace. You'll need a little bling." She scanned me, tapping a nail against her teeth.

I threw the pillow at her. "I don't want to give Stefan the wrong idea."

"What? That you're a woman?"

"Well, that I'm available."

"But you are."

"No, I'm not." I jumped up and brushed past her, plowing down the stairs. I zoomed into the kitchen and checked on the rice. Almost done. I turned up the heat under my frying pan and drizzled in some oil.

Clara followed and hovered behind me. "What do you mean you're not available? Are you telling me you're still married? That you married my dad and never divorced?" Her eyes begged for romantic fables, and her body tensed in anticipation.

I reached out and cupped her face in my hands, pulling her head down so I could kiss her forehead. "No. I never married. I've told you that."

How could those words drag so much failure from the swamp of my past? I cleared my throat and turned away. "I only meant I'm not interested. Not in Stefan. Not in anyone. It's not a real date. I just want info. Could you set the table?"

She hesitated. For a moment I feared we'd get back on the "give me more details" merry-go-round. Then she sighed and walked over to the cupboard above the sink. "So the few things you've told me . . . at least *those* are true?"

I dumped the veggies into the hot oil and jumped back as they spit and hissed. My temper splattered outward, too. "I've never lied to you. But I probably should have. I should have made up some great story about him going off to war and dying on the battlefield as he saved someone's life. Then maybe you'd let it rest."

I attacked the stir-fry with a wooden spoon, hiding the threat of tears in the steam. But Clara could read the muscles in my back. After she set the table, she came up behind me and wrapped her arms around my waist. "Sorry."

I nodded, not trusting my voice. After several deep breaths I got a hold of myself. "Could you get out the soy sauce?"

She moved away, rummaged in the door of the fridge, then handed me the bottle.

I grabbed it, but she didn't let go. My gaze lifted to hers. She gave a lopsided smile. "So you're telling me my dad wasn't in the army? At least that's *some* information."

I gave a bark of laughter and pulled the soy sauce free.

We resumed our truce and had a great supper. After I cleaned up, Clara took over the kitchen with her science books and notes. I went into the front room to practice some new repertory. The mood in the house turned so peaceful and normal, that I dared to bring a few books into Clara's room at bedtime, ready to resume our ritual.

She scooted over and patted a spot beside her. "I've got a new book for us to start reading."

"Really? Is it a classic?"

Our rule was that our read-aloud time was for great literature, not pulp drivel.

She held it up. "The cover says it's a classic. And the author's dead, so it must be. *Mere Christianity* by C. S. Lewis. He was a professor at Oxford."

Christianity? I stiffened. Not fair. Not fair. She was being sly again. Manipulating me.

On the other hand, the cracks in our relationship terrified me. If I could compromise a little, examine some of the things that interested her—it couldn't be worse than the whole cheerleading world.

"Fine. I'm open-minded."

"Thanks."

Her quiet word warmed me like fine wine and melted some of my prickles. She knew I didn't like delving this direction, so she appreciated me for trying. Her approval was a powerful barometer for how I viewed my parenting skills. That was probably all backward, but I couldn't help myself. Even from her infancy, when I coaxed a smile from her or sensed she was pleased with me, the affirmation strengthened me like nothing else.

She started reading, and I listened with one ear and kept a silent monologue going in my head. At least this guy didn't start out with a list of finger-pointing Bible verses, and he wasn't using a bunch of religious lingo. Just making some point about people's innate belief about right and wrong. *Blah, blah, blah.* One comment stood out, though. *"I do not succeed in keeping the Law of Nature very well, and the moment anyone tells me I am not keeping it, there starts up in my mind a string of excuses as long as your arm."*

Guilt. Excuses. I didn't need to hear about that. I was an expert already.

Clara finished the chapter. I kissed her good-night and hurried from her room as if the words were chasing me. My comforter offered me a place to burrow, but my pillow felt like a brick. Soon I was too hot and kicked off the covers. After watching my clock pass the time for an hour, I got up and opened my window. May air drifted in and cooled my skin. Outside, the moonlight struggled through the leaves of the maple on the side of the house, throwing speckles onto the neighbor's backyard. The moon's effort seemed futile.

"There's too much in the way," I whispered to it, resting my cheek against the window frame. I felt a sudden compassion for the moon—trying so hard to give a reassuring glow to the night, and only succeeding in softening a few of the shadows.

A sigh of air jostled the branches of the neighbor's tree. The breeze felt alive. Speaking. A speaking breeze that whispered a secret I couldn't quite hear.

I wanted to whisper back, to tell someone the truths I couldn't tell Clara, truths even Lena didn't know. Would the breeze understand? Would the moonlight forgive? Would the night air seep into my heart and untie the knots?

I slid the sash back down, shutting out the murmur in the wind. Then I pulled down the shade to silence the moon.

I had done my best to fix my mistakes. I'd made a good life for Clara and myself. That ought to count for something. I punched my pillow a few times and then crawled back into bed. I stared through the darkness in the general direction of the ceiling. "Okay, so what if I don't make any excuses? How does that help? I can't unmake my choices. All I can do is try harder now."

Trying harder was like climbing a StairMaster on heart-attack speed. No matter how high and hard I stepped, another step came at me. Futile effort. Waste of energy. I'd long ago given up on curbing my impatience with people who annoyed me, or tempering my frustration with artistic laziness. I'd stopped dreaming of having silky auburn hair waving around my face, or growing some long, slender legs. And I wouldn't try to muster interest in politics or local school board decisions. Wasn't going to happen.

But could trying harder make me a better mother? That would at least have some purpose. Could trying harder fill the hole?

Where had that thought come from? I didn't have a hole. I was doing fine, especially now that my career dreams were unfolding.

But I fell asleep and dreamed of doors that led nowhere and dark emptiness appearing in the space where my heart usually beat.

Tuesday night, Stefan arrived at the door with a single rose, looking dapper. In our living room he seemed even taller than he did at the theatre. "Clara, this is the concertmaster, Stefan Kronenberg. My daughter, Clara."

They studied each other, and I waited for a corny line from Stefan like, "You could be sisters."

Instead he waited for her to take the lead. She tilted her head. "Mom says you play a mean fiddle."

His laugh blasted like a trumpet, and he turned to look at me. "My thanks for the compliment."

Clara smiled and took the rose from me. "I'll go put this in water. Have a great time. Don't stay out too late; you've got rehearsal tomorrow."

"Yes, ma'am." I saluted sharply and watched her sashay out of the room. "She's getting sassier every day."

"She's lovely," Stefan said. "You must be proud. I wish I had children. But for some of us, we make sacrifices for the music, yes?"

"I have." I stiffened. How many times over the years had "real" musicians snubbed me?

Stefan didn't seem to notice my sudden irritation. He led me out to his Lexus and opened the door. His attentiveness soothed my bruised ego, and we picked up our conversation from the evening at the tapas bar as if no time had passed.

An hour later, we were still laughing and talking. A candle flickered over the white linen tablecloth, and we fought playfully over the last roll in the breadbasket.

Why had I avoided friendly dates for so many years? I was having a good time. "After all these years of teaching and playing for weddings, it's still hard for me to believe that I'm finally doing what I dreamed of." I took another bite of shrimp scampi.

"You must take what you want. I knew I wanted to be a concert-master from the first time I saw an orchestra perform."

"I know what you mean. I still remember seeing Rampal in concert. Incredible. And the Minneapolis Symphony is such a big step up for me."

A dark look passed over his Nordic paleness. "And for me a step down."

A step down? How dare he impugn the status of our symphony? "What do you mean?"

He took a sip of water. A self-satisfied smile hid behind the lip of his glass.

"We have a fine symphony." My voice came out too brittle. *Easy, Amy. The whole point of this dinner is to find out why someone is sabotaging him.*

"Of course it is. Forgive me." He leaned forward to cover my fingers with his.

I snatched my hand away.

Stefan laughed and attacked another piece of his steak.

This interrogation wasn't going my way. Time to try a new tack. "Do you think Peter Wilson could be the one trying to make you look bad?"

He tried for another laugh, but it came out strained. "Why would you ask that?"

"He has more access to the stage and backstage area than anyone. He doesn't seem to like you. He's tried to throw accusations my way, which is ridiculous and makes me think he's covering up something."

"Who can say? You know there are always rivalries in the music world."

I nodded. "Sure. Sarah is still prickly toward me. I can't understand it."

He chuckled. "That might not be musical rivalry."

"What do you mean?"

"She and I . . . well, we have gone out sometimes. If she has seen how I . . . appreciate you, I'm afraid it could make her less than warm toward you." Stefan turned away and signaled the waiter for a dessert menu. He lounged back in his chair with a contented sigh. He had the Casanova air that made me believe Sarah's gossip. I could see him breaking a second violinist's heart and flirting with Vicki and fueling Leonard's jealousy. And he'd just admitted to going out with Sarah. Probably kept a scorecard in his violin case. Maybe Sarah was a woman scorned and out to ruin Stefan. But I still thought another violinist was a better suspect. Maybe Peter had been married, and Stefan had an affair with his wife. Or vice versa. Or Stefan had a fling with Peter's sister (if he had one) and broke her heart, and she killed herself, and Peter blamed Stefan.

Mystery-solving energy began to surge through me. "Have you worked with Peter before?"

He shook his head. "Try the cheesecake. It's not bad for a bistro in a Midwestern city."

I waved that away. "So what's with you two?"

Stefan leaned forward, jaw clenched. "Ask him. He knows what he's done."

Okay, I'd been on the wrong track. It was something Peter had done to Stefan, not the other way around. And their feud may have nothing to do with the pranks.

"But Peter—"

"Do you want dessert or not?" Stefan's annoyance peeked through his slick amiability.

"No. I should get home in case Clara needs help with homework."

Lame reasoning, especially if he had known how little I remembered of calculus or European history or most of the other things she was studying. But he didn't question my excuse. He seemed almost relieved.

His willingness to cut the evening short was hardly complimentary, but I didn't mind. My strappy heels were raising blisters, the batik skirt dug into my waist, and the sparkly camisole Clara had lent me was scratchy. Casual dating was suddenly more exhausting than I'd remembered.

When we pulled up to the house, I threw the car door open before Stefan shifted into park. "Good night. See you tomorrow." I rushed up the sidewalk with my key out and ready and never looked back. Stefan's car growled as he pulled away.

Tomorrow we would move back into Symphonic Hall to begin rehearsals for the June Music Festival. A solid series and good reviews could raise our stature and help us get the funding we needed. Maybe there wouldn't be any more strange attacks on Stefan. But I'd keep my eyes and ears open. I ought to question Peter . . . but the way our last few encounters had gone, it might be wiser to keep my sleuthing under the radar for a while. .

CHAPTER

Modulation: Harmonic movement from one key to a related key.

ednesday afternoon my *check engine* light flickered as I drove to rehearsal. The weather had taken a sudden jump in heat and humidity, and my finicky car didn't like it any more than I did. The heavy air promised a spectacular thunderstorm before the day was over.

I thumped the dashboard. "Stop complaining. I'll get your radiator checked tomorrow." I wanted my first day at Symphonic Hall to be perfect. I'd sat in the audience countless times, and each time I'd dreamed of this day. A timpani rolled dramatically in my imagination as I drove into the parking lot behind the concert hall.

Right after I turned off the engine, Lena pulled her minivan into the space near mine. She saw me and jumped from her van, hitting her remote lock so that it chirped.

I got out of my Saturn, relieved to see a friendly face. "My car is acting weird."

"I'm sorry," Lena said, with an overload of compassion. If I told her I had a hangnail, she'd do the whole empathy thing with as much fervor as if I told her I'd been diagnosed with cancer.

"It's not that big a deal. Just annoying. I'll have to get it looked at tomorrow."

Lena sighed. "I'm so glad I have Ken. He always takes care of the cars."

She didn't mean it as a dig. She couldn't help being a constant reminder that I had no man to fix water heaters, tired cars, or cranky daughters.

I countered her cloying sympathy by squaring my jaw. "I like handling things on my own. It's good to be capable. Self-reliant."

"Of course."

Her sympathetic tone grated on my nerves.

We entered the stage door off the lot, and Lena led me through the brightly lit corridors to the dressing rooms. The smell of fresh paint made me sneeze.

"Hi, Snake." Lena gave a happy wave to a young giant with tattoos on both bulging biceps. "Wanna help me get my baby onto the stage?"

He grinned, snaggleteeth flashing through several days' worth of stubble. "Only for you, babe."

"Amy, this is Snake. He's the go-to guy for everything backstage."

"Um, hi." I didn't know whether to shake his hand or check him for weapons.

"So, Amy, whaddaya play?"

"Flute."

He grinned. "Smart. Why didn't this gal have your sense?"

Lena laughed. "Amy, choose any locker without a padlock, and make yourself at home. I'll see you later."

Snake and Lena headed back down the hall again to unload and transport her harp. I found an empty locker and threw my shoulder bag inside, snapping on the padlock I'd brought along. Then I carried my flute and music folder with me to do some exploring.

First, I found my way to the audience side of the stage. As I stepped into the familiar main-floor seating, I let some of my excitement well up and took a deep breath.

I'd enjoyed the Palace for its character, but Symphonic Hall was a far truer temple to music. Acoustical panels canted at scientific angles to prevent dead spots for the audience. Stark lines kept the eye drawn to the stage. The air vibrated with energy—the modern ventilation system probably helped create that sensation. No musty velvet or ancient set pieces here. The blond-wood stage, polished to a high sheen, carried the reflection of the grand piano, chairs, and music stands.

Snake invaded the sacred space, pushing a dolly with Lena's carefully wrapped harp. He whistled off-key and paused to scratch his ribs like a gorilla. But he unloaded the harp with care and took his time positioning it.

Lena came onstage. "Perfect."

"Yeah, you always say that." He waved and sauntered off into the wings.

I mounted the stairs at the side of the stage and walked over to Lena.

"Getting acclimated?" she asked.

I nodded, staring after Snake.

Lena giggled. "Makes quite an impression, doesn't he? He's got a heart of gold."

"And a couple teeth to match," I said under my breath.

"Guess what? He goes to our church. Isn't that cool?"

Her church seemed scarier all the time. I needed to have another talk with Clara. Hanging out with that crowd wasn't a good idea.

I found my chair in the flute section and assembled my instrument. In this holy place, I was almost afraid to try a note. Finally I closed my eyes and played one true, sustained C. As I held it, I let the vibrato grow and savored the way the sound swelled in the vast open space. I let the note soften before breaking it off.

I opened my eyes and indulged a grin. Pure heaven.

Sarah arrived and began bombarding me with instructions about the new pieces. The covey of violins and violas straggled in. Brass players began warming up. I could barely hear Sarah in spite of her shrill voice. Leonard and Vicki arrived, both moving awkwardly with their large instruments. Leonard stopped near the bassoon section.

"What's the definition of a half step?" He asked in feigned seriousness.

No one took the bait, so he grinned. "Two bassoonists playing in unison."

Laughs and groans added to the cacophony of sound.

Stefan strode in right on time, making a bit of an entrance. He paused to chat with several musicians in his section, glad-handing like a politician.

When Peter took the podium, my spine tightened. Was he holding a grudge? He'd been pretty mad after he tripped over me and then found me skulking in the storage room at the Palace.

The orchestra members settled and focused. Our first pass through "Rodeo" was rough. Peter chewed out the woodwinds, and I could have sworn he glared specifically in my direction. Maybe it was my imagination, but once, when he cut us off, he rubbed his elbow as if it were aching. That time I definitely caught a glower in my direction.

After some work, the beauty of the music began to shine. Personalities might clash; professional jealousies might seethe beneath the surface; disagreements about phrasing could erupt. But in spite of the conflicts, as a symphony we were one organism. One shared purpose. Polishing this new repertory was a pleasure.

The exuberant selection of Aaron Copland, one of America's premier composers, would open the Summer Festival concert, followed by a medley of songs from various nations. The At Home and Around the World theme let us show off a variety of styles. Repertory choices were lighter. The string quartet, which included Vicki and Stefan, would be playing mini-concerts on Nicollet Mall at lunchtime.

Halfway through rehearsal, Megan popped in to tell us that a crew would be filming throughout the week, doing candid interviews, and putting together a feature for a Saturday morning show on a local station. She spared us the pep talk this time. In fact, she seemed rather glum.

As soon as she trudged up the long aisle toward the lobby, Peter tossed us back into our work. Rehearsal ran long, and everyone scattered as soon as Peter laid down his baton. I swabbed out my flute and put it away, then grabbed my music and followed the others toward the wings.

"Ms. Johnson, could I see you for a moment, please?" Peter didn't look up from scribbling notes on his stand.

I was tempted to pretend I hadn't heard him and keep moving.

No. I wasn't the slink-away type. I marched over to him. "Look, I'm sorry about those triplets in the second piece. I've never tongued them in that pattern before. But I'll work on it tonight."

He glanced down at me, annoyed. "The triplets were fine."

"Oh. Well, if you're upset about us rushing the arpeggio, I—"

"If you'd let me get a word in . . ." He stepped down from his podium and squared off with me.

I blinked. "It's not the triplets or the arpeggio?"

"Forget the blasted arpeggio," he ground out. "What I'm trying to ask is whether you're available on Sunday morning. My friend needs a flute."

"What?"

"He's debuting a cantata he composed and his flutist got appendicitis. He only uses flute in one section."

"Let me guess. You've already asked everyone you know." Or maybe he really didn't trust me and wanted to keep an eye on me.

He studied me for a moment and his mouth quirked upward. "Does it matter? The point is, I'm playing violin for him, and I told him I'd ask around for a flute. Are you busy or not?"

"I guess not. I mean, yes. I mean, I guess I could do it. When is rehearsal?"

"Saturday morning—at the Basilica of St. Mary."

Shock and a bit of repulsion hit me. "A church?"

"The Basilica hosts lots of arts events. It's a great space. Airy, lots of marble. Bad sight lines, but great acoustics."

"But . . . church?"

He sighed. "They're performing the work between two of the morning masses as a special event for Pentecost. '*Veni Spiritus Sanctus.*' He's worked on the piece for months."

"My Latin's a little rusty . . ."

" 'Come, Holy Spirit.' "

A shiver spiraled up my spine and raised the tiny hairs on the nape of my neck. Spirit? That didn't sound good at all. Visiting Lena's church had already given me the heebie-jeebies—not to mention that book of Clara's.

Peter ignored my sudden silence, pulled some sheet music from his attaché, and handed it to me. "Be there by eight on Saturday morning, right?"

I suddenly resented his crisp accent—particularly when he was issuing commands. "Pip, pip. Cheerio," I muttered.

I didn't wait for his reaction but hurried backstage, then wanted to kick myself for again being surly and ungracious with the conductor. He'd asked me for help. If I had a knack for winning friends and influencing people, I could have built on this opportunity. I should have chatted for a while, asked him why Stefan was mad at him, followed the clues. Once again I'd let my temper take over.

I sighed. At times I could be a bit prickly, and normally that was fine by me. But it did make my investigation more difficult.

On my way down the hallway to the parking lot exit, I passed Sarah and Stefan in a huddled conversation. Sarah threw her head back and laughed. When she saw me approaching, she intertwined her arm with Stefan's in a possessive gesture and gave me a triumphant smile.

Stefan barely glanced at me.

Good. They could keep each other entertained, and maybe Sarah would be in a better mood tomorrow. She was probably hoping I'd be crushed at seeing her cozy with Stefan. I hid a grin. Boy, was she ever on the wrong page. I headed to my car, humming.

I buckled up and turned the key. Suddenly my cell phone buzzed from inside the glove compartment.

After some rummaging, I pulled it free and flipped it open. "Hello?"

"Mom! I've been trying to reach you." Clara's hysteria pierced my ears.

"Clara? What's wrong? What is it?"

She screamed and yelled something, but the connection cut in and out rapidly.

A giant fist gripped my heart. I swiveled, trying to get a better signal. "Are you there? Clara? Where are you? What's wrong?" I squeezed the phone and my hand trembled. Why hadn't I kept my phone with me at rehearsal? Who cared about stupid rules? She had needed me.

Another brief fragment of scream cut off into silence.

"Clara? Are you there? Hello? Clara!" I shouted into the phone as if my volume would restore our connection.

Dead silence answered me.

CHAPTER

 Accelerando: Gradually accelerating or getting faster.

I broke every speed limit racing toward home, hitting redial on my phone again and again. She didn't pick up. My signal bars were full, so something was wrong with her phone, not mine. Years of reading crime novels enhanced the torture of each minute. Scenarios chased each other through my brain.

Five thirty. She should be home from cheerleading practice by now.

Unless something horrible had happened to her. Buses got in accidents all the time. Or maybe she and her friends stopped at Baskin Robbins for ice cream on their way home, and the place was held up. Or maybe it was a fire. What if someone had set fire to the school gym?

Red brake lights filled the freeway ahead. Rush hour traffic was always a mess heading out of downtown, but today was worse than normal.

"Come on, come on." I saw an opening and swerved over a lane.

The cars in front of me slowed as well, and I swore. Finally, I pulled onto the shoulder and zipped past all the traffic. If the police stopped me, so much the better. They could follow me home to save Clara.

I reached my exit and barreled through several yellow lights. Good thing it wasn't raining yet. I skidded around a corner, barely keeping the car from spinning out. A car honked. A pickup hit its brakes with a squeal as I cut it off.

Only a few blocks from home. I was panting sharp, shallow breaths. "She's fine. She has to be fine."

But the "what if's" squeezed me tighter with each block.

I screeched to a stop on the street in front of the house, leapt from the car, and ran to the front door.

Locked.

I pounded. No response. I dug into my pocket for my keys—still in the car. I ran back to grab them, wasting precious seconds. Then I fumbled with the lock and dropped the keys. Twice.

Finally, I got the door open and raced into the music room then toward the back of the house. "Clara!" The kitchen stood empty, without the familiar clutter of her backpack.

No. She had to be here. She always took the late bus home after her practice. I galloped upstairs, checking each room, behind the shower curtain, under the beds.

Think, Amy. Think! She's in trouble. Where could she be?

Maybe she stopped at Miguel's to pick up a paycheck. She wasn't scheduled to work today, but . . .

I ran out the door and hopped in the car. Clara usually walked the same route between Miguel's and home. My car nosed forward, as I scanned each yard and side street. Up ahead, a long-haired, slim girl strolled down the sidewalk in a cluster of teens. My heart grabbed. She turned her head to talk to a friend. Not Clara.

When I reached Miguel's, I pulled along the yellow curb by his front entrance. The door jingled as I burst into the coffee shop. "Miguel? Have you seen Clara?"

He'd never seen me wide-eyed and frantic like this. He dropped his order pad and ran to meet me. "What's wrong?"

Hysteria swelled in my throat. My eyes stung. "I don't know. She called, and got cut off. But she was . . . she was screaming."

His dark eyes filled with concern. "Did you call the school? Did you check your phone messages?"

I shook my head. "I just stopped at home long enough to look for her. I was at the concert hall when I got her call. She hasn't answered since. Are you sure you haven't seen her?"

"No. Not today. You sit. Calm down. Let's call her friends."

"Okay. Okay. Sure. The school. Their number . . ." was in my address book, out in the car. I hurried out to retrieve it and saw my shoulder bag with my flute unattended on the front seat. I snatched it up and brought it with me. Miguel had grabbed a notepad. "Okay, first tell me any place she might be."

"I don't know," I wailed. "School, here, or home."

"Call the school."

I dialed and chewed the edge of a fingernail as the sound rang and rang. "They're not answering."

"Someone should be around after hours. A janitor. A coach. Let it ring. Meantime, let's list her friends."

Great. All the fluffy cheerleaders. What help would they be? "Let me try Janie. She knows everyone. And Clara spends lots of time with Janie's daughter, Ashley."

Miguel nodded, and I felt my first glimmer of hope. We would find her. She had to be okay. With Miguel's steadying influence I came up with several more names and phone numbers.

"Now, maybe you should go home to make your calls." He held the notepad out to me. "In case she is on her way there."

"Yes, but—"

"I'll call you if she comes here, okay?" He patted my arm. "Don't worry." But the furrows in his tanned skin belied his words. He'd been running a coffee shop in Minneapolis for twenty years. He knew the city's dangers better than most.

Feeling like I was running in circles, I drove the short distance back home. Then I wondered if I should have gone to the school instead. I couldn't seem to make a simple decision. The horrific images in my mind got in the way.

Clara in the trunk of a pervert's car. Clara bleeding from a knife wound in an alley. Clara hit by a stray bullet in a holdup on the way home from school.

Trembling, I forced myself to sit at the kitchen table. No one had answered at the school, so I hung up and tried Janie's house. All I got was a perky answering machine. My voice sounded like a stranger's as I left a message. "It's Amy. Clara's not home. I was wondering if . . ." My voice quavered. "Just call me please."

Next I tried Dawn Hanson. No answer.

Then Lena. At least she was home. "Clara's gone," I gasped.

"What?!"

I explained the strange call, the screams, and her disappearance.

"What can I do?" Instead of giving me gushy empathy, she became suddenly strong, controlled, firm. "Amy, it's going to be okay. Should I come over?"

She became my sandbar in the midst of a rushing, flooded stream. I was able to breathe again. Think again. "Not right now. She might call you. Stay by your phone and let me know."

"Did you two have another argument?"

"No!" *Please, God, no. Don't let her be in danger because she was mad at me.* "No, really. We settled that."

"Okay. Don't panic. I'll be praying."

I slammed the phone down. Praying? Lena could cover that base. There was no way I could talk to God about Clara. Besides, if she were harmed, it was probably to punish me for—

I pressed the heels of my hands against my temples. *No. You wouldn't do that, would you? Don't hurt her to get to me. I promise I'll . . .*

What? What did I have to trade? Nothing. Despair strangled me.

I resumed my calls, and finally reached Joy Selforth, the cheerleading coach. "She was leaving school when I saw her. Practice ran long, so a few of the girls were going to catch a city bus or walk home. They were all so excited about the—"

The back door rattled, and I dropped the phone and jumped up. Clara raced in, tossed her pack, and gave me a hug. "Isn't it great?" Her voice was still high-pitched with hysteria.

"Where have you been?" My terror did a quick-change into wrath. "Do you have any idea how worried I was?" I was shaking, and I grabbed her shoulders to still my wobbles.

She looked at me, startled. "I was at practice. I told you. We got the news, and so we stayed late."

"No, you didn't. You screamed and disappeared!"

Her mouth dropped open. "Oh, Mom. I'm sorry. I thought you heard me. I was so excited. We were all screaming."

"Why didn't you answer when I kept calling you?"

"My battery was dead." Pure teen nonchalance. I wanted to rip the cell phone from her pack and stomp it into the ground. I wanted to slap her.

"Do you have any idea what you put me through?" I shrieked the typical mom line I never thought I'd say. Then I noticed my cell phone resting open on the table. I grabbed it. "Sorry, Joy. False alarm. She's home now."

Clara sank onto a chair, eyes wide. "You were searching for me?"

I swallowed around a hard lump. "I went to Miguel's when you weren't here. And I've been calling the school. And Lena. And . . . Wait. I should call Lena back so she doesn't worry."

By the time I'd called Lena and Miguel and left a "never mind" message for Janie, my rage had bled away. I pulled a chair next to Clara's, wrapped my arms around her, and sobbed. I'm not sure if she stroked my hair, or I stroked hers. But somewhere in the hair stroking and gentle back pats, I was able to forgive her for the scare and find my equilibrium again.

"Mom, I'm so sorry. Especially when it was all because of such good news."

I wiped my tears and sat back, taking a steadying breath. "What good news?"

CHAPTER

Deceptive Cadence: A chord progression where the dominant chord is followed by a chord other than the tonic chord . . . The dominant to superdominant progression (V-VI) is deceptive to the listener, because the tendency is for the dominant chord to resolve to the tonic chord.

Clara sat safe, giddy, and beautiful across the table from me. Exhaustion settled over me like lead-lined coveralls as my heart rate returned to normal. With elbows on the table, I propped my chin, too weary to keep my head up. The fear of the past hour had pierced to the core of my darkest belief. I didn't deserve to be a mom.

Some music students at Juilliard saw my decision to drop out as a Grand Sacrifice. Others viewed it as the Great Betrayal to my music. They were both wrong. I was far from noble. And I didn't exchange my flute for a diaper bag. Instead, I charged forward with both identities—musician and mom—and came up short in both.

No wonder I kept expecting the worst. If there was a God like the one Lena had glommed on to, why wouldn't He steal my daughter away . . . if He did, indeed, know my secrets? And why shouldn't the god of music punish me for deserting my loyal pursuit of artistic perfection while I shared my attentions with Clara? I couldn't win. Either god would find me inadequate.

But at least this time my panic about Clara had been a false alarm. "So what was your great news?"

Clara lit up. She had no appreciation for the terror she'd set in motion earlier. "The squad is going to the big state cheerleading competition, and of course it was just going to be the old team, because the new members haven't learned all the routines, and they've been practicing for ages, but then Coach said it would be good experience and help build depth to let the new members be in the big number, and she checked with the committee, and they said since our original team was smaller than the limit we could add people for the big number, and so we all get to go."

And for this she had me envisioning her abduction or murder? I wanted to shriek at her, but that would require too much energy. "Wow. Exciting."

"Mom, you don't get it. This is like a once-in-a-lifetime opportunity. We're going to train like crazy, and you can come and watch us compete. June fifteenth, okay? Well, it's two days, but you've got to come see us Saturday night. That's the finals."

A halfhearted wave of panic rose up, propelling me off my chair and over to my calendar. "Good. No concert that night. It's our weekend off. I'll be there."

"You should see this new routine. It's so amazing. I'll be in the back with Ashley and Brittany, but who cares?" She continued to babble as she walked from the room.

I sat back down at the table and buried my face in my arms. This cheerleading stuff was going to be the death of me yet. I pushed my head up. "Hey, kiddo!"

"What?" Clara popped her head around the doorjamb.

"Your disappearing act? You owe me big time."

Her eyes narrowed. "What did you have in mind?"

"You're coming with me Sunday morning. I'm playing a cantata at the Basilica."

Her eyebrows lifted. "You're taking me to a church?" She ducked back out of sight. "And you say you don't believe in miracles."

"I heard that."

Her giggle was my only answer.

After a quick supper of omelets, Clara stayed in the kitchen to instant message all her friends about the cheerleading event. I settled into the music room to learn the cantata, which led to a review of the Copland repertory and some of the around-the-world composers. I hoped that Clara would be too tired for our reading time, but at ten o'clock she bounded into the music room. "Come on, Mom." She waved the C. S. Lewis book under my nose. "Time for our visit with the Oxford don."

Since it was my turn to read, I couldn't even zone out. The evening's chapter talked about two different ways of viewing the world: the materialist view and the religious view. Lewis closed the chapter with an in-between way of approaching the world—people who espouse a Life Force, a sort of tame god that you can switch on whenever you want. "All the thrills of religion and none of the cost," he wrote.

"At least I'm honest," I told Clara as I closed the book. "No messing around with in-between. I'm a solid materialist. This is what we've got to work with, and it's on our shoulders to figure out what to do with it."

She stared at me, her eyes dark, wise pools in the light of her bedside lamp. When she gave me a gentle smile, I braced myself for deep philosophizing.

"So, Mom. Do you like my hair better in a ponytail or two pigtails?"

I grinned. My daughter might be exploring the spiritual, but she was as solidly in the material world as I was. "You're adorable either way."

She rolled her eyes. "Mo-om. You're not helping. Coach Joy said a tight ponytail can look too severe. What do you think?"

I kissed her forehead. "You aren't an airhead like some of those girls. A more serious look suits you. Did you plug in your cell phone? I don't want your battery dying again if I'm trying to reach you."

"Yep. Sorry again. G'night."

"Night."

I padded across the hall to my room and crawled under the covers. Today had been long, and my body nearly shook with fatigue. But my mind wouldn't stop thinking and let me sleep. I kept reliving the terror I'd felt when Clara was missing. And the pleas I'd shot toward the sky like some sort of prayers.

So you believe in some sort of life force?

The thought slipped into the room like breeze through the window. That presence again. I turned my back to the window. Why should I believe in some God who despises me because of the things I've done?

You don't know me, but you believe I despise you?

I tugged my sheets upward with too much force, and they pulled loose from the mattress, creating a tangled mess. Sighing, I got up and remade my bed. What was my problem? I was tossing and turning while arguing with the inaudible voice of a being I didn't believe in. Maybe the pressure of playing professionally was shattering my nerves.

The next day Peter conducted rehearsal with a steady hand, as if the symphony were running smoothly, had abundant funding, and would thrive for years to come. Not a care in the world.

"Make the Strauss dance. Feel it in your bones. Percussion, watch for the tempo change. Strings, more staccato."

What was it about the musician's personality that made us thrive on direction? I'd seen the same thing at Juilliard with the actors and dancers. We all claimed we wanted artistic freedom. But we actually longed for a strong voice telling us which steps to take. A dancer friend told me she did a clean triple pirouette for the first time simply because her choreographer ordered her to do one at rehearsal.

I stopped pondering the question and surrendered to being guided, coaxed, and unified with other musicians to create the best music possible. I lost myself in the rapid waltz meter of "The Blue Danube." We raced toward the last page and ended with a flourish that left me breathless.

Megan, the ever-hovering development manager, coughed from the wings, drawing Peter's attention. She beckoned to him.

"Straight away," he called to her. Then he turned back to us. "Adequate." A smile stretched across his face. "And maybe a bit more."

He headed offstage and stood to the side talking with Megan and a visitor with a press badge. Lena left her harp and wove through the chairs to give me a hug. "I'm glad Clara was all right. I was so worried when you called."

"You and me both. Hey, she can't go to church with you this Sunday. She's coming with me to the Basilica. And get that gleam out of your eye. I'm only going because Peter's friend needed a flutist in a hurry."

Lena grinned. "I wasn't gleaming. Honest. Thanks for letting me know." Her smile faded. "Have you told Clara any more about Jason?"

"Why?"

Lena studied a button on her cuff, twisting it until I thought it would pop off. "She called me the other day."

"You didn't—"

"Of course not." She looked up suddenly. "But don't you think you're being unfair? She has a right to know more. Maybe she'll want to meet him one day."

"So she can admire him for the musical success he is, and she can lose respect for me by comparison?"

"Oh, Amy. If you believe that, you don't know Clara. She'll always respect you the most because of the choice you made. You've been there for her. He hasn't."

My throat closed up, and all I could do was shake my head.

"Do you want to go out for coffee? I've got an hour before the kids get home from school."

I couldn't. I was barely able to keep up the façade any longer. In my vulnerable mood, a cozy mug of coffee could pry open the locks, and I might find myself pouring out the truth. Lena, like Clara, thought I was the hero in the unexpected pregnancy story of my Juilliard days. I had to keep them both believing that.

"No," I croaked. "I've got a student coming."

Why not lie to my best friend? It was a small sin compared to my others.

CHAPTER

Tempestoso: A directive to perform a certain passage of a composition in a tempestuous, stormy, or boisterous manner.

Friday night I found myself in the wings of Symphonic Hall, avoiding the truth again. For someone with my tendency toward bluntness, I'd been doing a lot of dancing around the facts. "It's an honor to be part of a symphony with such a great musical history and solid repertory choices." I squinted against the harsh light over the reporter's shoulder and wished I'd done something with my hair.

When Megan had warned us that a crew would be filming a news feature about our move into the renovated Symphonic Hall, it never occurred to me that I'd be interviewed. But the newscaster wanted quotes from the newest members of the orchestra.

"And what do you think about the problems that have dogged the orchestra in the past month?" The young man shoved his microphone closer to my face. Avid curiosity brightened his eyes.

"It's a mystery, all right. My theory is that it's someone in the orchestra, because—"

Megan cleared her throat somewhere behind me.

Oops. "Anyway, that's not important. Every arts group goes through rough patches. That shouldn't diminish people's appreciation for our work. We're playing some amazing music. That's what it's all about."

"In fact"—Megan stepped into the light—"we need the public's support more than ever. With government cuts, and the tough economy, we need patrons to show that they believe in the value of the tremendous musical heritage of our Twin Cities."

The reporter sniffed and leaned closer to me. "And what do you think of the new conductor, Peter Wilson?"

I swallowed. "He's fine. I mean, the symphony has had some brilliant conductors over the years, so he has big shoes to fill."

"Do you think he's up for the job? Especially with the symphony in danger of closing?"

I glanced over at Megan. She was rubbing her temples and glaring at the floor. "He's a great conductor." I pulled my lips into a smile, wishing I didn't sound so much like a parrot reciting sound bites. "You should talk to him."

The reporter frowned, but I backed away, making it clear I was done answering questions. The young man told his cameraman to move to the next set-up.

I blotted sweat from my face and fled farther backstage. Lena snagged my arm and pulled me to a stop. "How'd it go?"

"Terrific. They'll probably show a clip on the evening news of me saying something inane or stupid, and the symphony will be in more trouble."

She laughed. "You're not important enough to single-handedly ruin the symphony."

"That's a comfort," I said wryly. "But if I don't go warm up, I'll never hit the high notes tonight. We don't need more problems, and Sarah doesn't need another excuse to snipe at me."

"Speak of the devil," Lena murmured.

"There you are. I suppose you think this is some kind of coup?" Sarah snapped at me—an incongruous, svelte, blond pit bull.

"You mean the interview? I didn't even want to—"

"Don't play dumb. I'm talking about the Takemitsu. I don't know how you talked Peter into giving you the solo. I'm supposed to chair our section."

Could I clock her over the head with a nearby music stand? Any jury would understand, wouldn't they? "What are you talking about?"

She narrowed her eyes. "Go check the board. He added a Take-mitsu flute solo to the Around the World series, and your name is on it."

Really? A delicious tingle spread from my lungs outward and through my limbs.

"We need to tune." Lena stepped between Sarah and me.

She was right. The bustle backstage had accelerated. Concert time raced toward us.

"This isn't over," Sarah hissed. But she hurried toward the stage. Even with her corks in a twist, she couldn't resist the inexorable pull of concert preparations.

The din of tuning notes calmed my jangled nerves. As pitches blended, I felt the unified vibration in the small bones of my ear. I blew gently across my mouthpiece, adding my two cents to the wealth of sound.

As Peter stepped to the podium, applause rang from the balcony and main seating area, surrounding us in encouragement. He dipped his chin toward the percussion section in unspoken reminder of the barely audible entry he had requested.

He surveyed the rest of us with a reassuring smile and gave us the count. The timpani began a muted roll that grew into magnificent thunder. The horns took us into the melody with joyful abandon. We woodwinds entered with a playful countermelody. Then the strings filled every empty space with resonance. Our music soared and expanded, so thick with power I wondered how we could breathe the air any longer.

In the midst of the triumph, a strange sound intruded. A snapping rubber band. A scraping *twang*. From the violin section.

No! Not again!

My heart screamed in protest. It was cruelty of the highest nature for anything to ruin the beauty of our music.

Stefan lowered his instrument. The bow in his hand looked as if it had exploded—horsehair spewing out like threads of a fiber-optic light.

Bowstrings could snap. But this?

David played undeterred. A stagehand slipped out and handed Stefan a spare bow. He ran his fingers down the hairs, tucked the violin under his chin, and leapt back in.

After the concert, Stefan's voice carried loudly from the stage-right wings where the reporter nodded with faux sympathy. "They were cut!" In his agitation, Stefan's w's sounded like v's. "I tell you, this has happened too much. No musician will allow this. I must leave."

"Quit the orchestra?"

"Of course. Damage to my bow. Damage to my career. This is a serious thing. They cannot hold me to my contract if they allow such attacks."

I groaned. Stefan made it sound as if the symphony invited vandals to hang around on a regular basis. He was drilling nails into the symphony coffin and tossing the press a shovel. They'd bury us.

Not now. Not when I've been tapped to play a solo.

I waited in the hallway and accosted Stefan as he headed toward the dressing room. "Show me."

He looked down at me. "They have gone too far." He held the bow out, as if presenting the lifeless body of a dear friend.

I pulled it from his hands. Clean breaks, all in the identical place, made it clear this was not defective equipment. "Someone nicked these with a razor or something. This is terrible."

"Yes, terrible. I should have left. But our esteemed Maestro told the board to hold me to my contract. This is his fault."

Stefan's temper had snapped like his bowstrings, and I didn't blame him. Why would Peter force a musician to stay when he was in danger?

"We need to find out who has a razor blade in their locker."

Stefan grabbed his bow back. "It doesn't matter now. I won't be back." He stormed past me like a drama king.

I wasn't about to give up that easily. Whether the culprit was David, the second-chair violin, or Leonard, the jealous husband, or Peter, the power wielding conductor, or even some spurned romantic interest like Sarah, there were sure to be clues somewhere backstage.

After changing into clothes I could skulk in, I locked my gear in my locker, slipped into the bathroom, and flipped open my cell phone. I was hoping to get voicemail, but Clara answered on the first ring.

"How'd it go?"

"Another sabotage. Stefan's bow was shredded. I'm going to stick around after everyone leaves and see if I can find anything to narrow the list of suspects."

"Mom, tell me you're joking."

"I just wanted to let you know I'll be a little late."

"Mom, no. You can't go lurking around an empty theatre—"

"Symphonic hall."

"What?"

"It's not technically a theatre."

"Whatever. Mom, think about it. How does Nancy Drew always get in trouble? It's the lurking. You read enough mysteries. You don't go meet the informant in a dark alley. You don't go into the scary building alone when the criminal just broke out of jail. You don't lurk. You should know—"

"Bye, Chicklet. Talk to you later." I slapped my phone shut.

It rang again immediately, so I turned it off and stuffed it into my pocket. Nancy Drew, indeed. I was a serious musician with a serious problem. The orchestra wanted to push the incidents under the rug to avoid bad press. Stefan wanted to give up and leave. But whoever had done these horrible things needed to be brought to justice. I had a moral imperative. Clara should appreciate that now that she'd found religion.

I threw the switch by the bathroom door, washing the room in darkness. The back corner stall provided a good hiding place. I listened to distant sounds of people leaving, doors banging, and keys rattling. The hall lights died outside, erasing the strip of light under the door. After the building went quiet, I made myself stay hidden for ten more minutes and willed my eyes to adjust to the heavy darkness.

Clues, here I come.

Tiptoeing through corridors barely illuminated by cold, red exit lights, my nerve endings twisted into a tight knot. The backstage rehearsal room was the logical first place to search. Musicians warmed up there, and Stefan might have set down his bow, leaving it unguarded for a moment.

Thankfully, rays from nearby streetlights pierced the windows, so I was able to pick my way around the dozens of metal chairs without bashing my shins. Broken reeds, wadded tissues, and bottles of valve oil littered the floor. I inspected the full perimeter of the room, looking for a razor, a knife, or some other weapon. The cabinets along the inside wall were securely locked. I pulled a credit card from my wallet and wedged it into one of the latches, but no amount of wiggling triggered the lock. An extra nudge forced the card's corner too far, and I couldn't pull it out. Finally, I wrenched it free, leaving a corner of plastic behind.

Okay, so I needed a few lessons on breaking and entering. I also needed a new Discover card.

I slipped from the room and tried the men's dressing room next. Most of my suspects were men, so I was bound to have better luck in there. I propped the door open so some of the hallway emergency lights could spill inside. A wadded sock lurked under a bench. A crumpled paper hinted at extortion or threats—but turned out to be a shopping list for a remodeling project: twelve two-by-fours, Sheetrock screws, two gallons of paint. I tucked it in my pocket anyway. A good detective doesn't dismiss any potential clues.

One by one, I investigated each unsecured locker. Those with padlocks were beyond my skill. But I carefully felt around inside each of the empty ones. Too bad I didn't keep a flashlight in my music bag. This room was much darker than the last. When nothing interesting turned up, I got down on my hands and knees and felt along the edge of the carpet. I backed my way along the wall toward the open door. The sound of breathing—not my own—hit me a second before the voice.

"Hey. Whaddaya think you're doing?"

I sprang to my feet and faced the dark silhouette in the doorway. Tall. Threatening. He blocked my only way of escape. I tucked my chin down and barreled straight toward him, hoping he'd step aside.

He didn't.

Powerful arms grabbed me, hefting me off my feet. The smell of tobacco and sweat surrounded me as I thrashed and screamed.

"Let go of me! I'm a—"

An arm across my windpipe cut off my demands.

"You're coming with me." The deep voice growled, hoarse and vaguely familiar. "Ow!"

My tennis shoe had connected with his shin, but it barely slowed him as he half-dragged, half-carried me down the hall. I struggled to bend my elbow enough to reach my cell phone. If I ended up dead for this stunt, Clara would kill me.

My vision grayed and it grew harder to breathe. My limbs felt too heavy to swing with any power. Over the loud throbbing of my pulse, I heard the heavy thump of pounding on metal.

My captor switched directions and dragged me toward the noise.

Great. He's got accomplices. Will the orchestra pay a ransom for a second-chair flutist? The thought of how little I was worth added depression to my panic as the man lurched up the dark hall with me in his grasp.

CHAPTER

23

Cantata: a choral composition, either sacred and resembling a short oratorio, or secular, as a lyric drama set to music but not to be acted.

Fresh air hit my face as the steel door to the parking lot swung open.

"Lena, what are you doing here?" my captor rasped.

"Lena?" I squeaked, twisting in his grip. Even backlit by the parking lot's motion-sensor lights, her willowy form was unmistakable.

"I came to find Amy. I thought she might have gotten locked in by mistake."

Rough hands pushed me out to arm's length. Snake glared down at me, the safety pin through his eyebrow flickering with menace. "Didn't know it was you. Sorry."

I pulled my arm free from his grip and smoothed down my sweatshirt. "No problem. But you could have asked." I rubbed my throat and swallowed, grateful that my voice still worked.

"That still doesn't explain what you were doing in the men's dressing room after hours."

I took a subtle step away from Snake. "Lena, how did you know I was still here?"

"Clara called me." She sighed loudly. "What on earth did you think you could accomplish?"

"No one else was doing anything." I crossed my arms and looked up at Snake, wishing I had a few tattoos to give me a tough appearance. "And just why were you lurking around backstage?"

He barked a low laugh that sounded like a Doberman about to bite. "You are a piece of work."

"We're really sorry for the mix-up," Lena said, reaching for my arm. "She's been worried about the sabotage."

Snake dug a hand into his long hair and shook his head as if it hurt. "That's why they hired me to hang out after hours." His gold tooth flashed with his grin. "Great overtime." Then his smile disappeared. He jabbed a finger into my shoulder. "You stay out of trouble, ya hear? I was about to call the cops. Then you'd really have some explaining to do."

"Let's go," Lena cut in before I could answer. She tugged me toward the parking lot.

I wished people would quit jerking me around. But to be fair, Lena deserved my gratitude for the unexpected rescue. I followed her meekly to my car.

She waited while I got in and started the engine. "Straight home. And call Clara. She's worried sick."

Fine. Then my daughter and I would be even. I waved at Lena and pulled out of the parking space. Shame hit me before I reached the first stoplight. Did I really enjoy the thought of having scared Clara? Of payback for the stress she had caused me? I was supposed to be the mom in our relationship.

Parenting: not a job for cowards. When I had dropped out of Juilliard, I set out to merge the intense and slightly neurotic life of a professional musician with the warm fuzzies of motherhood—a world I knew little about. To survive financially, I moved in with my dad. He was so preoccupied with his world of literature, he barely seemed to register my presence, other than to infuse the air with a vague cloud of disappointment. After all, I'd been destined for musical greatness, not unwed motherhood.

His attitude changed after Clara was born. Not all at once. In the early months, he'd shake his head at the sight of Clara shrieking and me crying just as hard as I tried to make her happy. Then he'd retreat to his office to research new acquisitions for the university library.

One night something changed. The smell of spit up and sour diapers had soaked into my pores, and I couldn't stand myself another minute. I left Clara sleeping in her Porta-crib in the living room so I could snatch a quick shower.

When I emerged from the paradise of lavender-scented steam and came back downstairs, Clara wasn't in the crib. Dad sat in the rocking chair with her bald, pink head nestled under his chin.

> *"If you can dream—and not make dreams your master;*
> *If you can think—and not make thoughts your aim;*
> *If you can meet with Triumph and Disaster*
> *And treat those two impostors just the same;"*

His voice graveled through the singsong words with amazing sweetness. I froze on the bottom step, not wanting to interrupt the familiar Kipling.

> *"If you can force your heart and nerve and sinew*
> *To serve your turn long after they are gone,*
> *And so hold on when there is nothing in you*
> *Except the Will which says to them: 'Hold on!'"*

My father had often been emotionally absent. But listening to him that night conjured a flood of gratitude for the things he'd been able to give me. A love for the arts, for books, for mysteries. The pursuit of perfection and beauty. And his genuine, if reluctant, support for me after I had failed.

> *"If you can fill the unforgiving minute*
> *With sixty seconds' worth of distance run—*
> *Yours is the Earth and everything that's in it,*
> *And—which is more—you'll be a Man my son!"*

I smiled at the gender error. My father would never allow the Politically Correct Police to rewrite a classic to make it inclusive. Clara gave a baby snuffle and burrowed against his neck. He looked up and gave me an apologetic smile, blinking against the fullness in his eyes.

He hadn't known how to love me. I didn't know how to love Clara. But he had given me what he could. I wouldn't have managed to cobble together a music ed. degree without his help. Somehow I raised my baby and completed my degree in stages so I could support myself and my daughter by teaching.

The freeway lights pulled me from my memories and guided me home with their pockets of illumination dotted between stretches of gray dimness.

When I walked into the house, I was subdued as I hugged Clara and apologized for worrying her. We headed upstairs for our bedtime snuggle, and I grabbed an old book of poetry from my bedroom. "Let's take a break from Lewis tonight, okay? Do you remember Kipling?"

Saturday morning I tiptoed into the Basilica for rehearsal, leery of religion slipping into my lungs like the stale smell of incense. I made it safely past the holy water, pews, and stained glass to the wide marble floor in the front of the church where a couple of music stands waited.

A pale man dressed in layers of black welcomed me. He tugged nervously at his blond ponytail and squinted into the distance as if he were listening to music none of the rest of us could hear. Dark shadows under his eyes told me he hadn't been sleeping much. Clearly the composer.

"I'm Amy. Peter said you needed a flute."

"Thank you, thank you." He grabbed my hand and pumped it. "You're saving my life. I'm Teige, but everyone calls me Tiger. We'll start in a few minutes."

Snakes, Tigers. The music world had become a jungle. I nodded a smile at the French horn player who was setting out his mute. An interesting but sparse selection of solo instruments.

Teige gazed past me and lifted a hand in greeting. "There he is. Okay." He clapped his hands together and rubbed them. "Let's get started."

Peter strolled toward us in jeans and a rugby shirt. How could a man in his forties look so boyish? His curls poked out in random directions as if he'd just rolled out of bed. He carried his violin case over his shoulder like a tennis racquet, casual and relaxed. "Glad you could make it," he said to me.

"I said I would." I took a seat and scraped the music stand toward me.

The man had practically accused me of causing all the symphony trouble. Half the time he ignored me like a piece of lint on a sleeve. Now he acted carefree and chummy?

I frowned at him. "Did you really force Stefan to stay with the symphony when he asked to leave?"

Peter's eyebrows lifted. He lowered his violin case onto a chair with slow deliberation. "Excuse me?"

"You're making him stay?"

He flicked the latches of his case open, then turned to me with some of his normal stiffness. "Of course. Stefan can't leverage his success with us into better offers and cut out whenever he wants. That's why we have contracts."

"And why did you assign me to play the Takemitsu? Sarah's furious."

"You don't want the solo?" A hint of teasing flickered in his dark eyes.

I sniffed and turned away. "Of course I do. But you could have warned me." Then I set up my music and turned pointedly away from him. If he was expecting me to thank him for the solo, he could wait.

Teige cleared his throat. "Okay. So the choir will be here in a half hour? I figured we'd run it through from the beginning?"

Was he asking our permission?

"Here. I don't think you all got copies of the libretto." He stumbled around our stands handing out a program. "Amy, sorry your name isn't in. Short notice, you know?"

"No problem." The way things were going, I wouldn't want anyone to connect my name with this.

Teige made his way back to the piano and bumped the bench so it screeched against the marble. "The theme is Pentecost." He shrugged. "Well, duh. But in case you aren't all familiar with the story we open with the disciples in prayer. Waiting. Even a little mournful. Jesus promised a Comforter and told them to wait. But no one likes waiting, right?"

He smiled at me. "So the flute carries the theme. The men's voices are singing 'Veni, Spiritus Sanctus.'" Teige was warming to his description and paced across the front of our music stands. "That's when the violin introduces the wind and flame. Can you imagine? God swoops in."

A whisper of sound seemed to breathe past my ear. My neck hairs prickled.

"The fire touches them. Soprano aria, of course. But then the response from the men's voices." Teige gestured toward the French horn player. "Lots of strength. Show the change it made. Anyway, it's mostly just the keyboard, voices, and horn after that. Should we try it?"

Teige perched on the piano bench and began playing.

He hadn't even given me a tuning note. I lifted my flute, exasperated, and eased into my part. Our first pass through the orchestration was a little rough. Each time we had to stop to fix something, Teige chewed his lower lip and cracked his knuckles. Why had I let Peter talk me into this? This composer was an ulcer waiting to happen.

On the other hand, the music was intriguing. I enjoyed his unusual intervals and the haunting minor key of my movement. I was able to study the program while he rehearsed the later sections of the piece.

An English translation of the Latin lyrics helped me follow the story line. Wind from heaven. Tongues of fire. Intriguing images. Something in this story resonated with me. As a musician I felt as if I'd been touched by fire and empowered by an artistic spirit. I'd told Clara I was an honest materialist, but maybe there was a deeper honesty to explore. Maybe something at my core—the same part of me that appreciated the magic of music—believed there was more to life than what could be seen and touched.

Whoa. Professor Lewis's bedtime chapters were getting to me.

I was relieved to see that Teige's nervous energy didn't hurt his keyboard technique. Music dripped from his fingers.

Choir members began to straggle in, some slouching in pews and listening to us, others chatting in small groups. Teige abruptly cut off the music and stood up. "Hey, everyone. Are we ready? Let's start, okay? There's a wedding coming in to set up in an hour, so we don't have much time."

The singers lined up on the steps facing the empty pews. Teige shoved the piano a bit to adjust the angle and prepared to direct from there. He screwed up his face, eyes tightly closed, and mouthed something. Then he began to play.

The flute was only scored for the overture and opening theme. I played a mournful descant line over the opening theme of the basses and tenors. Then I lowered my flute and listened as Peter conveyed flames and rushing wind. The cantata took on a new life as the voices told the story of Pentecost.

The beauty of the music was infectious. Free from the need to count measures, I could relax and fully listen to the cantata. Teige's piece had a classicism that spoke to me. I smiled as I followed lyrics about opening hearts and inviting God in. I'd heard those phrases at Lena's church, but they'd seemed cheesy and odd to me. Here in the towering Basilica, as professional singers shaped round tones that carried to the lofty buttresses, a strange emotion built under my sternum. My eyes tingled with a warning of tears.

If I asked God to open my heart, to come inside, what would happen? The music said that God's coming brought power, joy, peace, and life. As different from what currently lived in my heart as the powerful chorus being sung now was from my mournful opening solo.

A yearning that was part hunger, part loneliness, part recognition built into a throbbing pressure in my chest.

Are you there? Are you really pursuing me?

Just as the pull grew to an irresistible level, I remembered the slimy secrets that coated my heart. I could never coax it open and expose it, especially not to the God that inspired these soaring voices and lofty architecture. If He blew into my heart, His fire would burn me to cinders.

My fingers tightened around my flute, fluttering silently against the keys.

Peter glanced over, studied me for a moment, then politely turned away, leaving me privacy in my inner struggle.

I was barely aware as the cantata reached its powerful finale. After the last note, the choir members applauded each other and Teige. His sallow skin flushed with embarrassment and pleasure. "So everyone get here by eight-thirty tomorrow. There's almost no set-up time. We go right after the first mass, okay? Great job everyone. Thanks again."

The horn player was halfway down the aisle before Teige said good-bye. The choir members dispersed as quickly. I cleaned my flute and put it away, moving slowly and carefully. I was afraid that a move in the wrong direction would inflame the horrible pain I'd discovered within my rib cage. Peter and Teige murmured to each other, backslapping and jostling in the strange masculine conversation style.

"Bye, guys." I hitched up my shoulder bag and started down the aisle. When I reached the back pew, my feet slowed. Suddenly I couldn't face the glaring sunlight outside and the harsh emptiness of being alone with myself. I slipped onto a bench and stared at the altar where moments before glorious music tugged at my heart.

Teige exited out a side door. Peter walked past the rows of pews, slowing as he drew closer to me.

Go away. Keep walking.

"You okay?"

"I'm fine," I snapped. "Just thinking."

He nodded. "Yeah, it has that effect on me, too. Teige's a wonder."

I didn't answer.

Peter took a breath as if to say more but then shook his head. "See you tonight." And blessedly, he disappeared out the back of the church.

I leaned forward and buried my face in my hands. A few tears burned their way past my squeezed-shut eyes.

I can't invite you in. It's too ugly.

Unbidden, truth rose up in front of me as piercing as a high C. Like a car wreck on the side of the road, the memories demanded that I look.

Jason had suggested an abortion and then dropped out of my life. I'd let Lena think he was the supreme bad guy all this time. But I had no intention of having a baby.

I could still remember the smells of rubbing alcohol and anti-septic soap, the hushed, library tones of the clinic lobby, and the studied gentleness of the nurse who examined me.

"You must have a touch of flu. Or maybe we should do a strep test. You're running a fever, so we can't do the procedure today."

The procedure. I shuddered. The procedure I fully intended to have. The procedure that would have scraped Clara from my womb and ended her existence.

A week later, my fever was gone, and I planned to head back to the clinic. But that afternoon, one of my professors asked me to stay after a performance clinic. He reamed me out for my inadequate progress. "I recommend you transfer to a teaching program. It's kinder to tell you up front that you don't have a future in professional performance."

Pain and confusion chased me back to my dorm room. My pain at Jason's rejection was suddenly shown up for the imposter it was. That wasn't real pain. Not like this. Humiliation twisted me and doubled me over.

I ran to the bathroom and retched, coughing and crying. Then I sat on the cold floor, hugging my knees, sure that my life was over. My gut ached from the bout of heaving, and I rubbed it.

As my hand moved over my stomach—still completely flat and hiding any hint of the baby inside—I realized I had a way out. A way to save my pride.

I could leave Juilliard and raise my child. I'd be the poor abandoned woman. The sympathetic victim. I'd be the heroic single mother, putting her child before her artistic aspirations. Most importantly, I would not be thought of as a second-rate musician. No one would ever have to know that I had failed.

Yet, here I was, sixteen years later, trapped in time like this towering old cathedral. I lifted my head and looked up toward the seventy-five-foot ceiling. My smallness made me cringe. I couldn't keep carrying the weight of my lies. I'd never tell Clara I had nearly ended her life. But I needed to be honest with her about the rest. She blamed herself for my sidetracked life. She wondered about a father who didn't try to contact her.

But would the ugly truth make her reject me? This huge cathedral's God surely did.

CHAPTER

Tremolo: The art of performing or singing the same note over and over very quickly, executed most commonly but not exclusively on bowed string instruments. Tremolo may be measured or unmeasured and has the effect of adding motion to the sound.

Florists invaded the church to decorate for the afternoon wedding. I fled the building, but the searing glimpse of my past chased after me. Instead of heading to my car, I legged it across the bridge over the nearby freeway to the Minneapolis Sculpture Garden. Acres of green created a backdrop for a variety of modern art pieces, while also asserting an oasis of nature in the heart of the city. The gigantic Spoonbridge and Cherry sculpture looked even more ridiculously happy than usual. I frowned at the Minneapolis landmark, feeling much too dark to appreciate the whimsy. I wound my way past several other contemporary statues and entered the humid air of the conservatory. I hoped that the heavy, cloying warmth beneath the palm trees would wrap around the wounds I'd ripped open.

A bench gave me a safe place to mull.

I'm horrible. Wanting her dead. Then using her as an excuse. I glanced up at the sky through the wealth of windows. *I'm pure evil. I don't know if you exist, but if you do, I'm sorry.*

The huge glass fish in the center of the building sparkled as it seemed to leap upward toward the light. How had the sculptor captured so much movement? I suddenly thought of Clara's favorite childhood book, *Runaway Bunny.* When the baby bunny ran away to become a fish, the mommy bunny became a fisherman.

"Are you really there?" I whispered. "Do you want to catch me? Even when you know the truth?"

The warm silence was oddly comforting, and I stayed, allowing my breathing to slow and my mind to quiet.

Okay, if you're there, and you can forgive me, you'll need to show me. And I'm not gonna look for you at Lena's church. Sorry, but if that's how I have to know you, it won't work. Oh, and here's the deal. If I start letting you be part of my life, I expect your help with some things. Clara. The symphony's problems. Stuff like that. Oh, and I wouldn't mind being a little taller.

I dusted my hands, hitched up the strap of my shoulder bag, and pushed to my feet, satisfied I'd made my expectations clear in case anyone was listening.

That evening, I wound my way from the stage door toward the lobby. Dawn had called me during the week asking me to make reservations for herself and her seven-year-old urchin, Stephie. I wanted to check at the box office to be sure her tickets were waiting for her.

Megan paced the small room, cell phone pressed to her ear. "Bad enough when some of our foundations got twitchy, but now our reservations are down. What? No. No, I don't think we're going to bounce back."

I ducked back around the wall and waited in the hallway, hoping her voice would carry.

"What *can* we do? Cutbacks. And if things don't turn around soon, we'll have to close." Megan issued a few sighs and murmured agreements. "Yeah. Yeah. Bye." Her phone snapped shut, and my restraint snapped at the same time.

I stormed into the box office, a modern Hans Brinker trying to stem the flood of disaster with my finger in the dyke. "Megan, you can't close the symphony. We have to find out who cut Stefan's bowstrings. Can you get keys to the lockers? I'm sure if we searched them we could get to the bottom of this."

Megan wrinkled her forehead and her eyes scanned me up and down. "Who are you?"

"Amy. The new second flute."

"Oh, right. Welcome to the symphony."

I didn't miss the cynical edge in her tone. "Are the police investigating? Once the sabotage stops, we can rebuild the community's trust. Maybe we should bring in the F.B.I."

"Look, Annie—"

"Amy."

"Right. Look, the board is doing everything they can to support the orchestra. Why don't you concentrate on making music? Everything is being taken care of."

Was it my short stature that made everyone say things as if they were patting me on the head? I wanted to scream. But my screaming pitch was a quarter tone off-key, and I hated the sound.

Megan bustled past me and out the door. I checked the envelopes and made sure Dawn's tickets were waiting for her. Then I slumped onto a stool, glaring at the reservation rack. Tonight would be a slim house. We still had a good clump of season-ticket holders to fill out the main seating, but attendance was definitely low for a Saturday night.

Had all the mishaps caused this? Or was it the weeks of performing away from Symphonic Hall that had disrupted the flow? I rubbed my temples.

"Headache?" Lena stepped into the room and reached out to massage my shoulders.

I rolled my head from side to side, willing the stiffness away. "Still mad at me for snooping around last night?"

"Yes." She squeezed my neck muscles with unnecessary force. "I know you're worried, but you've got to let it go. *Que sera, sera.*"

I shrugged her hands away and turned to face her. "Easy for you to say." Then I took a slow breath. "Can I ask you something?"

"Sure."

"Have you been . . . you know . . . praying that the symphony won't go under?" I kept my gaze to the floor. If she got an eager, zealous expression, I didn't want to see it.

"Yeah," she said quietly. "I have."

"Then why? I mean, if He's there . . . is that out of His league? Or what?"

"He does exist, and His power is limitless. I believe that with my whole heart. But that doesn't mean He always gives us what we want."

I looked up and frowned at her. "Then what's the point?"

"The point?"

"Look, I understand quid pro quo. You fix up your life, He does stuff for you. If that isn't going to happen, what's the point?"

She smiled. "First of all, we can't fix up our lives. That's part of why we need Him. And second, He doesn't want quid pro quo. He wants a relationship."

My stomach did an uncomfortable twist. I glanced at my watch. "We better get ready."

"Yep." She gave me a quick hug, which I endured (since she was my best friend, and she hadn't pounced on me with a bunch of preaching) but as I followed her down the hall, I decided the whole exploring-God thing was a mistake. I understood cause and effect, crime and punishment, trade-offs. Relationships were much fuzzier. They'd never been my strong suit. If Lena was right and God wanted a relationship with me, things could get messy.

Stefan followed through on his threat and didn't show up. Because David had some notice, he was ready to take over as concertmaster and played well. In fact, he seemed to be in smug good spirits, almost as if he'd expected to move into the first chair all along. When I wasn't playing, I studied him, wondering if he could have caused the damage to Stefan.

Nothing went wrong, other than the many vacant seats in the audience. Dawn dragged her freckled daughter backstage to find me afterward, gushed about the music, and peppered me with questions while I tried to slip away and get home.

My mood wasn't helped when Snake walked up and stood near us as he rolled up a cable. He listened to Dawn bombard me with comments and smirked at me from behind her back. I was tempted to stick out my tongue at him, but if he reciprocated, he might reveal studs on his, and that was something I didn't want to see. If her second-grader hadn't started yawning and rubbing her eyes, Dawn would have kept me there until midnight. One little sewing meeting at Janie's house, and I was suddenly supposed to be best pals with all the cheerleading moms?

Grumpiness shuffled along with me, like Pigpen's cloud in the Peanuts comic strip. My mood tailed me out to the parking lot and filled my car's interior as I drove home. Nothing was going right. Megan's phone conversation made it clear the symphony was on the way to closing, and that would effectively close my hopes for a career. I'd toyed with the idea that if I "got religion," God might turn some things around for me, but Lena said it didn't work that way. And even without any promised brownie points from the Big Guy Upstairs, my conscience was insisting I come clean with Clara, which was not a conversation I was looking forward to.

I fumbled with my CDs and popped in Barber's *Adagio for Strings*. The funereal music was the perfect accompaniment to my drive home.

The living room was patterned with menacing shadows as I approached the pool of light near the fireplace. Clara looked young and fragile sitting with her back to me, her long brunette hair holding a sheen that reminded me of a cello.

I didn't know how to begin. Fear of her reaction wedged in my throat. "I'm sorry I haven't talked to you about this sooner." I finally forced the words out.

She didn't turn, didn't respond.

I stepped closer to Clara. "I didn't think you needed to know more than a few broad strokes, but I was wrong." I had to speak loudly now, over the sound of violin music. The muscles in Clara's back flexed and softened, her spine tall. "Clara, are you listening?"

She continued to ignore me, so I walked around the chair to confront her.

"Clara, I'm trying to tell you that it's not your fault. I'd decided to leave Juilliard anyway. I was failing. I didn't have the chops. Blast it, Clara, put down that violin."

Confusion rippled through me. Something wasn't making sense. Clara didn't play violin. We didn't own one.

Dark bangs snapped back off her face, as the bow continued to saw across the strings. She raised her eyes and gave me a coy smile. "You knew it couldn't last. Nothing good ever does."

I stumbled back a step. Clara's face had disappeared. Jason sat before me. "And you wanted to blame me all this time," he accused.

His fingers flew down the neck of his instrument, catching on one piercing note and holding it. "She'll never forgive you."

"Where is she? What have you done with her?"

Inexplicably, though his hand had stilled, the note continued until it filled my ears, my head, my world.

"Jason, she has to understand. I love her. I love her!" I shouted over the relentless tone.

He shook his head with regret. "You knew it wouldn't work." He tilted his head in a loving caress of his violin, and the piercing note grew.

I shot up from my pillow. My alarm droned a warning. Sunday morning. Time to go to the Basilica and face another opportunity to confront the persistent God that had been whispering to me, followed by the opportunity to make my nightmare come true.

Clara waited for me in the kitchen, munching a muffin and checking her e-mails.

"Good morning," I muttered, rubbing my neck.

She lifted a hand in careless greeting and resumed scrolling down the screen.

"Clara?"

She finally turned so I could see her. I walked closer and stared into her face, feeling a wave of relief. She was still Clara.

"Mom? Are you feeling okay? You look weird."

I turned away. "Did you eat the last muffin?"

"Yeah. So?"

"So, you could have waited for me. You could have shared."

She clacked a few keys and thrust to her feet. "Sorry."

Cold defensiveness sent a crack through the kitchen floor between us. What did it matter? There'd be a deeper gulf soon. "Are you wearing that?" Granted, her good jeans didn't have any rips, and her blouse covered everything important. But somehow I thought the Basilica would expect more.

This time she didn't bother to answer. "Let's go. We're late."

"Fine."

"Fine."

Yeah, this was going to be one terrific day.

We drove to St. Mary's in silence. When we climbed the wide stairs to the building, I paused to admire the stonework. Clara barely glanced at the breathtaking cathedral, sending an impatient glare my direction.

Inside, I found the choir room where we were gathering. The murmur of a large group of people speaking in unison carried from the sanctuary. The sound reminded me of a spooky movie, and I scowled at Peter, wishing he hadn't talked me into this.

"So this is your daughter." Peter strode forward like an old friend.

Grudgingly, I made the introductions. Clara brightened. "Mom's told me a lot about you."

My face warmed. I wished I were closer to my daughter so I could give her a warning kick.

Peter laughed. "I'm glad you came today. Teige's piece is remarkable. I hope you like it."

She shrugged. Then she turned to me. "See you later. I'll find a seat in the back."

I nodded absently, pulled my flute case from my bag, and preplayed my solo line in my mind.

"She gets like this," Clara said.

"Yeah. Musicians aren't easy to live with, are they?"

"Do you live with one?"

He laughed again. "Only myself."

I ignored them both and walked over to the rehearsal piano, where Teige was tugging at his suit jacket. I twisted the head joint onto my flute, tried a note, then twisted it again to adjust the tuning. "Can you give me an A?" I asked Teige.

By the time I was tuned, Clara had slipped away, and the choir members had all arrived. We warmed up with a few passages and reviewed a couple bits that had given us trouble yesterday. Teige looked at his watch.

"Okay, the mass is letting out. We can go up now. We take this back hallway. Follow me."

Suddenly I didn't want to walk back into the lofty space of domes, arches, pillars, stained glass, and God. I was a cancer patient terrified to be led into the CAT-scan room where all my tumors would be revealed. My knees locked, and I hugged my flute against my chest.

A hand touched the small of my back. Barely-there pressure. "Nerves?" Peter stood close enough behind me that I could feel his warmth.

"Of course not," I snarled. The irritation chased away my sudden panic and I was able to march after the choir and toward the sanctuary.

I heard Peter's low chuckle behind me, but as we stepped into the nave, I had the weird feeling soft laughter also filled the air above the altar.

CHAPTER

Dolce: A directive to a performer to play a certain passage sweetly, softly, with tender emotion.

With mental blinders, I shut out everything except Teige's direction and the music on my stand. Playing in my lower register, the rich melody introduced the opening movement. The men sang with deep yearning. A vibration answered from the core of my bones. I didn't simply play the plea, "Come, Holy Spirit." I embodied it. I prayed it.

When my part finished, I sat in concert position, straight-backed, still, with my flute in my lap. The cantata continued, and I braced myself against the impact it was having on my spirit. Then my control slipped, and I let my gaze travel to the rows of people facing us. Most seemed as transfixed by the power of the music as I was. Near the back a baby cried. A middle-aged woman in the front pew rummaged in her purse. If her cell phone rang, I'd walk over and snatch it from her hand and grind it under my heel.

Then my eyes caught on a white-haired grandma on my side of the church about three rows back. Instead of watching Peter as he stroked fire from his violin, she stared up at the altar. A light smile played across her lips, and a glow of reverence softened the wrinkles on her face. She nodded once, and her smile grew. She wasn't merely listening to the music. She was having a conversation.

Relationship. This must be what it looks like to have a relationship with God.

I wondered what she was hearing, what she was asking. I doubted she was telling God to make her taller. A wriggle of embarrassment tickled my back as I thought of the demands I'd sent skyward yesterday. My smallness impressed itself upon me again. Latin words floated upward, and part of my heart wanted to float, too. Goose bumps lifted on the skin of my arms. All this God-stuff was really getting to me.

I'd heard a conductor back in college once describe music as a prayer. He meant it—and I understood it—as a sort of touching the divine within ourselves.

But what if?

What if there was a spiritual being beyond human? What if our music was a way of speaking our hearts to that being?

I stopped fighting the stirring inside my rib cage and let the music guide me through feelings of exultation and triumph. The story might all be a myth, but if so, it was a grand myth, and I let myself enjoy the beauty of the art. The power of the music multiplied because of the audience. The enraptured faces shared the experience with the musicians and made this more than a performance.

Relationship. Music means more when the audience hears it.

The circle of giving and receiving captured my imagination. Maybe this was what Lena meant about God wanting a relationship.

As the last note echoed through the church, an indrawn hush held for several long seconds. Then the audience applauded, and the spell was broken. People hurried back to their real lives, the choir members chatted, and altar boys moved in to clear away music stands and prepare for the next mass. Clara came forward and waited while I cleaned my flute.

Peter patted Teige's back and then strode away from the piano toward us. "Would you like to grab some lunch together?"

"Great idea," Clara said.

"No," I blurted.

Two pairs of eyes turned toward me. Two sets of eyebrows flattened with disappointment.

No easy lie sprang to mind. "I mean, thanks, anyway. I need to talk to Clara about something. We're going straight home."

Peter gave a tight nod. "Of course. I'm sure it's hard to find enough family time. Wouldn't want to intrude. Thanks for filling in today." He turned and walked away before I could answer.

"Way to go, Mom," Clara complained. "What's with you lately?"

"What's wrong with a mom wanting to spend some time with her daughter?"

"Glad you feel that way," she said as we walked out into early June sunshine. "Joy's having a special parent meeting tomorrow night. It was just for the cheerleaders and parents involved in the big conference." She grinned. "Now that includes us."

"Okay." I fished my car keys from the bottom of my music bag. "That's fine."

Clara pressed the back of her hand against my forehead. "Are you coming down with something?"

I brushed her hand away. Clara was the most important thing in my life. I was about to risk her love by telling her truth that she needed—truth that painted me as a coward, a liar. But as fear flooded in and tempted me to change my mind, the strains of the cantata played through my memory and somehow fed me strength.

Maybe some of that Holy Spirit everyone had asked for in the music had actually drawn closer.

We got in the car and I turned to face her. "I'm ready to talk to you about your father."

She nodded slowly. "That bad, huh?"

"What do you mean?"

"You look sick. You've been crabby—I mean more than usual. It's gotta be bad."

"No. Well sort of. Let's go home."

"Fine." She reached forward and turned on the radio, finding a station of pop music. No wonder they called it bubblegum. It was as annoying as something sticking to my shoe. I refused to rise to the provocation. Instead I forced a smile and bopped my head in time to the music. That sight was so frightening that, after a few miles, Clara turned off the radio.

Neither of us was hungry, so by mutual consent we passed through the kitchen and settled in our chairs in the front room. Clara watched me warily.

"You're right. I've been tense lately. I need to explain."

"Let's hear it."

Now I couldn't speak. My brain froze, I felt like I was swallowing my tongue.

Clara scooted her chair closer and rested a hand on my arm. "Mom, it's all right. I love you."

Was she *trying* to torture me? Now my eyes began to sting.

"Jason Carrolli. Last I heard he was coprincipal violin with an orchestra in Brazil."

Small darts appeared between Clara's eyebrows. "What?"

"He doesn't know about you. I mean, he knew I was pregnant, but he assumed . . . I mean, he wanted . . . Anyway, he broke up with me long before you were born, and we lost touch after I left Juilliard."

I stared at the vacant fireplace, unable to watch the effect my words had on her. But I still heard the sharp intake of breath.

"And another thing. You think I gave up my dreams to take care of you. You can't keep blaming yourself. My music career was dead before I left Juilliard. Before you arrived."

"Dead?" Her throat sounded thick.

"The prof in charge of my program said I didn't have the chops. That's why I left. He told me I wouldn't make it in performance. But Jason . . . he made it."

Now words rushed to break free. "I didn't think you needed to know him. I wanted to protect you. He assumed I'd . . . get rid of you. And he didn't have room in his life for relationships. It was nothing but music for him. But you're right. You deserve to know. You can ask me whatever you want." I finally dared to look at her.

"Brazil?" Her voice cracked. "If you didn't stay in touch, how do you know?"

"Lena would sometimes see his name in her orchestra newsletters."

"Lena knew? All this time?"

"Not about me washing out. No one knew that. But yeah, she met Jason when we were dating, so of course she knew he was your father."

She pushed her chair back and stood up, swaying slightly.

"Sweetie, I'm sorry. I thought if you knew him, you'd want him instead of me. I didn't want him messing things up. Our life. I wanted you to myself."

"So you made the choice. For him. For me. If he had wanted to know me—" Her voice choked off.

I stood and reached out for her.

She held up a hand and shook her head. She opened her mouth, but after a tight breath in, closed it again. Then she turned and walked to the stairs. She didn't run. Didn't cry out. She moved like a ghost floating from my presence.

I wanted to run and grab her—make her talk to me, but I feared that my arms would go right through her and she would disappear completely. Couldn't she at least turn her head? Look at me? If I could see her eyes, I'd have hope.

But she didn't look my direction again. Carefully controlled, she stepped up each stair and out of my sight.

It would have been easier if she'd cried, or screamed, or yelled at me—anything to purge the mixed-up feelings tangled like barbed wire between us. I sank to my knees on the floor and rested my forehead on the cushion of her chair. It was over. I'd hurt the one person I never wanted to hurt. By my secrets. By my revelations. I couldn't win. A low groan tore from my throat. I clasped my hands over my mouth to stifle the sobs that wanted to escape. My body shook in silence.

After several minutes, I lifted my head and looked across the room toward my cabinet of flutes. I dragged myself to my feet, crossed the floor, opened the glass-fronted door, and reached out for my Pearl. My hand stopped inches away. The magnetism that normally pulled me toward my flute with inexorable force had lost its charge. I waited for something—some tug of longing, some familiar comfort. Instead, my hand withdrew, empty. A deeper level of hollowness sucked me downward.

I looked up the stairs. Complete silence glared down at me. Clara deserved time to process what I'd told her. I couldn't go running up there to seek reassurance, and I was the last person she needed comfort from right now. I slumped my way to the kitchen and made a cup of tea that tasted flat and stale. Instead of drinking it, I stared into the liquid.

That's where Clara found me an hour later. "I'm going to Ryan's." She wasn't asking permission.

"Okay." I looked up at her for clues. Was she crushed? Was she excited by the new information about her father? Did she despise me? Did she understand why I hadn't told her before?

She grabbed her purse, snugged a baseball cap over her hair, and reached for the back door. Her eyes still avoided mine.

I couldn't read her at all. "Are you all right? Should we—"

Again, she lifted one hand. A brief shake of her head was all she gave me before she slipped out the door. I heard a car pull into the alley. A door opened and closed and the engine revved quietly before disappearing.

My hands clenched around the mug of tea. My arms shook with a desire to fling it across the room. Instead, I played a modulating series of thirds in my mind until I could control the urge. Then I placed the cup in the sink and picked up the phone. "Lena? I told her."

"You did? Are you okay? Should I come over?"

My voice came out flat and calm. "No, I'm fine. . . ."

Half an hour later, I was sobbing, while Lena held me, rocking in a maternal rhythm she had picked up over the years. "It's okay. You did the right thing. Shhh. Just give her time. You'll be all right." We sat on the kitchen floor, her back pressed against a cupboard. I kept ending up on the floor. Somehow the weight of my pain dragged me straight down without the niceties of using furniture to support me.

Over and over she murmured soothing words. She hadn't seen me fall apart since college, when I told her I was pregnant and Jason had dumped me. I didn't let friends see me cry. And this was beyond crying. This was a Chernobyl-sized meltdown.

My hatred for feeling vulnerable finally reasserted itself, and I took a deep shuddering breath and pulled away from Lena. "I'm okay now. Want some tea?" I jumped to my feet, swiping at my wet cheeks.

"Tea?" Lena blinked up at me. "Um, sure."

"Stop looking at me like I'm loony."

Lena stood and pulled out a kitchen chair. "You? Loony?"

I sniffed. "Okay, so I've had a lot on my mind, and this pushed me over the top. I'm done now. No more hysterics."

"Amy, it's okay. You've seen me cry plenty of times."

I flicked on the burner under the teakettle. "Yeah, but that's you."

She raised her eyebrows. "Oh."

"I didn't mean it like that." I sat across from her. "I guess I've been holding this in for a while."

Her smile was soft. "I guess."

"There's something else."

"Go ahead."

I studied the scratches in the tabletop, tracing them with one finger as I told her the rest. The clinic. The planned abortion. The fever that postponed my plan for a week. I'd had enough of crying, so I forced myself to keep my voice level and calm. But I couldn't look at her.

When I finished, the teakettle gave a feeble whistle and spit some water onto the stove. I shut it off and sat down again, not bothering to get out cups or tea bags.

Lena's eyes were wide with sorrow, but held none of the revulsion that I had expected. "And you never told anyone?"

I shrugged. "But it proves it, doesn't it? Proves that I don't deserve her. And that I need to stay away from that God of yours."

"Or it proves He was looking out for both of you. He protected you both from your decision. And He keeps reaching out for you."

"Yeah, so He can hold my feet to the fire for what I almost did."

"Or so He can give you peace."

I jumped up, yanked open a cupboard door, and slammed two mugs onto the table. "What kind of tea do you want?"

"Whatever you're having."

I pulled out several boxes. The decision was too much for me, so I tossed them all on the table.

Lena stood and walked around the table. "Sit down before you break something." She coaxed me into my chair, poured the hot water, and chose a tea bag for each of us. Fragrant steam comforted my raw eyes and nose.

"Has it worked?" I asked between sips.

"Has what worked?"

"God. You were always pretty happy. Has this made you even happier?" I heard the sour tone in my voice but couldn't pull it back.

"I guess. But that isn't why I got interested in God. It's because of the questions."

"What questions?"

"You know. . . . Why am I here? What's the purpose of everything? How can music be so incredibly beautiful? Who thought it up . . . ? Those sorts of questions."

"And now you have all the answers?"

She laughed. "Right, that's me. Mrs. Guru." She tucked a strand of hair behind her ear. "Come on. You know it's not like that. There'll always be more questions. I'm just saying—" She stared into space. "Here's an idea. Ask Him for help."

"Even if I'm not sure He exists?"

"You can ask Him to give you faith. To help you become sure. To get to know who He is."

I sighed. "That's all I need right now. I have enough problems. By the way, I told Clara she could talk to you about Jason."

She nodded. "I don't have a lot to tell her, but I do see his name sometimes. It'll give her a place to start. I think he's been in South America the last few years."

"Brazil."

She gave me a sharp look. "But you haven't kept track."

"Go home. I need to get ready for tonight's concert. And . . . thanks."

"Anytime. That's what friends are for."

"If you start singing, I'll have to slug you."

She laughed and headed out. I stared through the window after her van pulled away. In spite of the fact that nothing had been solved, I felt lighter. Lena had heard the worst about me and was able to forgive me.

If she could forgive you, why don't you believe that I can?

That quiet presence again. Lately it felt less like a poltergeist messing things up in my life and more like the strength and flame that the cantata had proclaimed. Maybe Lena was right and He could care about me . . . forgive me. But could I let Him? And could I ever forgive myself?

CHAPTER

Syncopation: Deliberate upsetting of the meter or pulse of a composition by means of a temporary shifting of the accent to a weak beat or an offbeat.

Preliminary events begin Friday afternoon. The girls have to check in by one o'clock, so the bus will leave school property at noon." Joy bounced across the front of the classroom like a motivational speaker. "Girls, you'll want to eat before you get here. And bring all your gear."

How much gear could a few cheerleaders have? Apparently quite a bit, since the school was renting a separate trailer to accompany them to the convention center.

"Do pom-poms need lots of room to stay fluffy?" I whispered to Janie Biederbock.

She shushed me and adjusted a headband that held her honey-blond hair off her face. We both turned our attention back to Coach Joy.

"Parents, come early to get good seats—especially for the final events on Saturday. It'll be crowded. We'll be in Section F. First come first served. Those of you with booster sweatshirts, be sure to wear them. Or at least wear school colors."

"Red and gray," Janie whispered to me.

"I knew that."

"Right."

Janie of the perky flip and Laura Ashley living room could do sarcasm. I might have to decide to like her.

"Hey, I'm all about school spirit. I'm having my flute painted red and gray for the symphony performances next weekend."

She giggled. "Clara will love that."

Across the room my daughter jostled with Ashley and Brittany. Her eyes were bright. No one else would have guessed how withdrawn and subdued she'd been around me.

Yesterday, when she'd gotten home from Ryan's, I'd hoped for some indication of what she needed from me. A clue to what she felt. Instead, she was chillingly polite. "No, I don't feel like talking." "Yes, I'm fine." "No, I don't feel like reading tonight." "Don't forget the meeting tomorrow night."

She didn't slam her door. But it closed with the deliberate strength of a bank vault.

I didn't even have the luxury of a concert tonight to distract me. Instead I was once again in the surreal world of booster parents, fund-raisers, and handsprings.

"Now we have a treat for all of you. If you'll all follow us down to the gym, you'll get a preview performance of one of the competition cheers we'll be doing next weekend."

The girls squealed and started jumping as if they were on springs.

"Wow, they've got a lot of energy." Dawn Hanson followed Janie and me at a more sedate pace down the hall. "Hey, Stephie is still talking about the concert. You made quite an impression on her."

"What's it like?" Janie stopped short, letting other parents pass us. "Doing something special? Something that matters? Having a gift?"

The question confused me. "It's like . . . being a misfit."

Janie and Dawn laughed as if I'd told a clever joke. "No, really," Janie said.

I followed the sound of clapping and stomping ahead of us and started walking again. "Really. I eat, drink, and breathe music. I don't know how to French braid hair. I don't keep up with the dirty laundry. I make a mess out of parenting. Half the time I'm making mistakes and the other half I'm trying to clean up after them."

Janie threw an arm around my shoulder. "Just like the rest of us."

"Don't give me that. You're like the queen bee of moms."

"Oh, honey, you've gotta hang out with us more often. We're all just muddling through. That's the *definition* of parenting."

Suddenly the domestic-diva moms didn't seem so annoying. I still didn't fit in, but I forgot to think about that. Instead, I clapped and cheered, genuinely impressed by the gymnastic routine that the cheerleading team performed.

However, when Clara did a series of cartwheels, I cringed. She could sprain her fingers, or her wrist. How would she play piano then? I hadn't surrendered my hope that one day she'd get focused about her musical talent.

The demonstration ended, and Brittany and Ashley bounded over to their moms. Clara followed in their wake. She glanced at me as if gauging my reaction, but then looked away.

"That was great." I stabbed my fist in the air and tried to copy Janie in her ability to enthuse. On me, the move looked like a parody.

Clara narrowed her eyes. "Thanks." Her lips flattened.

"Did you see that Jessie almost dropped Rowen when we did the throw?" Ashley's words spit past her braces at turbo-speed.

Clara lit up. "I know. I just about died. And I totally blew the reindeer jump."

"You did not."

Clara and her friends moved away from us, chattering in the lilting cadence of teen girls, with high-pitched upswings at the end of sentences. Something twisted under my ribs. I pressed my hands against my diaphragm as if I were fighting to hold back hiccups. Maybe pressure could stop the bruising pain. Clara's exuberant energy around her friends emphasized the contrast to her bland tolerance around me. Would I ever regain her trust?

"You okay?"

Janie was too observant by half.

"Sure. I've just had a lot on my mind. The symphony's been having some problems."

Dawn edged closer. "Yeah. I read that it's going under. That would be a shame. But hey, then you'd have time to do more teaching. Stephie is thinking about taking up the flute again."

I ground my teeth. As if a seven-year-old student would be adequate comfort after losing my dream job. My moment of bonding with the cheerleader moms dissolved.

"Clara!" I yelled. "Time to go."

The next day when I arrived for rehearsal, Sarah pulled into the parking lot right before me. I found a space as far from her as possible and waited in the car to give her a head start into Symphonic Hall. My strategy didn't work.

A sharp knock on my window made me jump. "Hi, Amy." Sarah scanned the humble interior of my Saturn and wrinkled her narrow nose.

Sighing, I pushed the door open and scrambled out. "I'm coming."

"How'd the churchy thing go? I felt so bad when I couldn't help Peter out."

"It was fine." I refused to let her rub it in that I was always a last-resort choice. "Did you have a good day off yesterday?"

She led the way toward the entrance with mincing steps. "Sure did. I made good use of it, too. Got tapes and résumés sent out to four orchestras."

I skidded to a stop. "What?"

"Oh, come on. You're new, but you aren't stupid. Read the writing on the wall."

"You really think it's hopeless?"

She yanked the door open. "Of course it is. And Megan told me the board is making your boyfriend the scapegoat."

"My *what*? Who . . . what . . . ?" Did she still think Stefan and I were an item?

"Everything started going wrong when they appointed him as head conductor." She smirked. "I knew he was trouble when he fought to get you hired. We had three other candidates with lots more experience."

Not Stefan. Peter. *Not that again.* I trailed after her, sputtering as I tried to put two words together.

"Well, it doesn't matter now, does it? He'll be out of work soon, too." She smiled again and then hurried on toward the stage.

I forked my hands into my hair and shook my head.

"Need an aspirin?" Snake slouched in a doorway and grinned at me. "Not planning on snooping around after hours today, are you?"

I huffed, spun on my heel, and stalked down the hall. The announcement board snagged my attention. Staring at my name on the list of solos eased the throbbing behind my eyes. My dream was crumbling to dust, but a thrill of joy shot into my veins like a drug when I saw my solo listed for the summer repertory.

A fluorescent printout caught my eye. *Attention. Due to shortfalls in funding, the board is scheduling additional benefit programs. Please add these to the schedule.* A complex listing of small ensembles, solos, as well as extra full-symphony performances covered the page.

Megan was clearly hard at work setting up events to coax patrons out of more money. *Good for her.* I pulled out my pocket calendar to jot the new dates in.

I scribbled down the first event without thinking. Next Saturday at the Minneapolis Institute of Arts. My solo would be featured. I couldn't wait to casually mention that to Sarah.

Then I stared at my calendar in horror. The cheerleading competition. Saturday's final event was scheduled at eight. Exactly when I was supposed to be playing for the newly scheduled benefit event.

"No. No, no, no." I moaned.

"Something wrong?" Peter appeared at my side.

"No. I mean, yes. This new event . . . I thought we had this weekend off. Never mind. I'll figure it out."

"I'm sure you will." He smiled and leaned a shoulder against the board. "Have I mentioned how much I appreciate your willingness to jump in and help? You wouldn't believe how many musicians refuse to add anything to their schedule. I knew when I met you that you had commitment."

I swallowed hard. "It's what I want to do." It's all I *ever* wanted to do. I wouldn't say anything to jeopardize that now.

"Did Clara like the cantata?"

"Yeah. I guess." Why was he still standing there? The sleeves of his blue denim shirt were rolled up, and he had ink smudges on his hands.

"You didn't ask her?"

"We kind of had other things to talk about."

He gave a slow nod. "Everything all right? You seemed . . . upset on Sunday."

I had a sudden picture of myself pouring out my worries, strong arms reaching out to hold me, gentle lips kissing my hair and whispering that everything would be okay. Heat raced across my skin. Horrified, I slammed down a metal door on that image.

"Everything's fine. I've gotta warm up."

"Sure. But if you need . . ." He dropped his chin and cleared his throat. "I mean . . ."

"Yeah. Thanks." I hurried away. Even sitting by Sarah was appealing now. Anything to get away from the confusing non-conversation and the weird feelings it stirred.

The pre-rehearsal chatter hovered at a low volume on stage. Leonard stood up in the trombone section. "Why are conductors' hearts in high demand for transplants? They've had so little use." The answering laughter was halfhearted.

Vicki raised her bow from the cello section. "What's the definition of a gentleman? Someone who knows how to play trombone and doesn't."

This time a few more musicians chuckled, with Leonard's chortles the loudest of all.

Another of the trombonists tugged his stand close and gave Leonard a pointed stare. "Or someone who knows all the musician jokes and doesn't tell them."

"Poor Leonard and Vicki," Sarah whispered toward my ear. "Hard for them to find two openings in the same orchestra. I'm lucky I can pull up stakes and land anywhere."

I brushed my hand across my ear as if batting away a mosquito.

Sarah laughed low in her throat. "Oh, sorry. I forgot. You've got a kid. You probably don't have many options, either, do you?"

I turned in my chair and squared off with her. "The symphony isn't closing. The only thing that would ruin us now is if we all start believing it's hopeless."

"I hadn't pegged you for a Pollyanna."

She had it all wrong. I didn't have a Pollyanna curl on my head. I wasn't driven by optimism but by desperation. I had to believe the symphony would survive this.

Peter tapped his baton on his music stand, and conversation broke off. "Ladies and gentlemen, shall we begin with the Bartok?" Musicians pulled music from their folders without enthusiasm. The Hungarian portion of the Around the World theme wasn't a favorite.

Stefan marched in, stirring some whispers. He ignored the reaction and began tuning us. Had he changed his mind and decided to help us all get back on track? Or had he been arm-twisted? What coercion had they used to bring him back? His face gave nothing away. He smiled at the horns, winked at the cellists, murmured a comment to the violin section. If he was worried about further sabotage, he gave no hint of that fear.

When the orchestra was ready—toes on a cliff's edge like a hang glider about to take flight—Peter set his baton down on his stand. "Before we begin, I want to address some concerns."

Although Peter showed passion in his conducting, he was never mushy or emotional in his leadership. I liked that about him. But now he looked like Papa Conductor about to reassure his children.

I bit my lip. Couldn't we just get on with rehearsal? It was the best cure for what ailed us.

"As you are all well aware, we've taken a few hits in the press in recent weeks. But we don't play for the press. We've lost a big grant. But that isn't our worry. The board and development staff will find solutions. Our job is to make amazing music. Breathtaking music. When you walk onto this stage you leave any concerns at the door. There isn't room for distraction, for nerves, for apathy." His gaze lingered a bit longer on the first violins. "Now, let's get on with it."

In spite of my disdain for win-one-for-the-Gipper pep talks, I felt strangely heartened. Peter wouldn't have made this speech if the symphony closing was a foregone conclusion. I clung to that hope throughout rehearsal.

By contrast, Sarah grew more out-of-sorts. She criticized my vibrato and mocked my phrasing—all normal behavior. But I could tell her heart wasn't in it. The cause for her bad mood revealed itself during our break. Sarah's posture tightened when Stefan strolled past us with Vicki. The two were deep in conversation about the string quartet schedule and appeared oblivious to their effect on Sarah.

When we prepared to resume the rehearsal, Sarah's tone turned shrill as she played a coda. I echoed her, but with the round, full tone appropriate for the Strauss waltz. She didn't comment, and I realized that she wasn't listening. Her eyes narrowed as she watched Vicki adjusting the bridge on her cello. I glanced behind us to where the brass players were entering to take their places. Leonard slouched in his chair, idly moving his slide in and out while his trombone rested in his lap. The bags under his eyes were no longer hidden by the round cheeks of a gregarious smile. Even when other musicians settled within earshot, he didn't crack any jokes. He just stared with basset hound sadness in the direction of the cello section.

As we left the stage after practice, I stayed close to Sarah. "I have a conflict with the Saturday gala. Would you be able to play the Takemitsu solo that night?"

"Sorry. I'm not scheduled, so I won't be there. Other plans." She tucked her flute under her arm. "Call Megan," she tossed over her shoulder as she hurried away.

I found a quiet corner and pulled out my cell phone. I dialed the orchestra offices and after a few transfers, reached Megan. "Hi, this is Amy Johnson. I saw the new schedule, and I have a conflict with the Saturday night gala."

"Hold on." Papers shuffled and static attacked my ear. "I'm back. Who is this?"

"Amy Johnson. Second flute. I'm scheduled to do a solo Saturday."

"Right, right. I've got it here. Congratulations. Peter said it's an unusual piece and we're lucky you know it."

"Yeah. I'm honored. But I have a problem. I have another commitment—"

"No, you don't."

"I'm sorry?"

"I've got your sheet in front of me. You didn't list this Saturday as a conflict."

"Well, this came up since then, and—"

"No way." Impatience edged her tone. "We've got one of our biggest corporate donors coming, and he especially loves Japanese composers. Why do you think we added it to the repertory? You're playing the Takemitsu."

"Can't one of the other—"

"No. Gotta run."

The dial tone drilled into my skull. My temples pounded. This was not good.

I hunched my shoulders and headed out to my car. *Always tackle the difficult passages of music first. Don't avoid it. You've got to tell Clara right away.*

In spite of my intention to get it over with, I drove well below the speed limit on the way home. When I walked in the back door, the first thing I saw was a strange man's back as he leaned into the pantry. Shock raced through me, but my instincts swooped in to help me. Chill calm took over, and I lowered my music bag silently. Glancing around, I spotted a tightly wrapped umbrella left on a hook by the back porch. I grabbed it in both hands and tiptoed toward the intruder.

"Hold it right there," I shouted in a gravelly voice.

The man spun to face me, and Clara gasped from behind him.

"Don't shoot. It's me." Ryan threw his hands up. He was a lot less menacing now that I could see his freckled face.

"Mom, what are you doing?" Clara tugged my weapon from my hands. "Do you take classes on ways to embarrass me?"

"What were *you* doing?" I countered.

She turned away to hang up the umbrella, so I looked at Ryan. His freckles darkened, and he stared at the floor.

"Ryan came over to hang out. Okay?"

I glared at the boy in question. "In the pantry?"

Clara sighed. "I was looking for some potato chips. He was . . . helping." She had the grace to blush.

"Look, I better get going. I promised Mom I'd mow the lawn today."

Clara made moon-eyes at him. "You don't have to—"

"Good idea, Ryan. See you later."

He grinned. "Nice to see you, Mrs. Johnson." Then he paused in front of Clara. "Call me." His hand touched her face, and she walked straight into him for a hug that looked far too easy and customary.

He escaped out the back door, and I planted fists on my waist. "Clara, I don't want you having boys here when I'm gone."

"He's a friend, all right? I thought you liked him." Then she dismissed my worries with a toss of her hair. "So how was rehearsal?"

The bandit in the pantry and the Lothario chasing my daughter had been a happy distraction. Now my headache rushed back. "Well, I've got some good news and some bad news."

CHAPTER

27

Sforzando: Sudden strong accent on a note or chord.

It was official. My daughter hated me. Oh, she lied about it persuasively, but I was no idiot.

Her exact response to my bad news was, "Mom, don't sweat it. You don't have to be there."

"But, sweetie, it's a big deal. I want to see you. I tried to get Sarah to cover, and I called Megan, and if—"

"Hey—" her lips twisted into a half smile—"at least you have a better average than my dad. He's never seen me in anything." She went into the pantry and came out with a bag of chips. "Of course, he might have tried, if he'd known about me." She tore the bag open. "But you didn't give him that choice, did you?"

After that surgical strike, she smiled benignly and fled the kitchen with her chips.

"Wait just a minute." I stomped after her. "He had a choice. When he found out I was pregnant."

"Just because he dumped you doesn't mean he wouldn't have wanted to know me . . . be part of my life."

"Trust me. He made his feelings clear."

"Trust you?" She dropped the bag of chips on the piano—even though I never allowed food near the cherished instrument. "That's the point, isn't it? I can't."

This time I didn't follow her when she left the room. I pulled out the music for the Takemitsu solo and started practicing. Let her chase down her reluctant father. See if he'd sew her cheerleading costumes and go to meetings and watch loud competitions. I might have my flaws as a mother, but I'd given birth. I'd nursed her, read to her, made a life for her.

I'd see her cheer on Friday night, but I wasn't going to risk my dream job to be at the finals on Saturday. She ought to understand the honor I'd been given. A virtuoso solo at the gala.

I overblew a harsh note across my mouthpiece. After a deep breath I pushed forward into the challenging intervals. The unsettling music matched my churning stomach. My life was fragmenting just like the melody line. Everything that had been held together in a cohesive chord was suddenly breaking away.

The phone rang, interrupting a soft low note. I ignored it, waiting for Clara to answer, but she didn't. When it stopped, I started the piece over, only to be interrupted by the ringer again. I marched into the kitchen and grabbed the receiver. "What?" I barked.

"Amy?"

I'd know that British accent anywhere. "Peter. Sorry. I was practicing. I get cranky when—What do you need?" *Drat.* I was sounding breathless again.

His low chuckle made me feel warm and off-balance, as if I'd had too much wine. "Megan said you had a problem with Saturday's concert. I wanted to tell you that if you're feeling insecure, don't be. If you can play the piece half as well as you did in the audition it'll be perfect."

Another liquid tingle moved up and down my spine. "Th-thanks." Should I tell him that wasn't the reason I had called Megan? What would he think if I told him the truth . . . that I had wanted to get out of the performance so I could go to the cheerleading competition?

"Good. Glad that's settled. You've . . ." He cleared his throat. "You've added a lot to the symphony."

"Well, thanks." Uncertainty numbed my tongue, and I couldn't think of anything else to say.

"Are you up for another lecture-demo next month? Megan has me booked to speak at the Duluth Music Festival."

"Duluth?"

"Right. Bit of a hike, but I can drive us both."

"Sarah's busy?" I said with a bit of inadvertent sourness.

He made a sound something between a *harrumph* and a sigh. "You're my first choice." I could hear his mood begin to stiffen. "But if you'd rather not, you are certainly under no obligation. It's not an official symphony event like the gala."

"No, no. I'd be happy to do it."

His words reminded me that this weekend's gala *was* a mandatory event. One I better not evade.

When I hung up, I felt a bit of adolescent giddiness, but I convinced myself it was about being respected as a musician by my conductor. It had nothing to do with the thought of driving up to the North Shore with Peter next month.

Wednesday afternoon we had a short rehearsal scheduled, then would break before our evening concert. The performance would be the last of the Three B's series and the last before our weekend off. Next week we'd begin performing our Summer Series.

I studied my suspects as they arrived for rehearsal. David Tanner settled into the second chair and frowned at his music. His silver hair probably reminded him each morning that he was at a place in his career where he'd risen as far as he could. He couldn't help but resent Stefan and the concertmaster's cavalier flamboyance. Vicki sat straighter and a small smile played across her face when Stefan walked onto the stage. She enjoyed playing quartet pieces with him, but was there more going on? Leonard sulked behind his trombone, his supply of jokes exhausted as the symphony's morale sagged under rumors of closing. Would he really risk harming the symphony just to get back at Stefan?

Stefan faced the violin section. He made a comment that I couldn't hear, and several women in his section giggled. I could well imagine the jilted second violin player from last season learning of his casual flirtations and plotting revenge. Sarah watched Stefan and sniffed to herself. She was meanspirited enough to be the culprit. And she didn't care about the symphony closing, since she had plans for moving on.

"Ready?" Peter barked at Stefan when he stepped onto the podium.

"Of course, Maestro." Stefan dripped sarcasm from the title, instead of the admiration the term was supposed to indicate.

Peter had refused to let Stefan out of his contract when a new offer came along. But was there enough animosity between the men for Peter to sabotage one of his own musicians? I hated to believe that was true.

Means, motive, and opportunity were what criminal investigators looked for. But so far I had too many choices. If Stefan's violin had sustained serious injury, I would have had to eliminate my entire suspect list. No true musician would damage an instrument. Oiled tuning pegs, nicked bow strings, altered sheet music, and even the clove oil all caused reversible damage. Almost on the level of pranks. Unfortunately, the effect they'd had on the symphony was much more serious.

I'd let myself become distracted lately. Wrestling with my conscience, allowing questions about God-stuff to roil around my brain, revealing the past to Clara, even learning how to navigate the cheerleading mom's world—all had kept me from solving this case. From now on, I'd be on high alert, Stefan's secret shadow.

When rehearsal ended, I made a beeline for the lanky, blond violinist. "I'm glad you decided to stay."

He gave me a benign smile. "*Ja*, well, my lawyer recommended. Not good to break my contract over what has happened."

"And the trouble seems to have stopped. Are you taking precautions?"

"Of course. I'm bringing only a secondary violin tonight."

"But you're doing the solo concerto."

He rubbed the back of his neck. "Yes, but I can't take the risk."

"I'm sorry." Sadness filled me at the thought of him being forced to use a lesser instrument. He created magic with his premier violin—especially in the solo concerto.

His formal nod accepted my compassion as his due. "Thank you. Congratulations on your solo this Saturday. You have unusual talent."

I beamed. "I'll need to rehearse every spare second to be ready."

"You'll be fine."

Gratified by his reassurance, I crossed the stage, smiling to myself. When I reached the wings, Peter was talking with Snake about positioning the special percussion for the new repertory.

"No hiding out after hours tonight, understand?" Snake said with a grin.

"Give it a rest," I snapped.

Peter didn't say anything, but I could feel his thoughtful gaze bore into my back as I walked away. Let him think what he wanted. He'd thank me once I solved the case.

I kept my detective radar finely tuned that night. I hovered near Stefan as much as possible, earning annoyed glares from several women in the orchestra. Megan buzzed around backstage while we prepared to go on. I heard her comment to Peter, "We have a good house tonight. Let's get back on track." Then she hurried over to Stefan. "The *Pioneer Press* sent someone to do a feature on you. Keep it upbeat. They'll take a few photos during intermission. Talk up your solo, all right? And say something reassuring."

"Of course." He traced a flourish in the air with his bow. "I know the game."

"Places, places." Our stage manager, Chris, snapped at our heels like a terrier, and we took our places on stage.

The first half of the concert flew by. My stomach still knotted, and each number left me breathless. But I had begun to feel at home in Symphonic Hall. I belonged here. Even Sarah couldn't convince me otherwise.

During the intermission, I watched from nearby when the reporter directed her photographer to get a few pictures of Stefan in the rehearsal hall. The other musicians vacated to some of the small practice rooms. Since the room had several doors, I was able to hover in one entrance and keep an eye on things.

After a few poses, Stefan handed his violin to David and drank from a bottle of Evian. The reporter asked a few questions, jotted more notes, and pulled Stefan away from the chaos to get a photo of him against the stage curtains.

I followed at a discreet distance, watching everyone near Stefan. Whoever was out to get him wouldn't get close without me seeing him. I was positive I'd uncover the culprit tonight. I almost grabbed Leonard's arm when I saw him reach into his jacket pocket. For a second I was sure he was about to pull out a gun. Instead, he opened a packet of Juicy Fruit gum. When he noticed me staring at him, he offered me a piece, but I shook my head.

"Enough." Stefan gave a good-natured wave of his hand. "I must prepare."

The reporter thanked him and turned to talk to the photographer.

Stefan disappeared into the rehearsal room. I wanted to follow, but the journalists blocked my way in the hall.

"Excuse me." I nudged my shoulder between them.

"No!" Stefan bellowed from beyond the doorway. The photographer ran forward, already snapping pictures. The reporter jogged into the room just in front of me.

Stefan's hands were lifted and frozen in shock. He stared in horror at the table where his open violin case rested. I ran closer, slipping in my low-heeled pumps.

His violin was in the case, but the wood splintered out from a wound. A huge butcher knife had been driven between the f-holes, right above the bridge. A hammer must have been used for added force, because the blade pierced all the way through to the sound post and was lodged there. The brutality of the attack shocked me. The instrument was beyond repair.

Stefan turned wild eyes toward the reporter. "I don't understand. Who could do this? I've tried to continue, but this is too much."

Chris trotted into the room.

I dragged my gaze from the injured violin. "Call the police. Hurry."

Stefan only moaned.

Chris pulled out his cell phone. He gave a terse report to the police, slapped the phone shut, and looked around the room. "The rest of you, get out on stage. We still have a concert to finish."

Stefan pulled out a chair and sank into it, shaking his head. "Why?"

I rested my hands on his shoulders. "It's all right. Don't touch anything. The police will figure this out."

The reporter knelt near Stefan with avid interest, and the camera clicked with frenetic energy. "What's your reaction to this latest attack? Do you think it's personal?"

"Get back to the stage." Chris waved his arms, shooing the people in the hallway away from the rehearsal room.

"Wait! Shouldn't we make a list of where everyone was at the time of the crime?" I tried to stop people from moving, and at the same time memorize who had been closest to the doorways. Leonard had been quick on the scene. Sarah peered in from the second doorway near the women's restroom. Anyone could have ducked into the room while it was empty and then gone out a side door.

Peter stormed in through the entrance closest to his office. Could he have been in the rehearsal room while Stefan was being interviewed?

Chris glared at me. "We'll let the police do the investigating. Go on. Get ready." He grabbed the reporter's arm. "I'll have to ask you to leave now."

Stefan moaned again, and the photographer took one more picture on his way out the door.

Peter shouldered past me and stared at the violated instrument. "Chris, make the announcement that we won't be doing the concerto tonight. Tell them . . . tell them they get a sneak preview of the Summer Series. We'll play the Aaron Copland."

He scanned the people nearby. "Where's David?"

"Here." The older man stepped from the shadows near the storage cabinets. Had he been hiding there?

"You'll take over as concertmaster for the second half." Peter's brusque orders pulled everyone from the shocked tableau around the table.

It killed me to leave evidence unprotected and suspects unquestioned, but Peter was right. The concert must go on. And his idea of surprising the audience with a preview was brilliant. They wouldn't feel shortchanged because of the missing concerto.

I should have hurried out with the rest of the musicians, but Stefan's face was so stricken I was worried about him. "Stefan, do you want to play the second half? Use one of your rehearsal violins?" Making music always helped me when I was traumatized. Maybe Peter shouldn't have assigned David to take over.

Stefan shook his head slowly, staring again at the violin and shuddering.

"We'll find out who's doing this. We will." I patted Stefan's shoulder twice.

Peter took my arm. "Amy." When I didn't answer, he tugged. "Amy. Onstage. Now."

I yanked my arm free and glared at him. "I told you. You weren't taking this seriously enough." I lowered my voice. "I was trying to watch out for Stefan, but with the reporters back here, I lost track. Did you see what happened? Stefan handed his violin to David. He must have set it on the table. The room was only empty for a few minutes. Who was closest?"

"Amy." Peter barked my name with no hint of patience. "You're not helping."

"But—"

His caramel eyes turned hard as toffee, and I clamped my lips shut. Fine, if he wanted to ignore an experienced observer, let him solve the case himself. Resentment dogged my heels as I made my way toward the stage. He was probably keeping me from helping because he knew I was too close to the truth. Stefan had been disrespectful numerous times toward Peter, not bothering to hide his irritation that Peter had forced him to stay when a better offer came along. Maybe Peter had begun to harass Stefan as payback.

As Peter strode across the stage to pick up his baton, I glared at him.

Confident, focused, he led us into the music, showing glimpses of his connection to the melody in his smiles, frowns, and animated movements.

As music surrounded me, directed by his hand, my anger melted. I simply couldn't believe that a gifted conductor like Peter had anything to do with the crime. Maybe I was wrong. I hadn't had much experience with men in the past fifteen years—and my experience in college showed only poor judgment. But all my instincts told me that Peter wasn't a bad guy.

I sat up straighter and took a deep breath before attacking the next woodwind melody. Now I just had to convince him to let me help.

CHAPTER

 28

> *Da Capo: A directive to the performer to go back*
> *to the beginning of the composition. This directive*
> *is abbreviated D.C.*

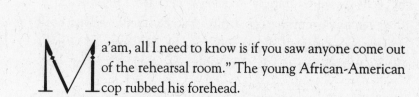

M a'am, all I need to know is if you saw anyone come out
of the rehearsal room." The young African-American
cop rubbed his forehead.

I'd informed the police about the conflicts within the symphony
and all the research I'd done so far. "No, I didn't see anyone. But
David was the last one to hold the violin. Of course, I don't know
if he's had experience with clove oil. I doubt it was the former
second violin because no one has seen her around. But Leonard
was nearby. I wish someone had checked his locker for razor blades
when the bowstrings. . . . You're not writing this down."

"You can go. I'll call if we have further questions."

"But I still haven't told you about the bow markings."

"Ma'am, we're just questioning people about the violin tonight.
We're done with you."

Deflated, I packed up my belongings and left Symphonic Hall. How were the police going to find the criminal with such a cursory investigation?

When I got home, I barely sniffed at the lilacs pouring over my neighbor's fence and hardly glanced at the clump of ferns by the back porch light that usually made me smile. I slammed into the house, wishing I played cymbals so I could crash out my frustration.

"Rough day?" Clara looked up from her book. She lounged across two kitchen chairs and was working her way through a bag of tortilla chips and a bowl of salsa.

I straddled a chair across the table and rested my forehead on the back of it. "Another attack. And the police won't listen to me." Clara passed me the chips, and I indulged in a satisfying series of crunches. "I can't believe I missed him. I was this close to catching him. I barely took my eyes off Stefan."

Clara went back to her book, probably trying to cut me off with her cool disinterest. I wasn't that easily deterred. I filled her in on the evening's events and gradually her face lifted from her book and her eyes widened. She couldn't help but be impressed with the drama of the latest attack. "The violin was stabbed?"

"I know. It's like a murder."

"Mom, you said it happened when Stefan was being interviewed. Who knew that he was going to be distracted and lured away? He had to have planned it. No one carries around a butcher knife."

My heart pumped more rapidly. "The usual suspects, of course. And Megan. She set up the interview." I gasped. "Do you think . . . ? But what would she have to gain?" I struggled to remember if she'd been around during the other incidents.

Clara's interest fed my analytical skills. We brainstormed for a full hour. In the end, we couldn't come up with a plausible reason for Megan to be involved. I didn't even know if she knew enough about music to have changed the bowings.

"I'll have to cozy up to her and find out what I can. Maybe I can get into the orchestra offices in Bloomington. I went there when I signed my paperwork."

Clara leaned forward, her eyebrows puckering. "Mom, be careful."

The warmth that seeped up from my toes was almost enough to erase my desperation to save the symphony. She cared. She was worried about me. Did my career even matter that much when set against her love?

Yes, it did. I was a symphony flutist. It was what I was meant to be.

Clara slumped back and turned a page of her book. Smudges under her eyes and a subtle droop to her lips hinted at fatigue.

I stood to pull a carton of ice cream from the freezer. "Are you okay?"

She held a finger in the page and looked up. "What?"

"Something wrong? I mean, besides . . . the obvious."

She watched me for a long moment, then tossed her book aside.

"Okay. Here's the deal. I was helping Brittany with her algebra, but she has to take a summer school class, and she wants me to keep helping her. But I'm working more hours, and it's summer, and Ryan and I want to spend time together, right? But when I tried to explain, she went ballistic."

The familiar panic flared when the be-a-wise-mom floodlight turned on me. "You helped her all this time, and instead of thanking you, now she's mad when you need to stop?"

"Exactly." She sounded relieved that I understood. That someone took her side. What had Janie said? All parents had to muddle through. Maybe I did a better job at this than I gave myself credit for.

"She doesn't sound like much of a friend." I passed the chocolate-mint ice cream across the table.

Clara stared at it with dull eyes. "Yeah, but that's the point. I thought she was."

When she still didn't move, I plunged the spoon into the carton and waved the ice cream in front of her. "Sweetie, you've gotta face it. People will take everything you've got and then gripe that you aren't giving them enough. You need to quit being so nice."

"You're a cynic." She grabbed the spoon and popped it in her mouth, rolling her eyes with pleasure as she swallowed.

"It's smarter not to count on anyone but yourself. People let you down." I stared hard at the table, letting guilt twist a painful course through my veins. "Like me. The finals on Saturday. I hate disappointing you."

"Lena's pastor said something like that. Said we could only count on God."

Oh, no. We were *not* going back to that topic. "My point is, protect yourself."

"How's that working for you?"

I grabbed the spoon from her hand and drove it into the carton. "We're not talking about me."

She smirked for a second, but then the muscles of her face fell back into melancholy planes, and shadows curved beneath her eyes again. We chatted while we polished off the pint of ice cream, but I wasn't able to coax any further animation from her until bedtime.

"Oh, I forgot to tell you." She came out of the bathroom with a toothbrush in her mouth and foam on her lips. "There's gonna be a big party at Ashley's Saturday after the competition. Okay?"

"Sure, but remember, no drinking, no sex, no drugs."

She disappeared into the bathroom and spit. "Yeah, yeah, yeah."

I followed her. "I mean it. And I read in the paper that some kids were playing Chubby Bunny and one of them died."

She toweled her face. "Huh?"

"It's some game where kids see how many marshmallows they can stuff in their cheeks. Don't do it."

"Got it. No drinking, no sex, no Chubby Bunny."

I grabbed a hand towel and flicked it at her. "Don't give me your sass."

She shrieked and jumped out of range, then tossed a handful of water my direction. We chased each other around the upstairs until we collapsed on my bed breathless with giggles.

"Chubby Bunny?" She started laughing again. "Where do you get these things?"

I sobered up. "I worry about you."

"I know. But I'm not a kid anymore. Give me some credit for common sense."

"I do. I'm just . . ."

"You're just a mom."

Satisfaction added to the flush of our playtime. "Exactly."

Clara's restored affection should have erased my worries about missing the Saturday cheerleading competition. Instead, it had the opposite effect. I fretted all day Thursday that I would miss her team's biggest event of the year. In between wrestling guilt, I wrestled the difficult Takemitsu solo.

And in the pockets of time that remained, I worked on the case. I made a chart of all my suspects and clues. Nothing jumped out at me. I tried calling Stefan to go over the details of Wednesday night, but he didn't return my messages. Friday, I dropped Clara off at the school just before noon, with a promise to see her that night in the first-round competitions. She'd spend the afternoon in classes and clinics.

I needed more clues to break the case. Dressing in sneaky black clothes and rubber-soled shoes, I drove to Symphonic Hall.

Snake opened the back door at my knock. "Whaddaya want? There's no rehearsal today."

"I know, but I left some music in my locker. I need it for the gala." I couldn't meet his eyes, although his stained and tattered work boots didn't provide a reassuring view, either.

"Fine. I'll come with you."

Not part of my plan. He stuck to me like polish on silver no matter how hard I tried to brush him off. After I went through the charade of opening my locker, I remembered that I didn't have any music inside at all. "That's funny. I was sure I left the copy of my Takemitsu solo here. Did you hear that I'm doing a solo? Well, sorry for wasting your time. You go ahead with whatever you were doing. I'll see myself out."

His formidable tattooed limbs blocked my way. "Can't con a con, lady. Whatcha really doing here?"

A sudden brainstorm helped me ignore my tight throat. I crossed my arms and glowered. "Snake, do you have a criminal record?"

He scowled past his overgrown whiskers. "What's that got to do with anything?"

"I mean, do you know how to break into a locked building?"

He stepped closer, towering over me. "So now you want to blame the violin on me? You've got a lot of nerve."

I backed up until my back hit the locker door. "No, no, no. You misunderstood. I need your help."

His gold tooth gleamed as his lips parted in a slow smile. "What's cookin' under that copper-top of yours?"

"This has to stay between us."

He held up three fingers. "Scout's honor."

I snorted. Like he had ever been a Boy Scout. "I have a theory. I'll spare you the details, but I need to get into the symphony offices over in Bloomington to check out a few things."

"So, go there Monday morning. Don't they open at nine?"

"Don't be thick. I need to get in when no one is around."

His grin stretched wider. "You want me to help you break into the offices?"

I waited, excitement building. If I could get an ally like Snake, nothing would stand in my way.

He took a deep breath, threw his head back, and laughed.

"Hey, I'm serious—"

He laughed harder. "You think I'd—" The words choked out, but hooting noises took him over again. Finally he wheezed to a halt.

He held up a hand. "Please. I'm begging you. No more." He gasped in another breath. "You're the limit—you know that? Now go home before I call the men in white coats."

"But I—"

"Go. Now. Otherwise I'm calling the powers-that-be."

When I got in the car, I wanted to pound my fist against the dashboard. But I didn't dare bruise my fingers. Finally I banged my forehead against the steering wheel.

CHAPTER

*Inversion: The position of a chord when the
fundamental is not the lowest note. When the lowest
note is the fundamental, the chord is said to be in root
position. When the third of the chord is in the lowest
voice of the music, the chord is a "first inversion,"
and when the fifth of the chord is in the lowest voice,
the chord is said to be a "second inversion."*

Echoes bounced off the concrete walls in the convention
center, amplifying the screeches of excited girls. In the
auditorium, music blared, feet stamped in disconnected
rhythms, and groups chanted inane phrases in sporadic bursts. I
stared, openmouthed, at the crowd. No wonder the cheerleaders
were excited. This was a huge event and the finals weren't even
until tomorrow night.

A distorted voice sounded over the loudspeakers, welcoming the
teams from around the country. The greeting necessitated more
stomping, screaming, and yelling as each school was named.

"Amy, over here." Janie Biederbock waved from a row midway up Section F.

I climbed the steps, heart pounding in protest. I really needed to get more exercise one of these days.

"We saved you a seat." Dawn Hanson pushed up the sleeves of her booster club sweatshirt. Her attention was tugged away by a cheerleader below us who started a wave. Dawn swept up and down with a whoop of glee, along with seven-year-old Stephie beside her and all the other parents in our section.

"Here." Janie pushed foam animal ears onto my head. "I brought extra."

"Gee, thanks." Why did Clara's school have to be the Wolverines instead of something that made sense, like . . . Come to think of it, none of these team names made much sense.

I hadn't had trouble coming up with gray slacks and a gray silk blouse. Red was harder to find. Clara had to lend me a vest from her closet. Unfortunately, it was leather with a wide metal zipper and very tight.

I looked like a short Katharine Hepburn at a biker bar . . . with wolverine ears.

Janie, on the other hand, could have been a J.Crew model. Perfectly put together with a red polo shirt, and a gray sweater tied around her shoulders. "Isn't this exciting?"

"Thrilling."

She elbowed me. "Come on. You're having fun. Admit it."

I smiled and joined in the next clapping rhythm because I didn't want to get into an argument.

The sensory overload eventually numbed my brain into a dull throb. After a few minutes we were no longer cajoled into clapping, stamping, and shouting, and the first team took the stage. The music was too techno and way too loud. But the athletes flew into the air, ignored the laws of gravity, and contorted their bodies into amazing shapes. I'd always loved classical ballet, and if I squinted my eyes and tilted my head and ignored the noise, I could find similarities.

By the time Clara's team bounded up the steps to the platform, I was clapping and whooping with the best of them.

The other cheerleaders disappeared into a background haze as I stared at my daughter. She kicked the air with fierce energy that made me fear she'd rip out her leg muscles. When she jumped, she was spring-loaded and joyous. My neck muscles tightened as she gripped hands with a teammate while a tiny girl shot up and stood on their shoulders. Clara's smile never wavered. I leaned to the side when other cheerleaders blocked my view of her in the back row. Where had this talent come from? Not from Jason—a pale melancholic. Not from me—dogged, focused, and cranky. She punched the dance moves with confidence. Energy that was unique to her shone from her face. Vibrant, she cartwheeled into her identity.

When the number ended, my face was wet.

The parents around me screamed with so much abandon that no one noticed.

"They nailed it!" Janie grabbed me, jumping up and down. "Wasn't it great?"

"Amazing," I said quietly. Once the uproar calmed, I stood and picked up my purse.

Janie grabbed my arm. "Where are you going?"

"Well, they're done, right?"

"Honey, you have to stay to hear the scores. And three more teams have to compete before they announce the teams that will advance."

I winced.

Janie stood up. "Come on." She guided me down the steep steps and out to the ladies' room in the hallway. The noise faded to a muffled roar.

In the bathroom I splashed water on my face. "Thank you."

"You looked like you needed a break. Are you okay?"

I forced a half smile. "Sure. No. I don't know."

Janie handed me a paper towel and waited.

"I have to play at a gala tomorrow night. I can't come to the finals, but I hate letting Clara down. Things have been a little tense lately."

Janie laughed. "Something would be wrong if you had a teenage daughter and no tension. Cheer up. If they don't rank high enough, they won't be performing in the finals."

My mood lifted. "Really? That would be great."

But a half hour later, an announcer named the teams continuing to the finals, and our section went ballistic when they heard the Wolverines would be advancing.

That night, Clara was flushed with victory. The team didn't go out to celebrate, because Coach Joy insisted everyone go home and get a good night's sleep. But based on the adrenaline pumping through Clara's veins, I guessed no one would get much rest—including me.

"So did you see how great we did on the lift? And Amber did a full twist on her roundoff back handspring. Remember that tricky part I told you about? We nailed it."

I had to peel her from the ceiling to get her to sit down over mugs of cocoa. I smiled through my whipped cream as she talked herself out. When only chocolate dregs remained in our cups, Clara leaned on her elbows and sighed. "So, really. What did you think?"

I matched her posture, meeting her eyes. "I'm proud of you. You're really good at cheering, and I was impressed with the team."

She gave me a grateful smile and sighed again.

"The music could use some help," I continued. "I get the driving rhythm thing, but couldn't they use something with a decent melody? And are you being careful? You've got magic hands at the piano. You don't want to sprain something—"

"Mom." She held up a hand. "Quit while you're ahead."

"I'm just saying."

"Yeah, yeah. I know. Can't help yourself."

I sobered and put my hand over hers on the table. "I really wish I could be there tomorrow night. I tried everything to get out of the gala."

"It's okay." She said it like she meant it as she pushed her chair back. She walked around the table and pressed a quick kiss on the top of my head.

As she headed up to bed, I stared at the kitchen wall. How many times had she used those exact words? *"It's okay, Mom. I'll give our neighbor the popsicle frame I made for Father's Day." "It's okay, Mom. I know we can't afford a trip since you had to get a new flute." "It's okay, Mom. I'll color in the kitchen while you teach. We can play dominoes later." "It's okay, Mom. I know you need to practice. We can talk tomorrow."*

My self-doubts moved into pure loathing. I wasn't merely an inept mother. I'd been selfish. Since she didn't act out, didn't scream out her demands, it had been too easy for me to believe that she had no needs. The truth was, I hadn't wanted to see them, since I didn't know if I could meet them.

Clara popped her head back in the room. "Mom, did you really ask Snake to help you break into some building?"

I put on my most innocent face. "What?"

"He told Lena."

"Oh. Well, it's not like it sounds. I . . . I . . ."

"Mom, how could you? He's on the praise team at church. Lena said he used to do drugs and served some time, but now his life is turned around."

"Oh, please. Don't all criminals say that?"

"He's not a criminal. He's a person. A person who made mistakes and a person God forgave." She turned on her heel and disappeared again.

So God liked Snake, huh? Then maybe I had a shot at God liking me, after all. Something to think about later. Right now I had a different dilemma. How could I let Clara know I loved her when I was missing the most important event in her world?

On Saturday night I glared up at the imposing stone lions by the side stairs of the Minneapolis Institute of Arts. Then I circled to the front entrance and yanked the door open. Sure, part of me felt tingly at the thought of debuting a flute solo. But I couldn't focus. I kept hearing the pulsing rhythm of Clara's cheerleading number and seeing her electric smile.

I found the room where the musicians were gathering and grabbed a program. Gold embossed letters listed the numbers. I traced my name with one finger. Stefan was scheduled to play a movement from his violin concerto, followed by the string quartet, then a brass ensemble, a cello solo, then my flute piece.

So while fat cats sipped champagne and listened to our pieces with as much discernment as my mechanic, I'd be missing Clara's finals.

Suddenly, I knew I couldn't stay. If I left I would jeopardize my job, Peter's respect, any future chance at solo work. But I wanted to be with Clara. I needed to be there for her.

I gathered my things, tucked in my chin, and charged for the door.

A form blocked my way. "Whoa. Where are you going in such a rush? They're almost ready for—" Peter reached out and almost touched my arm. "Amy? What's wrong?"

I blinked hard and stared at the floor. "I can't stay."

"Nerves? This group isn't—"

"No, of course not. You don't understand. Clara is in the finals of a cheerleading competition, and I have to be there. I know it sounds silly, but I've let her down in so many ways, and she needs me, even though I didn't think so, and now I know, and it's so important, and I'm really sorry, and it's not that it isn't an honor, and I really tried to find someone . . ."

Peter took a slow breath.

I braced myself. He'd tell me that the symphony had taken a big chance on someone with my lack of experience, and I should appreciate the opportunity, and that someone with my lack of commitment should not bother to return Monday morning.

"I guess there's only one thing to do."

I closed my eyes.

"We'll move your piece to the beginning. Get out there and play. Will that give you time to get to Clara's event?"

I jerked my head up and looked at him, then at the clock on the wall. "Yes." Breathless, off-center, I felt my eyes well up. I forced the tears back and squared my shoulders. "Yes," I said firmly.

Peter gave me a slow smile. Why had I ever thought he was stiff or cool? His dark, flecked eyes had the dangerous warmth of a campfire near dry timber.

He stepped aside. "Good. Off you go."

I played with subtle phrasing and confident dynamics—not that anyone but the other musicians would appreciate it. Although my heart seemed to flutter, my breath support was strong. I fought the impulse to rush the tempo. The music deserved every stretched fermata and lengthy rest. Sometimes the most important part of the music was the silence. Yearning, hope, and budding exhilaration floated from my flute into the air. Perhaps a few of the listeners even recognized and absorbed the emotions.

When I finished, I nodded sedately to acknowledge the applause, gestured a thanks to my accompanist, hurried to the back room, disassembled my flute, and tore out of the building to my car.

Back streets or the freeway? Which would be quicker? I gunned the engine and zipped through some yellow lights on my way to the freeway entrance. I pulled around a lumbering city bus, zipped past a station wagon waiting to turn left, and then screeched to a stop at the next red light. My fingers skittered along the top of the steering wheel and a flash of color caught my eye.

The engine light.

"No. Oh, no. Oh, God, let my car keep running. Just until I reach the convention center. Please, please, please. I'm finally doing something right. You've gotta help me."

When the traffic light turned green, my motor sputtered and almost stalled. Then it roared back to life and propelled me forward.

A weird tingle spidered across my skull. Was the engine recovery a coincidence, or was God really giving me a hand? I wanted to laugh off the question, but my heart felt so full of gratitude there wasn't room to mock. "Thank you," I whispered.

It wasn't until I parked near the convention center that I realized I'd left my music on the stand. My articulation notes and phrasing were priceless to me. I ran along the sidewalk while I called Megan's cell phone. She'd be buzzing around backstage or courting the press.

"Hello?" Her voice was barely above a whisper, and I heard a violin in the background.

"It's Amy," I panted without slowing my pace. "I forgot my music."

"Yeah, Peter grabbed it for you. He said he'd leave it at Symphonic Hall in his office, if you want to pick it up before Monday."

I thanked her and jogged the rest of the way to the convention center doors. The auditorium vibrated with the excitement of the competition. The Wolverine section was packed with parents, so I didn't try to find a seat. I stood near the railing where I had a great view.

"Wow, you really dress up." Janie nudged my side.

I looked down at my floor-length black gown. I hadn't even remembered what I was wearing. Now I felt silly surrounded by jeans, sweatshirts, and booster-wear.

"Did I make it in time? Have they been on yet?"

Janie gave me a sideways hug. "Relax. You made it."

She stood with me and gave me a running critique of each group. Unison, amplitude, dynamics—there were as many things to watch for and appreciate as there were in a symphonic performance. I was ready to burst with excitement and nerves by the time Clara's team jogged onto the stage to compete. I screamed myself hoarse and blocked out every thought but rooting for Clara. Was this what love felt like? This intense, telescopic focus? This powerful desire for the well-being of the loved one? My love had never felt quite this true before.

The Wolverines came in third in their division. But the girls beamed like triple-A first-place winners. During the trophy ceremony, Clara's gaze swept the parent section. She smiled and waved at some of her friends' moms. Then she spotted me down by the rail. Her eyes widened.

I blew her a kiss, then joined back into the applause, hands held over my head so she could see them.

Her smile grew, and my heart stretched. I'd finally gotten something right.

After the formalities, Clara leaped down the steps and ran to meet me. She was sweaty and smelled of hair spray, but she felt wonderful in my arms. "I love you, Clara-bird."

"Thanks, Mom." She squeezed the breath from my lungs.

Shrieking friends pulled her attention away. Ryan waited with his freckles and letter jacket to congratulate her.

I held on. "Do you need a ride to the party?"

"Naw. Brittany's driving. I'll be home by midnight."

"I could pick you up." But I was talking to empty air.

Janie sighed beside me. "I know it doesn't look like it, but she'll always remember that you were here for her big moment."

I clung to those words on my lonely drive out of downtown. The radio clock claimed it was nine o'clock, but that couldn't be right. I felt like I'd lived through a decade in the last few hours. Now I had nothing to look forward to but an empty house.

On impulse, I turned and headed toward Symphonic Hall. I could pick up my music. The gala performance would have ended by now, and Peter was likely to stop by his office. I decided not to think about why an excuse to pop into his office made me cheerful.

CHAPTER

30

Fermata: A notation marking directing the performer or ensemble to sustain the note of a composition affecting all parts and lasting as long as the artistic interpretation of the conductor allows. The fermata is marked above the note or rest to be held. Also known as a hold or bird's eye.

You again? Whaddaya want with me now? Planning a bank heist?"

"Hi, Snake." I chewed the inside of my cheek to hold back a snide comment. I deserved his teasing. "I left some music at the gala. Megan said Peter would leave it in his office."

Snake shrugged, bulging biceps shifting under his shirts. "You know the way."

"Not going to follow me?"

He threw his head back and laughed. "Promise not to cause any trouble?"

"Scout's honor."

He laughed again and walked away shaking his head. I started down the dim hall, my toes complaining about a whole evening of standing around in dress shoes. I'd sacrifice for my music, gladly, but blistered feet were useless suffering. I slipped out of the pumps and left them near the door. The cold concrete felt delicious under my soles. I padded silently toward Peter's office.

A light from the rehearsal room detoured me. Some of the other musicians must have come back after the gala. Had the rest of the program gone well? Were the important patrons convinced to continue their support of the symphony?

I veered toward the open door. My foot came down hard on a discarded reed, and I stopped to rub away the bruise.

"*Ja, ja. Ist nicht schwer.*"

I froze. Stefan was in the rehearsal room talking to someone. I didn't want to stumble into one of his trysts.

Silence followed, then more German from Stefan. He must be on the phone.

"*Ich werde in zwei Wochen in Stuttgart sein . . . Nein.*" His laugh showcased his ego—full of self-assuredness and an undercurrent of mockery for anyone who had the misfortune not to be him. "*Mein Rechtsanwalt hat mir gesagt, sie müssen mich von dem Kontrakt entlassen.*"

I continued down the hallway. I'd admired Stefan—both his music and his courage in overcoming all the attacks. But I'd known too many people like him who were consumed with their own brilliance.

I tapped on the doorframe of Peter's office.

His back was to me, his feet on his desk, hands linked behind his head as he stared at the ceiling. "Come in."

"How did it go?"

His feet hit the ground in one smooth movement as he rotated his chair. "Great. Except for all the people who wanted to meet the new flutist who played the Japanese composer."

My stomach tightened. Was I in trouble?

Then he smiled. "How did Clara do?"

"Amazing. They got third, but the judges were favoring stunts instead of technique. Their unison was the best in their league. I guarantee the other schools weren't using brand-new members." I'd absorbed a little while listening to Janie. "Clara is definitely the strongest of the new sophomores. I wouldn't be surprised if she ends up as captain when she's a senior." I stopped to breathe.

Peter's eyebrows disappeared under his curly bangs. "Listen to you."

My face felt hot, and I curled my bare toes under.

His teeth flashed. "I like it. I've seen the dedicated musician, but this . . . It's nice to see."

The strange flutter in my stomach annoyed me, and I clamped it down. "So will it be enough? The gala. Was it the damage control Megan hoped for?"

Peter's smile disappeared. "Maybe. Hard to say. Stefan is being released from his contract, so maybe all the problems will go away when he does."

"The symphony?"

He rubbed his right shoulder and winced. "Don't know. Honestly, even without any more problems, we've lost a lot of ground. I wish we'd found out who was causing this. Having some answers would restore the public's confidence."

I perched on the battered folding chair near his desk. "At first I thought it was Leonard. Or David. Or Sarah." I looked down. "I even suspected you for a while. But no real musician would stab a violin."

He didn't seem to be listening to my analysis. "Where are your shoes?"

I shifted and tucked my feet up under me. "I left them by the door."

Peter scowled. "Were you snooping around again?"

I sighed, dispirited. "No. Although I did hear Stefan talking to someone in German. Anyway, then I thought it was Megan, because I heard she's planning to leave. But why would she—"

"German?"

Why couldn't he concentrate a little better? "Yes. At least I think he was speaking German. He said something about Stuttgart. Anyway, I couldn't figure out how Megan would have—"

"What did he say? Stefan. What did he say?"

I shrugged. "Something in German. What difference does it make?"

"Try to remember."

"It sounded like cereal."

"Cereal?"

"Yes. You know, Müeslix." Peter seemed really worked up about this. *Good ear, don't fail me now.* I struggled to remember the sounds from his last phrase. "Something like Müeslix, and then a word that sounded like contract." I squeezed my eyes shut. "And something that sounded like ant lasso."

"Ant lasso? *Entlassen?*"

I opened my eyes and made an apologetic face. "That's what it sounded like."

"Is he still here?"

"Who?"

"Stefan. Where is he?"

I frowned. "Who cares?"

Peter's eyes narrowed. "I'd like to know who he was talking to."

Adrenaline rose in my veins like a high tide. "I could distract him. You could—"

"Hit redial." He sprang to his feet.

Devious, clever, tracking down clues—I could fall for this guy. Of course, once again he was distracting me from solving the important mystery, but I could play along.

Peter sat down again. "But what would that prove? He's made no secret of wanting to leave."

I nibbled my lower lip. "Hey, if you want to know who he was talking with, I don't mind helping."

He stood up with less energy. "I suppose. We might find out something. Not that it can help now."

I jumped up, but my feet tangled in the long dress and I started to fall.

Peter caught me in an awkward bear hug and propped me up. His arms lingered for a second, and I felt his warm breath near my face. We broke apart quickly.

"Okay." He cleared his throat. "You chat him up."

"Check. But first I need to grab my music bag so I don't forget it again."

I scanned his office.

"I had Vicki put it by your locker in the women's dressing room. I figured you'd check there first."

"Wait here." I ran lightly on the balls of my feet and blamed my racing heart on the unexpected exercise. I retrieved my bag, gathered up my skirt, and ran back to Peter's office. "Let's go."

"Lead the way, Miss Marple."

"That's Sherlock to you, Watson." I stomped off to the rehearsal hall, only to find the lights off and the room empty. "Where did he go?"

"Did you forget your magnifying glass?" Peter kept walking and pointed to the door of the men's dressing room, where light crawled from beneath the door.

"I can't go in there," I whispered. "If you want me to distract him, you gotta get him out of there."

"Snake said you were poking around in there last week."

"That was different. No one was around."

Peter rubbed his temples. "Do you honestly believe in your logic?"

I glared and held my ground.

"Fine. Barmy flutist," he muttered under his breath.

He disappeared into the dressing room and soon I heard the rumble of men's voices. A minute later Stefan and Peter emerged.

"I disagree. The concerto is more impressive at that tempo." Stefan made no attempt to hide his disdain.

"But the composer's intent has to be considered in those choices." Peter froze with his hand on the door. "I need a tissue. I'll be right out."

A tissue? He needed to read some of my mystery novels so he could come up with better dodges than that. "Hi, Stefan. How did the gala go after I left?"

"Fine." He smiled. "Good job on the Takemitsu. Were you nervous?"

"Of course. But—"

"Stuttgart?" Peter barreled out of the dressing room holding a cell phone in front of him. "That's what this has all been about, isn't it?"

I looked back and forth between the two men. Animosity flared from Peter. Stefan sneered.

I felt like I'd stepped into the wrong Megaplex theatre after going out for popcorn. "Um, guys? What's wrong?"

Stefan studied a callus on his finger, then smiled at Peter. "I warned you not to stand in my way." If his voice hadn't been so calm and reasonable, he would have sounded like an arch villain in a melodrama.

"So you went to all this trouble. You figured enough sympathy would get you released."

I didn't like being ignored. "All what trouble?"

Stefan shrugged. "The Stuttgart Orchestra is a huge opportunity. Recording contracts. World class."

"All what trouble?" I shouted.

"Tell her," Peter said.

When Stefan didn't say anything, Peter turned to me. "We'd invested months of P.R. budget when he was hired. Committed to a long-term contract. And a few weeks after he arrived, he wanted to leave for another offer."

"Yeah, you told me. But . . ."

Stefan yawned. "So a few months later when Stuttgart's new concertmaster didn't succeed and they contacted me again, I found, this time, a way to accept."

Confusion and frustration played a tarantella behind my eyeballs. "But how could you accept when you knew the Minneapolis Symphony would keep you under contract? It's only because of the sabotage that they finally—" I gasped and stumbled back a step. "No. Tell me you didn't."

"Anyone would do the same."

I fumbled with my bag. "The cut bow strings? The allergy? The tuning?"

He lifted his chest with something like pride. "Clever, *ja?* Now I leave with no hard feelings."

From the rage radiating from Peter, Stefan hadn't begun to experience the hard feelings in store.

I shook my head. "But I ruled out musicians as suspects once the violin was stabbed. No musician would damage an instrument."

He gave a regretful nod. "Very sad. If this man had listened to reason, it would not be necessary." Then he shrugged. "But it was a rehearsal violin, and insured."

"But you were out here talking to the reporter."

"I had a moment alone when I went into the rehearsal hall. Time enough. I carried the knife with me."

Nausea curled under my ribs at the pure, careless evil Stefan was revealing. I'd shared tapas with him, and musical opinions, and a sort-of date. I turned away, sickened.

"It's the Maestro who destroyed the symphony, not me. None of this would have been needed if he had listened to reason."

My toes curled against the cold concrete. I rounded on him in a coiled bundle of fury. "Reason? How dare you talk about reason when you betrayed all your fellow musicians?"

"You would have done the same. You understand sacrificing all for your art. You could not pass up such an opportunity."

I stared up at him with complete conviction. "Yes, I could. Some things matter more." And I was proud of myself for knowing that.

Then I jabbed a finger into his chest, lifting my chin to glare at the tall blond. "You are going to speak to the press and let them know what you did. Before you fly to Germany you're going to apologize and take the blame for all the problems the symphony has been having." I turned to Peter. "That'll help, won't it? We'll win back some of the patrons and grants when the truth comes out."

Peter's eyes held admiration as he watched me, but his nod was sad. "Yes, it would help."

So why wasn't he excited that we'd broken the case?

Stefan chuckled. "Why would I do that? Better for my career that I was driven from my last position by a crime spree . . . so typical for this violent American country."

"But Peter and I both know the truth. We'll tell the press if you don't."

"And your proof . . . ? *Auf Wiedersehen.*" He smiled, almost gently, and walked away.

"Stefan, stop right there." I used the voice honed over fifteen years of parenting. Both men looked at me, startled. "I've got all the proof I need."

CHAPTER

31

Stefan turned back and smiled at me with condescension. Peter put an arm around me. "Come on, Amy. Let him go. With time and hard work the symphony will rebuild."

I shrugged away from Peter and glared at Stefan.

"I never would have believed you could do this—hurt so many people. But when Peter said he wanted to find out who you'd been talking to, I figured it might be an interesting conversation." I reached into my music bag and pulled out my Dictaphone. Finally, my Perry Mason moment. "I've got your confession right here."

Stefan stared at my recorder and moved closer, realization turning him pale.

I held the small recorder over my head. "Don't know what it's like where you come from, but I'm guessing the police would be a little upset at being called in by a fraud."

Peter pulled his amazed look away from my Dictaphone and smiled at Stefan. "And I believe a false insurance claim is a crime, isn't it, Amy?"

Stefan reached for my hand, and for a moment I thought the evening would end with a brawl. Would a violinist be that desperate? Would he risk hurting his fingers by punching someone?

I skittered back a few steps, and Peter got between us. "Hard to fly to Stuttgart when you're awaiting trial."

Stefan forced a laugh. "I haven't filed an insurance claim yet. The rest was a prank only. I cannot be arrested for that."

"Maybe. I'm calling our contact at the newspaper right now, so you can give them a statement. Otherwise we turn you over to the police and let them sort it out."

Stefan's jaw lifted with stubborn arrogance. Anger crackled through the air. I braced myself to catch Peter if he got slugged.

Off-key whistling interrupted us. Snake ambled down the hallway from the set shop. "Need some help?"

I'd never been so glad to see gold teeth and tattoos before.

Peter shoved his sleeves up, as if longing for a fistfight. "Thanks, Snake. Take this pathetic git to the rehearsal room and keep him there. I've got some calls to make."

"No prob." Snake began to steer Stefan down the hall. The concertmaster decided not to try his luck beating up Snake. Instead, Stefan's shoulders sagged. He glanced back at me, pale and stunned. I almost felt sorry for him.

Not.

Peter strode toward his office.

I scampered behind him. "My toes are cold."

He veered into his office and grabbed the phone. "Megan? Yes, I know what time it is. Don't give me that." He filled her in on what we'd learned and told her to roust the woman who had been doing interviews. The lucky reporter was about to get a new slant on the story. "No, she's got to come down here. We'll wait. No, I want her to hear Stefan in person . . . Too right. Yes."

He hung up, swung around, and grinned at me. "Sorry, you were saying?"

"My toes are cold."

Peter looked confused.

Let him think I was odd. A chilly vibration moved through me. Was I shaking? How weird. The backstage area was cold, but not this cold.

"Daft girl. Running around without shoes." He crouched to dig through a duffle bag under his desk. "Here."

A ball of socks pelted me in the head and dropped to the floor. I stared at them, dazed, and couldn't seem to move. My brain had stopped working, and I couldn't process why I was in Peter's office and why he was throwing socks at me.

Peter straightened and took another look at me. "Blast. You've gone white." He grabbed a cardigan from a hook on the wall, wrapped me in the scratchy wool, and guided me to his desk chair. "Sit down. You're so pale I can see your freckles." He knelt and pulled his oversize socks onto my feet. "Are you all right?"

"It's true? We really solved the case?" I wished I could shake off the out-of-body feeling that fogged my brain.

"*You* solved it."

A slow smile tugged my lips. "Wow." Then I frowned at him. "I don't have freckles."

He grinned. "There she is. There's the gal I know. Went a bit wobbly?" Then his smile faded. "Is it only shock? Or something else? Did you and Stefan . . . ?" He cleared his throat. "Better for you to know now."

"Stefan?" My head began to clear. "He stabbed a violin! Who does something like that?"

Peter straightened and sat on the edge of his desk. "And you got the proof. How did you ever think of recording him? You're brilliant."

"I am, aren't I? Must be all those mysteries I read." The shivers had stopped, and a sense of triumph blossomed in my chest. "We did it, didn't we? It'll help, won't it? The symphony? Once people realize what was going on?"

Peter smiled. "Bound to help. I'd say your Case of the Corrupt Concertmaster is well and truly solved. Congratulations."

He held out his hand and I took it, but after a crisp handshake, he didn't let go. "You can tell me. Is Stefan . . . is your relationship . . . do you want . . . ?"

"You can't be serious." I snatched my hand away. "I went out with him once only, and that was to collect clues."

Peter laughed. "I should have known you'd be trouble when I heard you play the Mozart."

"Trouble? Me? I've been *solving* the trouble. What are you—"

"Later." His eyes met mine, and the last of my chill melted. "One of these days I'll tell you all about how much trouble you are." Then he shook himself. "Now, let's listen to the tape."

"Tape?" I swallowed hard.

"Your recorder. Your genius plan."

I pulled the cardigan tighter, even though I was growing very warm. "Well . . . let me explain it this way. Have you ever played poker?"

He nodded slowly. "Why?"

I hunched my shoulders. "I was bluffing." I held out the Dictaphone and popped it open. "No tape."

His mouth opened as if I'd played a run from a Sousa march in the middle of a Grieg overture.

I tossed my head back. "I couldn't let him get away like that. But . . . there's no recording. "

A grin spread across Peter's face. "Well, we'll just keep that to ourselves."

"It's really going to be in the paper?" Lena looked satisfyingly impressed as she sat in my kitchen Sunday afternoon.

"Have a doughnut." Clara pushed the box across the table to Lena.

I intercepted the box and snagged a chocolate éclair. "Peter said I might have saved the symphony."

The glow of solving my first official case still had me floating. On top of that, Clara was touched I'd made it to her cheerleading finals, and Lena was smiling at me with approval.

"The reporter got Stefan's confession, but she also interviewed me. I told her how I'd been analyzing all the incidents. You know, musicians notice more details than normal people. I figured out everyone who had a motive. And it's my musical background that helped me remember the phrase I heard Stefan saying in German—and that's what gave it away to Peter."

"But you never suspected Stefan." Clara licked frosting off her fingers and grinned at me.

"Maybe I did. I don't tell you everything."

Her impish face sobered. "No kidding."

"So, church was great this morning." Lena blurted, twisting a strand of her long hair. "Are you coming with us next week?"

I swiveled my head and pretended to look for someone behind me. "Me? You talkin' to me?"

"Mom, you got used to the cheerleading moms. You could get used to church."

"No, thanks." I crossed my arms. "Subject closed."

Clara and Lena exchanged a look. Lena gave a small shake of her head.

They were sharing unspoken communication, and it made me mad. That was part of my special relationship with Clara.

"So, Mom, I need to tell you something." Clara's eyes darted over to Lena again.

"You don't have to look at her. If you have something to tell me, just do it."

Clara sighed heavily. "Lena found out where my father is, and I Googled him."

"You what?"

"Did an Internet search. I want to write to him."

I choked on my pastry and reached for my coffee. "No. Not a good idea." Jason's rejection had nearly killed me. I didn't want her to go through similar pain. Music consumed him. He'd have nothing to offer her. I knew how that felt—and not just from Jason. My dad had preferred the dusty stacks of the university library to the complex puzzle of getting to know me.

"I'm just going to send a letter. It's not like I'm flying down to Brazil to meet him."

I looked at Lena. "Did you encourage this?"

Lena's face puckered like a damp tissue. She turned panicked eyes toward Clara.

Clara banged her fist against the tabletop. "Don't pick on Aunt Lena. This was my idea."

"Careful of your fingers."

"I think I should let you two discuss this." Lena pushed back her chair, but Clara and I both ignored her.

"Did he beat you? Is he violent? I don't understand. What are you so afraid of?"

"I'm not afraid of anything. Why mess things up? We have a good life."

The door clicked quietly behind Lena as she left.

Clara took a deep breath, stared at the ceiling, and muttered something. It took me a minute to make out what she was saying. She was reciting one of her inane cheers over and over. Finally, she flattened her hands onto her lap and met my eyes.

"Mom, this isn't going to get between us. He's not going to steal me away."

Tears stung my eyes. I must have been overtired from the events of the weekend; my control was slipping. "Okay, I'm scared," I whispered. "I don't want to lose you." The truth of the words brought relief even as they shamed me.

Clara leaned back, forehead pinched. "I know. But I'll be leaving for college in a few years. I won't always be here."

When I didn't answer, she smiled gently. "You're getting used to sharing me with Ryan. And cheerleading."

"And God." I slumped into a pout.

She gave a surprised laugh. "Him, too. And you haven't lost me."

"Feels like it. You talk to Lena more than me. We haven't played together in ages." We used to while away evenings with Clara at the piano and me trying some new composer or enjoying old favorites.

Clara's eyebrows climbed.

"Okay, okay," I said quickly. "I've been busy, too. I just . . . I don't want this to get between us."

"Then don't fight me on it. He deserves to know he's a father." She frowned. "I don't know why, but even if he never talks to me, it'll feel better for me if he knows I exist."

I chewed my éclair for a minute. Maybe she was right. And maybe I'd feel better, too. Could some of the guilt I'd carried all this time include the niggling worry that I should have let him know about my choice?

"Fine. I don't have the energy to fight you, anyway. You are the most stubborn person I know. Don't know where you got that from."

Clara stood up. "Want to play a few duets?"

She loves me. Even though I'm an unconventional mother. Even though I kept the truth from her for so long.

"I guess. But I get to pick the music. Hey, wash your hands. No playing piano with sticky fingers."

CHAPTER

32

Fine: An indication of where a composition ends when there is a repeat of some section of the composition in such a way as to make locating the ending confusing.

Musicians arrived for Tuesday morning's rehearsal with the animated noise of a tree full of grackles. When I walked onto the stage, Leonard hefted his bulk from his chair and pushed his way toward me.

"Is it true? It was Stefan all along? I read it in the paper yesterday, and then Megan posted it on the symphony Web site this morning, but I couldn't believe it."

I tossed my choppy bangs back from my eyes. "I heard his confession with my own ears."

Leonard grinned. "I won't deny I've had fantasies of doing the guy in. Who would have guessed that he was attacking himself?" He looked over at Vicki, who was studiously sawing away at her cello, trying to tune. Then he smiled at the empty concertmaster's chair. "What do you call a concertmaster with half a brain?"

I sighed. "I give up."

"Gifted." Leonard winked. "Good riddance to the guy."

"I'm still mad that he made the whole symphony look bad. Good thing I was on the case."

But Leonard had already waddled back to the trombone section. David Tanner came in and sat in the violin section's first chair. We were lucky to have him to step into the breach. He wasn't flamboyant like Stefan had been, but he was a consistent and solid musician and a leader who had no desire to create drama.

As I settled into my chair, Sarah looked over at me with an expression more sour than usual.

"What's wrong?" May as well pretend to be polite, even though I didn't really want to hear her answer.

"My contract was up for renewal. I thought we were going under." She shifted the angle of her music stand and frowned at the music.

"So?"

"So, I didn't renew. I resigned."

Glee rocketed through me, but I kept my face still. "So where are you going?"

"Probably Atlanta. I'm tired of the cold weather here anyway. But if I'd known . . ."

"Yeah, that's rough." I was amazed at my ability to fake sympathy when my innards were doing a jig. Without Sarah around to belittle me, the symphony would really feel like paradise. I played a quick arpeggio to hide a giggle.

Peter walked sedately to the podium and waited for the chatter to die down. I loved how he commanded attention without a single gesture. When silence held for a full second, he looked up from his music stand and smiled. His dimples could be registered as lethal weapons. Why hadn't I noticed them before? Why was I noticing them now? I quickly picked up a pencil and chewed on the eraser while pretending to study my music.

"So, you've undoubtedly heard the news." He glanced over toward the string bass player. "Or some of you haven't heard anything."

A few people snickered, but the bass player just looked around and blinked in confusion.

Peter smiled again. "I want to thank someone who has fought hard for this symphony and wouldn't give up when all the problems were going on."

I gnawed the pencil end harder, feeling a blush traveling up my neck and tingling my earlobes. What if he asked me to come to the front and say something? What should I say?

"So, let's get her up here and thank her."

I shifted, preparing to stand.

Peter turned toward the wings and gestured toward Megan. She jogged out and took the podium.

"Thank you, Maestro."

Megan? Had she been interviewing suspects and lurking in dark shadows? Had she thought of using a Dictaphone to trap the villain? No! Lena had told me that Megan had been sending out résumés for a new job. I bit the eraser right off my pencil.

"I also thank all of you for your patience," she chirped. "I know this has been a difficult stretch with being out of our space for several weeks and the uncertainty about funding. I spoke with one of our corporate patrons after the news broke, and he is doubling his commitment for this coming season. I suspect this will be the beginning of lots of renewed support. Our development team is applying for a major Minnesota Arts grant. Now, have a great Summer Festival."

Polite applause answered her, and the string players tapped their bows on their stands. Peter resumed his place and again waited for silence. "Most of you have read about our former concertmaster—if not, there is a report on our Web site. But what many of you don't know is that his scheme might never have been exposed without the efforts of one musician who took it as her personal responsibility to find out who committed the sabotage. We all owe her our deepest gratitude."

His dark eyes found me, and I felt my skin flush to match my hair.

"Amy Johnson, thank you." Peter smiled and began to clap. The woodwind section joined in enthusiastically. The brass section shouted a "Hoo-yah" and launched to their feet. The strings all began tapping their bows and also stood. Soon the whole orchestra was giving me an enthusiastic ovation.

Only a few months ago, I was plodding along teaching music, endlessly practicing an audition piece with little hope that my dream would ever come true. Now I was not only a symphony flutist but a hero. The whistles, stomps, and applause were as exhilarating as Beethoven's Ninth.

That afternoon, Clara and I ordered a pizza to celebrate both our triumphs.

"So Coach Joy thinks that next year we'll be going to the nationals again. Can you believe it?"

"Yes, I can believe it. I saw you cheer. Remember? You guys are terrific. And I've got news, too. After rehearsal, Peter asked me to come to his office. He wanted to talk to me about Sarah leaving. The principal flute position will be vacant."

"Did he want to move you up?"

I huffed. "Get real. I'm good, but I'm not that good. No, but he asked me to sit in on the audition panel." I rubbed my hands together in anticipation.

"Oh, no. You're gonna be scary, aren't you?"

I grinned. "Musicians are tough. They can take it."

"Mom, I have a question."

I snatched the last piece of pizza and took a bite. A perfect blend of grease and cheese and tomato rolled around my tongue. "Hmm?"

"Are you finally going to be busy enough so that you stop looking for mysteries to solve?"

I threw my shoulders back. "I don't go looking for mysteries. I've never gone looking for them. I just happen to *notice* them and want to do something about them."

Clara moaned. "You're sick. It's a sickness."

The empty pizza box made a satisfying sound as I whacked her over the head with it. "Respect your elders. Don't they teach you that at Lena's church?"

"Not fair. You don't get to preach at me if you don't go to church."

I gathered up our plates and walked to the counter. "About that." I stared out the kitchen window. Hien Nguyen and a couple of his ten-year-old friends blitzed down the alley on their bikes. "I wonder what they're up to tonight?"

"Mom? Hello-oh? Your train of thought jumped the tracks."

I busied myself scrubbing the sink so I wouldn't have to face her. "I was thinking we could go sometimes."

"Huh?"

"Church. But not Lena's. It gives me a headache. Can we find a different one? One with some good music?"

"I guess. I like the youth program at Lena's church, but they have a service on Sunday nights that I can go to." She came and stood beside me at the sink. "Look at us. We're exploring our spiritual side. You're finally moving forward in your career. I've got the cheerleading team, a boyfriend, and . . . I'm finding out about the father I never knew. If there is a God, He sure seems to be guiding our lives in new directions."

I tugged the kitchen curtains shut. "Don't push it. That's still a big *if*."

Except if I were honest, I'd already crossed that threshold. The tugs I'd felt at my inner spirit in the past months, and the discussions with Lena and Clara, had already led me to a grudging acceptance that there did seem to be an entity that set the world in motion. My struggle now was making my boundaries clear to Him. I might believe in His existence, but I didn't want Him to meddle in my life.

Clara and I began to argue about which churches to try, but the phone rang and interrupted us.

Janie Biederbock's voice caroled a hello. "Are you busy?"

I wasn't ready to be roped in to more sewing. "Well, um . . ."

"Ashley told me that Clara told her that you saved the symphony. I thought that required some celebrating. Have you tried the Cheesecake Factory at Southdale yet?"

Clara had disappeared behind the computer screen, fingers clacking messages to friends. "I guess I could get away for an hour or so."

"Great! Meet you there in . . . half an hour?"

"Wait. One thing. Promise me: no talk about the car wash fund-raiser."

Janie giggled. "Promise. Besides, we'll get that all planned at the meeting on Thursday."

I groaned, but she had already hung up. "So, I guess I'm going on a mom date."

Clara glanced up. "Good. I can get some piano practicing in without you poking your nose in to comment on my phrasing every two minutes."

"I don't—"

"Yes, you do. Relax. I still love you."

I replayed her words through my head all the way to Southdale Mall.

Janie waved to me as I walked down the hallway from the parking lot. Dawn and two other cheerleader moms were with her. "There she is!"

When they squealed and gathered around to hug me, I almost turned tail and ran for my car. But Dawn held my arm. "You guys have got to hear this woman play. The symphony is incredible."

"We want to hear all about how you solved the mystery." Janie bounced as she turned her gaze to the other women. "And no talk about the cheerleading squad or fund-raisers tonight."

"Or our kids," Dawn chimed in.

Oh, great. What would we have to talk about?

Surprisingly, we found a wealth of topics. The women had interesting lives hidden behind their cheerleader-mom exteriors. Janie's quilts were going to be displayed in an art show in Uptown. Dawn was writing for a local paper in between shuttling her kids to various lessons. And they were avid listeners as I shared my symphony adventures.

Clara was right. My mom-and-daughter-against-the-world bubble needed to expand. Filled with coffee and cheesecake, I felt an expansive openness to new people. The sensation was a surprise, and I mulled it over as I drove home.

As a teen, I'd pictured myself living a Bohemian life. A walkup garret and empty cupboards wouldn't have bothered me a bit. I'd stay up all night practicing my flute and cadge a cup of coffee off a friend the next morning. Recreation would include arguing about music with other musicians and sometimes exploring old bookstores for a change of pace. But because of Clara I had needed stability. Like the saying goes, "Life is what happens when you're making other plans."

When Jason dumped me, and I fled Juilliard, I lost more than the picture of how my dream life would look. Something had shriveled inside of me and I'd created a tight pocket of safety around Clara and myself, guarding it like an ill-tempered bulldog.

During my drive home, I glanced upward. "So if you're there, show me how to let people in." Then I checked the back seat to be sure no lurking carjacker was hiding to hear my fledgling prayer. The embarrassment would have killed me.

When I got home, a bouquet of daisies and sweet peas greeted me from the kitchen table. Clara's Chopin swirled from the living room but cut off abruptly when she heard me close the door.

"Are these from Ryan?" I didn't think a football player would have that kind of sensitivity.

Clara leaned against the doorframe. "Naw. They're for you."

I picked up the tiny card. "With gratitude. Looking forward to our trip to Duluth. Peter."

My eyes widened.

Clara laughed. "I think he's into you."

"Don't be silly. It was probably Megan's idea."

"And what's this about a trip to Duluth?"

I waved a hand dismissively. "It's just work."

"Uh-huh. Now say that without blushing."

"I don't blush."

She was still teasing me when we got ready for bed. "Mom, admit it. He's a cutie."

I tugged the belt of my bathrobe tight. "That's sacrilegious. No one calls a conductor a cutie."

Clara smiled. "Uh-huh. My turn to read tonight." She picked up *Mere Christianity*.

I rolled my eyes, then remembered that I had decided to be somewhat receptive to finding out more about God and settled down beside Clara on her bed. I was an educated, cultural woman.

I could handle exploring theology without getting bent out of shape. Besides, trying to be good—telling Clara the truth, letting her contact her father, being pleasant to acquaintances, offering to go to church—felt kind of nice.

I listened with one ear as Clara read, until words snagged me—words that were such a specific response to my thoughts that my spine prickled. " 'That is why the Christian is in a different position from other people who are trying to be good. They hope, by being good, to please God if there is one; or—if they think there is not—at least they hope to deserve approval from good men. But the Christian thinks any good he does comes from the Christ-life inside him. He does not think God will love us because we are good, but that God will make us good because He loves us.' "

I sat up straighter and grabbed a pillow to hug—wanting to hold on to something as the planet seemed to wobble beneath me.

" 'And let me make it quite clear that when Christians say the Christ-life is in them, they do not mean simply something mental or moral. When they speak of being "in Christ" or of Christ being "in them," this is not simply a way of saying that they are thinking about Christ or copying Him. They mean that Christ is actually operating through them.' "

Clara lit up. "Isn't that radical? I asked Him to come in, and He's inside me. At least that's how Lena explained it."

I pulled the book from Clara's hands. "Okay, it's been a long day. Bedtime."

She gave me a hard look but didn't argue. "G'night, Mom."

I kissed her forehead and padded across the hall to my room. There, I propped against my headboard and hugged my knees. Mysteries didn't frighten me. I thrived on them. Crimes that needed to be solved. The mystery of how a series of notes could create music that touches the soul. The awe of a tiny life growing inside me, bursting into the world, and becoming her own person. But this

"Christ in me" notion was a mystery that went so deep it made my head hurt.

"God, I thought I was meeting you halfway, here. I'll believe you exist, and try to be good, and you leave me alone."

Would you have left Clara alone?

Terrific. God didn't want to settle for my vague definition of faith. He wanted a relationship. And it seemed like Clara already had a head start on building her own relationship with Him.

I punched my pillow and curled on my side, staring at my photo of Clara on the nightstand. Some relationships were worth the effort. Maybe this one would be, too.

"As long as you understand, God. I'm set in my ways. Do you know what you're getting into?"

The curtains moved as a breeze slipped through my window like a low chuckle.

Veni, Spiritus Sanctus.

The melody of Teige's cantata played through my mind, and I whispered the lyrics. Then I pulled my quilt up around my shoulders. "All right, all right. I'll look into this whole theory about Christ. Personally, I don't think it makes much sense. But I'll check it out. At least for a little while."

After my declaration, I expected dread to well up in my soul. Instead, I felt a tingle of anticipation. I might just have stumbled across one of the most intriguing mysteries of all.

ACKNOWLEDGMENTS

My *deep gratitude goes to:*

Every wonderful person at Bethany House, but particularly the stellar editors Charlene Patterson, Ann Parrish, and Karen Schurrer.

Agent Steve Laube.

Writer friends from ACFW, Mount Hermon, MCSG, Word Servants.

My Book Buddies.

Early readers and critique partners like Camy Tang, Sherri Sand, Jill Nelson, Nancy Brown, Jonathan Friesen, Bill and Cheryl Bader, Carol Oyanagi, and Chawna Schroeder.

Branson Brainstormers, who were there when scenes were tiny ideas on three-by-five cards.

Mary Beyersdorfer for sharing her beach home with our Church Ladies. I made lots of progress during that vacation visit, and went home refreshed enough to tackle the rest of the story.

The Colorado Stelzer reunion that inspired many ideas for this story.

Nettie McCortney, Dottie Burroughs, and Caleb Green—gifted musicians whose advice honed key points. Any errors are mine, not theirs.

Deb Kellogg for help with German.

All the music teachers, band conductors, and choir directors over the years, your passion for music touched me and made a difference in my life.

The large musical Hinck clan.

My friends in the real world who pull me out of my writing cave from time to time. St. Michaels, Logos Bible Study, Life Group, Church Ladies, and other pals.

Flossie Marxen for reading, proofing, and encouraging.

To the musicians closest to me: Joel, Kaeti, Josh and Jenni—no mother could be prouder of the way you use all your gifts, including music.

Ted, you make my heart sing.

Father God, for music, for family, for forgiveness, for mystery.

READING GROUP
DISCUSSION QUESTIONS

1. Lou Holtz said, "I believe in God, but I do believe that everybody has something that they worship—sometimes it's materialistic things. Sometimes people worship money. Sometimes they worship power. [Everybody] has something that they are willing to put above everything else." Do you agree? What are the things you put first in your life? What is important to you?

2. Do you think Amy Johnson is a good mother? Why or why not?

3. How did Amy's secrets affect her relationship with Clara, with men, and with God?

4. During the span of the story, what changes were developing in Amy and Clara's relationship? Do you have relationships in your life that are going through changes? Children moving toward more independence? Friendships growing closer or more distant?

5. Can you identify with Amy's passion for her dream? What are some of your longings and passions?

6. Amy feels like a misfit when she's around "normal" people. Have you ever felt like a misfit? What groups are you comfortable with? Uncomfortable with? Which settings are difficult for you?

7. Amy initially disdained the cheerleader moms. Have you ever stereotyped a group of people? Did anything challenge your initial assumptions?
8. Amy has avoided dating relationships for sixteen years. What is different about Peter? Do you see a future for them? Why or why not?
9. Can you list some of the relationships and experiences that God uses to woo Amy toward a relationship with Him? What ways have you heard God whisper to you?

ABOUT THE AUTHOR

SHARON HINCK is a wife and mother of four children who generously provide her with material for her books. She has a M. A. in communications from Regent University and has served as the artistic director of a Christian performing arts group, a church youth worker, a classical ballet teacher, and a professional choreographer. She has played a variety of instruments, including college study of piano and church organ. She lives in Minnesota with her family. To learn more about her writing, visit her Web site at *www.sharonhinck.com*.

Be the first *to know*

Want to be the first to know
what's new from
your favorite authors?

Want to know all about
exciting new writers?

Sign up for Bethany House newsletters at
www.bethanynewsletters.com
and you'll get regular updates via e-mail.
You can sign up for specific authors or
categories so you get only
the information you really want.

Sign up today